PARIAH

DONALD HOUNAM

CORGI BOOKS

PARIAH
A CORGI BOOK 978 0 552 57440 2

Published in Great Britain by Corgi Books,
an imprint of Random House Children's Publishers UK
A Penguin Random House Company

Penguin
Random House
UK

This edition published 2016

1 3 5 7 9 10 8 6 4 2

Penguin Random House is committed to a sustainable
future for our business, our readers and our planet.
This book is made from Forest Stewardship Council® certified paper.

MIX
Paper from
responsible sources
FSC® C018179

Set in Baskerville 12/16.5pt by Falcon Oast Graphic Art Ltd.

Corgi Books are published by Random House Children's Publishers UK
61–63 Uxbridge Road, London W5 5SA

www.**randomhousechildrens**.co.uk
www.**totallyrandombooks**.co.uk
www.**randomhouse**.co.uk

Addresses for companies within The Random House Group Limited
can be found at: www.randomhouse.co.uk/offices.htm

THE RANDOM HOUSE GROUP Limited Reg. No. 954009

A CIP catalogue record for this book is available from the British Library.

Printed and bound by Clays Ltd, St Ives plc

For
John and Katie

Order for the detention and trial of Francis Joseph Sampson, issued on the 5th of October 2015 by the Holy Office of the Inquisition of the Society of Sorcerers.

Whereas you, Francis Joseph Sampson, aged fifteen, son of the late Joseph William Sampson, were denounced to this Holy Office for summoning without official authorisation the demon Cimerez, a marquis of Hell ruling twenty legions of spirits:

The Society being determined to proceed against the disorder and mischief thence resulting, the Board of Discipline suspended your licence to practise sorcery and sentenced you to undertake a pilgrimage to the tomb of our founder, Saint Cyprian of Antioch, in the Holy City of Rome; and, upon your return, to perform an act of sincere contrition before the assembled members of the Society.

Since you have disobeyed this injunction and have aggravated your delinquency, the Tribunal of this Holy Office has determined:

That your licence be permanently and irreversibly revoked.

That, following your arrest by the Knights of Saint Cyprian, you will be remanded to the custody of this Holy Office until your trial on charges of insubordination, disobedience and the practice of black magic.

That, if found guilty of these charges, you will be burned at the stake, your ashes cast into the River Isis, and your name stricken from the records of the Society of Sorcerers.

And so we say, pronounce, sentence, declare and ordain.

Signed:
Ignacio Gresh, Grand Inquisitor of the Society of Sorcerers

CHAPTER ONE
Floating Balls

A ny sorcerer will tell you: once there's a demon in
the room, all bets are off.

Funnily enough, though, the demons aren't the
problem. So long as you say the right words, make
the right smells and remember to duck in the right
places, it's easy enough to avoid getting mashed up.

It's the people you've got to watch out for. One of
the first things they taught me when I was a novice sorcerer: you can never predict or guarantee any human
behaviour in the presence of a demon.

You want proof? OK, here it is: a tall, middle-aged
man staring back at me from a magic circle that's all
that's keeping him from being torn apart and dragged
off to hell . . .

Three weeks ago he was the dog's bollocks. The king
of the castle. The fairy on the top of the tree. The
Superior General of the English branch of the Society
of Sorcerers.

My boss.

He used to be all smart dark suits, beautifully polished shoes and cashmere overcoats. Now he's wearing a stained, crumpled linen robe, tied at the waist with a ripped silk scarf. His grey hair used to be neatly tonsured – you know, shaved into a small, round bald patch at the centre as a reminder that in the eyes of God we're all arseholes. Now it's long and straggly, and it's turned white, like the ragged beard covering his face.

He used to be in charge of everything. Now he can't even stop his own hands from shaking like twigs in a hurricane. The nails are long and black with dirt. I can see where he lost the little finger of his left hand . . .

His name's Matthew Le Geyt. He was my Master and he taught me everything I know. He fed the missing finger to a demon, seven years ago, to save my life – maybe my soul, if I had one.

We're underground, in the secret sorcerer's lair that lies beneath the Bishop's Palace in Doughnut City*. It's like the inside of a circular church, about twenty yards across, with a domed ceiling and a sort of arcade round the perimeter.

There's mashed-up furniture; and magical gear scattered all over the place: candlesticks, braziers, a sword, various knives, silk squares, spilled herbs and

* Look, I know there is a lot to take in. So I've stuck a glossary at the back. A bit of history, a few jokes . . .

4

spices. The chalk lines across the black-tiled floor are all smudged, apart from a small double circle around the Boss, scattered with symbols. He's got a single white candle burning in a silver candlestick, a paper bag containing more candles, a box of matches ...

And even if he *is* the Superior General of the Society of Sorcerers, he still needs to go to the lavatory, so he's got a metal bucket with a lid.

The place stinks. Like someone shut a herd of cows in a small barn and fed them on baked beans, cauliflower and lentils for a month. We're talking serious farting, with a heavy note of sulphur and a bitter edge of herbs and spices.

That's because we've got a demon.

His name's Alastor. He's this bloody great huge bastard, the best part of seven feet tall, with bright golden eyes, like a bird's, and the traditional goat's horns. In one hand he's swinging a scourge with a dozen chains ending in sharp hooks. In the other he's clutching an axe. All he's wearing is a studded leather belt; and the only reason he's wearing that is so he has somewhere to park an evil-looking dagger with three serrated blades.

So he's a bloody great huge *dangerous* bastard, and he'd be snacking off my head if I didn't have a silver pentacle hanging around my neck on a gold chain.

Basically, what we've got here is an unresolved magical

event, like a juggler's been called away and left all the balls just floating in mid-air . . .

About three weeks ago I realised that the Boss was involved in all sorts of murky stuff involving unlicensed sorcery and murder. Unfortunately, Matthew realised I'd realised. He's way too old to do magic himself, so he got this tame sorcerer to summon up Alastor to chew me up and spit out the bits.

That pissed me off. Big time. But I turned the tables and I was seriously tempted to feed the Boss to his own demon—

But I couldn't, could I?

The grimoires – the magic books – are very clear about this: if a demon manages to get its talons on you, it'll turn you inside out and unravel you. Then it'll whisk you off to hell and put you back together in a different order so all its chums can have a laugh. Why? Because demons are miserable bastards who got booted out of heaven, and the only thing that makes them feel better is if someone else is in even more pain than they are . . .

I know it doesn't make sense. And even if it does, it's so incredibly out of order that I'm damned if I'll believe it.

Except that maybe I'm wrong. I'm wrong about most things, yeah? So if there's even the *tiniest* chance it's true, I couldn't condemn Matthew to that.

Which left me with a problem: what *could* I do with

him? Couldn't let Alastor have him. Couldn't risk letting him go, because he'd just trot back to the Society and see about having me stuck on the end of a fork and toasted.

So I ducked the problem and left him stuck down here in a protective circle with Alastor bouncing around outside.

It's a mess. But hey – it's my mess.

I've been down here for at least an hour, just sitting on the floor with Alastor blowing green smoke over my shoulder, wondering how the hell I sort it all out.

'It's obvious,' says Matthew. 'You have to let me go.'

'And then what?'

'We can work something out.'

'Like what?'

I sit there until he says, 'So do you have anything to suggest?'

Absolutely not. And I've got other stuff to worry about. I can't think about this any more – not tonight, anyway. If I keep him here, it's like I've got a fishhook through my own entrails and I'm dragging them out, inch by inch. If I let him go, the Society will do the entrail-dragging for me.

It's hopeless and my head is starting to hurt.

'What about Kazia?' he says. 'I assume you're looking for her.'

'No.'

He smiles. It's not a real smile – he's in too much pain for that. It's the sort of smile that says, 'You can't fool me, sunshine. I know more about you than you know about yourself.'

And he's right. Of course I'm looking for Kazia.

Full name: Kazimíera Siménas. Nationality: Lithuanian. Age: 16. Profession . . . well, none officially, but she summons demons in her spare time. And there's a rumour going round that I'm in love with her.

Which reminds me . . .

I check my watch. It's four o'clock in the morning and if I'm ever going to find her I have to see a man about a dead shark. I get to my feet.

There's an arch at the bottom of the stone stairs that spiral up towards the real world. I stop and check the charcoal symbols scrawled down the stonework each side, to prevent Alastor from leaving.

He's standing right behind me.

'Are you sure I can't take care of him for you?' He demonstrates by dragging one of the razor-sharp blades of his knife across his own throat. I close my eyes as thick black liquid spurts out. When I open them again, of course he's uninjured and standing there grinning down at me. 'Just trying to help,' he says.

In the library at the top of the stairs, I stop to reset the spell on the cellar door. It grumbles a bit and calls me a few names, but at the end of five minutes it's securely locked and invisible to anybody who enters the room.

I could just sneak out of the palace the way I sneaked in: through the gardens and down to the path along the river. But tonight . . . I dunno, maybe I'm just in a funny mood.

I open another door and follow a long, dark corridor to the front of the palace. I manage to avoid falling over any of the furniture and waking up the household, and I find myself standing on the black-and-white chess-board tiling of the entrance hall, craning my neck to peer up into the stairwell.

That's where I glimpsed Kazia for the very first time: hanging over the banister, two floors up, staring back down at me like she knew a twerp when she saw one.

One of the things you learn as a sorcerer is to *envision* things. Whatever you're trying to achieve – find buried treasure or lost dogs, cause naked maidens to dance on the table, summon up a demon to rub somebody out – requires an *intention*.

I have a powerful intention: to find Kazia. Unfortunately, I'm pretty sure she has an equally powerful intention of her own: not to be found.

I close the front door of the palace silently behind me. The porter at the gate is fast asleep. I trot off along the Palace Road, under the railway bridge and up the hill towards the Hole . . .

CHAPTER TWO

Grown on Trees

I've said it before, so I'll say it again: there's a lot I can do with a dead shark. I just didn't expect Dinny to turn up with anything so bloody big.

'What am I supposed to do with this?'

''Ow should I know?' Dinny does his special French shrug. 'You are the magician.'

'Sorcerer. Magicians do card tricks.'

'So make trick with two 'undred pound.' Dinny doesn't like to be reminded that he was a sorcerer himself, until his Gift vanished.

We're in an upstairs room in the remains of one of the old university colleges, slap-bang in the middle of the Hole.

Not *a* hole. *The* Hole.

That's why they call it Doughnut City. After the college wars, eighty-five years back, there was nothing left in the centre of Oxford except an enormous pile of rubble, still oozing magic. Nobody who mattered wanted to move back in there; but there were plenty of poor people who couldn't afford to mind if their skin came out in boils or an arm fell off, and they drifted in, moved the wreckage around and made the best of it.

Most of the magic that did the damage had a short half-life, so these days only the occasional finger or toe still falls off. The Hole has turned the clock back to the Middle Ages: wood and tin shacks, piled on top of each other in the shells of the old buildings; open sewers; a population who don't need magic to dismember and disembowel each other.

There's the sound of gunfire and a lot of screaming. Nobody gets much sleep in the Hole. One day the army'll move in and clean it all up; but tonight there's just a small gang of us up here glaring at each other: me, my mate Charlie Burgess, Dinny Saint-Gilles and a couple of his goons.

I'm placing two small silver pentagrams on the marble mantelpiece, above a gaping cavity in the wall where the fireplace used to be. I'm not quite sure what they're supposed to save me from. They certainly won't protect me if the sagging ceiling decides to fall in.

Water runs steadily down the crumbling brickwork where the oak panelling has been torn out for firewood; it forms a puddle on the floor, then trickles out under the door and down the stairs. On top of the stench of rotting rubbish drifting in from the street through the broken window, there's this stink like urine coming off

11

the shark. It's about four feet long and it's lying on a sheet in the puddle, with the sawn-off tip of some sort of spear still sticking out of its side.

'I mean, how'm I supposed to get it back to my place?'

Dinny does the shrug again.

'But all I wanted . . .' I hold up my hands, a couple of feet apart.

'Sharks,' says Dinny. 'They do not grow on trees.'

'And you said fifty quid, anyway.' I don't think we agreed a price, but that's all I've got in my pocket.

Dinny lost both hands a couple of years ago. The light from the lantern glistens along two steel hooks as he waggles them under my nose. 'Two 'undred.'

'You'll have to take it back.'

''Undred fifty.'

I decide to let that stick to the wall for a bit. I crouch beside the shark to inspect the snout. I need time to think. I'm desperate, but I haven't got that kind of money.

'Where'd you get it, anyway?'

'Fell off the back of a boat,' one of Dinny's goons sniggers. Big bloke with a tiny round head like a billiard ball.

My money's on a private aquarium. I've got the shark's mouth open. Not a pretty sight, but most of the teeth are present and correct and in better shape than Dinny's. For the procedure I have in mind, all I need is the barbels – the two fleshy whiskers growing from

12

each corner of the mouth; but I'm sure I can find something useful to do with the teeth, the eyes, the heart, the liver . . .

Useful rule of thumb: no sorcerer ever turned his nose up at a dead animal.

Charlie used to be a sorcerer too. He's sitting quietly on a broken chair, rolling a cigarette. He's this little bloke with curly hair, bleached white. He's post-peak and can't do proper magic any more; but he can still handle elemental work for the jacks – the police.

He's a good mate, because he catches my eye and pulls the corner of a banknote out of his jacket pocket. He holds up three fingers; I hope that means thirty . . .

'OK.' I get to my feet. 'Here's the deal. I pay eighty quid tonight, after you've helped me get it back to the monastery—'

'Are you taking the mickey?' Billiard Ball is so outraged that his glasses fall off. He just manages to catch them and sticks them in his pocket.

'Then tomorrow night you come and take what's left away, and I pay you another twenty.' I guess I can find it somewhere. 'That's a hundred quid.'

'No, no!' Dinny waves his hooks madly. 'I don't take less than one 'undred thirty.'

My heart's in my boots. I've got to have that shark if I'm going to find Kazia.

''Undred twenty.' Dinny manages not to stab himself as he folds his arms. 'Final offer.'

So I'm standing there, wondering whether I've died and gone to Another Place where I'm doomed to spend eternity haggling over a dead fish with a French psychopath with no hands—

When the door bursts open and two uniformed jacks burst into the room.

'Freeze!' one of them yells, waving a pistol.

Another thing I've said before and I'll say again: there's something wrong with me. And here's the proof: I stand there like furniture while everyone else makes a bolt for it. Charlie and one of the goons vanish out of another door. Dinny pushes Billiard Ball out through the window ahead of him. The two jacks split up and go after them. There's a crash from outside – the sound of shots—

Which leaves just me and the shark. You can tell which is which, because I'm the one who's still blinking when a small figure, dressed in black, marches into the room.

CHAPTER THREE
Tatty

Marvo stops dead in her tracks, staring at me. 'I thought you'd gone,' she whispers.

After I locked Matthew in the cellar with only a pissed-off demon for company, I realised it was only a matter of time before the Society missed him and started prodding me with sharp objects to see if I knew where he was. They'd already ordered me to make a pilgrimage to Rome, so I got myself seen climbing aboard a train and leaving town.

'I came back.' I do my best smile. 'You're looking very smart.'

Her days of dressing like a deckchair are gone. Detective Constable Magdalena Marvell is dressed all in black: coat, scarf, trousers and shoes, like she's making some sort of statement. She was always skinny – even more of a shrimp than I am – but now she's lost even more weight. With her hair cropped short and bleached, like all the CID wear it, she looks like a small, sad tree after a snowfall.

She'll never make detective sergeant, by the way, because she's a tatty. And tatties get used and discarded, not promoted.

'I came looking for you.' Her eyes dart around the room, taking it all in. 'At the monastery.'

'And?'

Her face has gone blank. 'You weren't there.'

Actually, I was. That train I got on? As soon as it was clear of town, I jumped off and sneaked back. I've spent most of the time since then hiding out in my studio, which I've got wrapped in a cloaking spell. It's not just invisible: people can't remember that it was ever there. And if they really try to think about it . . .

Well, Marvo's clutching her head like it's about to explode.

It's dead clever, a cloaking spell. But to tell you the truth, the fun wears off after a while.

'I'm here now, anyway.' I raise one hand and make a shape with my fingers – not real magic, by the way; more like hypnotism.

A flicker of light from the stone in my ring darts across Marvo's eyes. Her face relaxes. Her eyes drift closed . . . and I'm just stooping to pick up the shark and tiptoe out of here when there's the sound of shots outside and her eyes flutter open.

'What's that?' She's staring at the shark.

'My lunch.'

'Don't be a prat.'

'It's what I do best.'

'See what I mean?' She leans over the shark and sniffs – tatties sniff things a lot. Her face wrinkles up. 'That's disgusting!'

'*Ginglymostoma cirratum*,' I say. 'The nurse shark. Fully grown it can reach a length of fourteen feet. It's a common inshore bottom-dwelling shark, found in tropical waters—'

'What's it for?'

'I'm planning a seafood risotto. What do you *think* it's for?'

One of the jacks stumbles back in, mopping sweat from his forehead with a snotty handkerchief. His name's Carter and he's close to retirement, if he doesn't have a heart attack first. 'Bastards got away,' he gasps.

'You don't say,' Marvo mutters.

'Can we get out of here?' Jacks are scared of the Hole, especially at night.

'What about Hasnip?'

I assume that's the other jack. There's a flash of light from outside, followed, a moment later, by the sound of an explosion.

Carter jumps. 'Did you hear that?'

Marvo flaps a hand at him. 'In a minute.'

'What are you after Dinny for, anyway?' I ask.

17

'For Christ's sake, Marvell!' Carter's at the window, staring anxiously out into the darkness. 'It's not safe.'

'I said, in a minute!' Marvo turns back to me. 'The chief thought he might know something.'

'He knows where to get a shark. Know something about what?'

'We've got this dead kid.'

There's the sound of running footsteps overhead. Lumps of plaster fall from the ceiling. Carter jams a pair of thick spectacles on his face. He pulls out his revolver and flips the cylinder open.

'Stupid bleeding tatty!' he hisses. 'Get us all killed!' An empty cartridge case rattles off across the floor. Carter's eyes are rolling behind his glasses like goldfish in a bowl. He fumbles with a fresh round, moving his head backwards and forwards, struggling to focus—

It's called the Blur. Medical name, presbyopia.

You're fine as a kid; you can see everything sharp as a knife.

Around twenty, your eyes start to act up. You can still see stuff in the distance, but your close vision goes to hell and you get these blinding headaches. There's nothing healers can do about it . . .

By the time they're twenty-five most people need strong glasses to make out anything less than a room away.

Thirty: those lenses are like goldfish bowls.

18

The banging overhead is getting louder and Carter's beginning to panic. He's dropped his gun and he's down on his hands and knees fumbling for it.

'Here.' Marvo steps across, picks it up and hands it to him.

'Bloody tatty!' He holds the gun at arm's length, eyes screwed up. After a bit more fumbling, he jams the new round into the chamber.

I catch Marvo's eye. She just shrugs. She doesn't expect any thanks. Tatties don't get thanked.

If you're a grown-up and you're Blurry, any kid with half a brain can find a dropped gun, thread a needle or read stuff out for you. Tatties, though . . . they're special. They're sharp. They can't just *see* clearly, they can *think* – clear and fast. They'll walk into a room and notice things that anybody else would miss. They'll spot the connection between two shreds of information that nobody else could've seen.

That's why Marvo's giving the orders, even though she's only sixteen.

Uniformed jacks like Carter, they can't stand tatties.

'This dead kid,' I say. 'The Crypt Boy, right?'

After three weeks locked away in my studio, all I know is what I read in a newspaper that I picked up. The police found some kid's body stuffed into a secret chamber underneath a derelict church.

19

'Nothing to do with Dinny,' I say. 'He wouldn't hurt a kid.'

'But he'd know people who would.'

I'm about to say that I don't think so, and that maybe Marvo might like me to look at the body—

When there's a final, deafening crash overhead, and we all look up in time to see the ceiling cave in and Hasnip come tumbling down in a cloud of shattered wood and plaster.

Like a good mate, Carter breaks his fall.

After that, nobody says anything for a bit. Marvo gets Carter on his feet, and together they pick up Hasnip. I've got the shark, wrapped in the sheet. I grab my pentagrams from the mantelpiece, and we're out of the room, struggling down a shattered staircase. The shark weighs a ton, but I'm holding it over my head because there's this horde of children hanging over the banister a floor up, yelling and screaming and chucking stuff down at us.

The kids in the Hole – they'd give most demons a run for their money. I see a brick bounce off Marvo's shoulder, but then we're over a pile of rubble and out of the building, dashing across the street towards a waiting police van.

The driver's waving a gun. 'Come on!' He fires into the darkness.

The ruins of the old college buildings loom over us like a crumbling wedding cake. Opposite, there's open ground with a couple of dogs rooting around in the rubbish. Street lights? You must be joking! Bonfires burning in the distance . . .

We can stand around admiring the scenery another time. Right now, the bricks are still raining down. Glass smashes on the cobbles and a trail of fire roars towards us. As I pull Marvo out of the way, another flaming bottle flies out of the darkness. Carter's got his arm under his mate's shoulder and his gun out, firing wildly as a mob of kids swarm out of cover and the entire street is engulfed in flames and oily smoke. The horses scream and rear up, almost throwing the driver off the box.

Out of bullets, Carter throws Hasnip into the back of the van. The shark is finally getting bored with bouncing around on my head. I can't hold it with just one hand, but as it falls I manage to shove it in Marvo's direction. She catches it, stumbles backwards and falls inside the van. I trip on the step and land on top of them both. I hear more breaking glass and shooting, and when I look over my shoulder the van door is on fire.

Carter lets off a couple of final rounds, then throws himself on top of the pile. We all roll around on the floor as the van takes off, trailing flames and smoke.

Yeah, you can see why the jacks steer clear of the Hole.

CHAPTER FOUR

Strawberry and Vanilla

'Where'd *you* crawl out of?' The receptionist at the mortuary stares at me over his spectacles. 'I thought you'd gone.'

'I missed your welcoming smile.'

'Smartarse! Anyway, I can't let you—'

'I'll sign him in.' Marvo's been clutching her shoulder ever since we ditched Carter and Hasnip at the infirmary. I told her to let a healer look at it, but she said she wasn't going to risk me getting away. She winces with pain as she grabs the pen and turns the logbook.

'What happened to you?' the receptionist asks.

'Nothing important.' She's left a smear of blood across the page.

'Stupid—' He breaks off as he finally notices the shark. 'What's that?'

'Evidence.' Marvo turns away from the desk and just walks into me. 'Come on.'

I used to work here, until I got fired for getting up

22

too many people's noses. I lead the way across the lobby and into a corridor.

'Autopsy room's that way,' says Marvo.

I manage to raise the shark in my arms. 'Can I park this first?'

There are three forensic amphitheatres in the city mortuary and I used to have the run of one of them. Just outside it is my old robing room. At least they haven't messed with the door: I brush my fingers down the wood; it sighs like maybe it's missed me and swings open.

I lay the shark on the floor and turn to Marvo. 'Let's have a look.'

'What?'

'Your shoulder.'

'I'm fine.' But she knows she isn't. She hisses and pulls faces as she wriggles out of her coat and drops onto a stool.

One good thing about my robing room: I've got an electric light. It hasn't been used since I ran off, so the battery's fully charged, and now that Marvo's sitting down I can see dark roots where the bleach is growing out of her hair.

It's a CID thing, the bleach. They seem to think it makes them look special or clever or something. I never thought Marvo would fall for it, and I suspect she only did it to wind me up. Since then, maybe she's forgotten or just couldn't be arsed. Maybe she's depressed. She doesn't look very happy.

'So.' I open a cupboard and grab a porcelain jar. 'Pleased to see me?'

She frowns. 'Haven't decided yet.'

'Surprised, though.'

'Not really.' She nudges the shark with her foot. 'Something special in mind?'

There sure is, but I don't want her laughing at me. Not yet, anyway. I change the subject: 'I thought you'd put in for a transfer.'

'Changed my mind.' And before I can ask why: 'The dead kid – the Crypt Boy – there's weird stuff . . .'

'Like what?' Her grey cotton shirt hasn't ripped, but there's a dark patch of blood soaking through it.

'Sorcery or something,' she mutters.

'Yeah,' I say. 'But every time there's something you don't get, you make this jump – like it's always sorcery.'

She's undoing her sleeve button. 'Try not to rip it this time,' she mutters.

Me and Marvo . . . we've got form, as the jacks say. Every time we meet up, she seems to manage to get herself hurt.

'You'll have to take it off,' I say.

'Nark off!'

'Loosen the neck, then.'

She opens a couple of buttons. 'Gimme that.' She grabs the jar and sniffs at it.

24

I grab it back. 'Has to be me.'

'A likely story!'

I stick my fingertip in the jar, fish out a dab of goo and hope it hasn't gone off. 'Hold still.' I slide my hand under her blouse.

I'm not just *any* sorcerer; I'm a forensic sorcerer. OK, so I got the push a while back, but when I touch human skin, I'm used to it being cold and dead.

I think I prefer it that way. Clear signals. I'm trying to pretend that Marvo's skin isn't soft and warm. My hand follows the line of her collarbone towards the shoulder—

'What's the strap?'

'Are you stupid?'

I'm actually blushing. 'I live in a monastery, remember?' I'm very relieved when my fingertip encounters the sharpness of her shoulder and the sticky wetness of blood.

She hisses with pain. 'Get on with it!'

'In the name of Adonai the most high. In the name of Jehovah the most holy!' I smear the salve around the place, chanting away and making shapes with my free hand.

'Are you done?'

'Don't rush me. In the name of the Lord who healeth the sick.' I pull my hand out, carefully again. 'Once a prat,' I say, 'always a prat.' And when she gives me this angry look, I specify: 'Carter.'

'Christ!' She's glaring down at the shark while she does her buttons up. 'That thing stinks.'

Can't argue: the pissy smell is overwhelming. 'You're welcome.' I'm at the basin, washing my hands.

'It was your fault I got hurt in the first place.'

'But you're all right now . . .'

'Yeah, I'm fine.' She moves the arm in a circle. Her voice softens. 'Thanks, Frank.' She's on her feet, pulling her coat on.

Moment over: 'Can we look at this kid now?'

Down a flight of stone steps and along a lamp-lit corridor that gets colder with every step, I put out my hand to open a door.

'Hang on,' says Marvo. Her hands are trembling as she pulls a flat, round silver case out of her pocket: her scryer. 'Gotta call the chief.'

'Can't it wait?'

She turns her back on me. She's got the scryer open and she's tapping the inside with her fingertips.

'Hey,' I call after her. 'This was your idea.'

She's walking back the way we came. Doesn't even look round; just flaps her hand at me and blows on the surface of the mirror inside the lid. 'Yes, Chief,' she says into it. 'I'm at the mortuary.'

Whatever. The door closes behind me with a faint sigh like an old man sitting down. I shiver.

I never come down here if I can avoid it. They call

26

it the children's ice room, which sounds, I dunno, sort of strawberry and vanilla, you know . . . .?

It's more like a wide corridor than a room. About twenty yards long and five across, with another door at the far end. The floor is flagged stone, slippery with ice. One wall is just dark-red brick. Stretching all the way along the other side is a row of doors, dozens of them, each about three feet square. They're made of silver, with magic symbols etched into them. Below them, through a metal grille, I can see the ice stacked up.

It's freezing cold.

Halfway along it opens out into a sort of circle, with a desk in the middle. There's a sour-looking middle-aged bloke huddled behind it, with a little kid on a stool beside him. They're both wrapped up in fur coats, wearing gloves and hats, with silver amulets hanging around their necks. Their breath forms clouds in the air.

You see this combination all over the place. A grown-up because they're supposed to know what they're doing. A kid because the grown-up can't actually *see* what they're supposed to know how to do.

The bloke's got his glasses off and he's staring up at me. 'Name?'

Like he doesn't know.

'Frank Sampson,' I say. The kid pulls off one glove and writes in a big ledger.

'Occupation?'

27

'Forensic sorcerer.' Not strictly true. Like I said, I got fired.

'Here to see?'

'Dunno his name. The Crypt Boy . . . ?'

The kid opens another ledger and runs his finger down the page. The bloke sticks his glasses back on his nose and squints. They come off again as he gets up and comes round the desk. 'Over here.'

His official job title is 'diener', which is just a fancy word for mortuary attendant. He leads me to the far end of the room and opens one of the metal doors. He puts his amulet to his lips, then grabs two handles and pulls. There's the rumble of wheels and a steel tray slides out. The body of a child lies on it. A girl aged maybe five or six; a white silk sheet, embroidered with symbols, drawn up to her neck.

'No!' Back at the desk, the kid is gesturing madly. 'Number sixty-seven.'

The diener slides the tray back and slams the door. He opens the compartment to the left. The tray is empty. He turns to the kid. 'What are you playing at?' He strides back to the desk and shoves him out of the way. The glasses go back on. He peers and pulls faces as he runs his finger down the ledger.

I shiver as a whisper of icy air blows through the room. I close the door on the empty compartment and open the next. A boy a couple of years older. Curly red hair. Freckles. Half his face smashed in.

The reason the mortuary has a dedicated children's ice room is because Doughnut City's got a lot of dead kids. Like I said, apart from tatties and sorcerers, pretty much everybody's half blind by the time they hit twenty-five. If they're going to hold down a job where they've got to make out anything closer than the other side of the street, they need a kid to do the seeing for them.

There's a lot of people who really don't like that. So who better to take it out on than the kids themselves?

The diener is making heavy weather of flicking through sheets of paper, his eyes rolling like a fairground ride. The little kid's come over and he's looking up at me, wide-eyed. He whispers, 'Are you really a nekker?'

I'd rather he didn't call me that. 'Nekker' is short for necromancer, and raising the dead to get racing tips is one of the things the Society of Sorcerers definitely draws the line at.

Think bonfires.

'He's in the autopsy room,' says the diener.

'Thank you.' I close the door on the dead boy.

The kid tucks his hands under his armpits and whispers enviously, 'I wish I was a nekker.'

'It's not all it's cracked up to be,' I say.

'Better'n this.'

The diener steps up and whacks him round the head.

The kid's got a point.

'Skinny little freak!' the diener mutters as the cold draught shepherds me out through the door at the other end of the ice room.

CHAPTER FIVE
Scarification

Several corridors later, Marvo still hasn't caught up with me. I push open the door to the autopsy room.

It stinks of burning herbs. At the centre, half a dozen electric lights glare down on the body of a boy with a gold-embroidered, blue silk sheet pulled up to his neck. He's lying on a silver slab: legs out straight, his arms by his sides. He's maybe ten or eleven years old, but it's hard to tell because his face is sunk in, like he's been starved. Skin as white as ash. Eyes closed.

Standing over him, a tall figure we've all come to know and love. Ferdia McKittrick has dark, perfectly tonsured hair. He's dressed to slice and dice, in a pale blue rubber apron over black silk overalls and exorcised latex gloves. He's got a small table covered with a white linen cloth; and a brazier on a tripod with a haze of smoke rising from it.

He looks up at me, surprised. 'I heard you'd left town.'

'That's what I heard too. Yet here I am.'

Ferdia frowns and turns to open a drawer.

There's someone else in the room. The jacks are on the case, so of course there has to be a data elemental to remember everything. He's standing against the wall with a sad smile on his face . . .

I call him Mr Memory. He looks like Charlie Burgess. That's because Charlie built him – like he builds data elementals for every major investigation. Always the same: a weary-looking little man with white, curly hair, wearing a crumpled dinner suit over a white shirt and a blue, food-stained bow tie.

Ferdia's back at the table with a small tray covered by a black silk cloth. The cold light glints on the instruments laid out on it: scalpels, shears, forceps, scissors, clamps, a saw . . .

'Caxton know you're back?' he asks. That's Marvo's chief, the one she stopped to scry.

'Nah. Marvell dragged me in.' I look round. Still no sign of her. What's she playing at?

Ferdia picks up a hazel wand and waves it over the body. 'In the name of Adonai the most high. In the name of Jehovah the most holy.'

I hear the door open behind me; I assume it's just Marvo rolling in at last and I say over my shoulder, 'So did Caxton have anything useful to say?' And when Marvo doesn't say anything: 'Didn't think so.'

Still no reply. I look round and of course it's her:

Detective Chief Inspector Beryl Caxton. She's wearing an utterly hellish shiny grey jacket over navy trousers and brown shoes. Her spectacles dangle around her neck on a frayed cord. She's got a much better bleach job on her hair than Marvo, but it's not a pretty sight.

She sticks a huge fist in her pocket, pulls out a silver amulet and kisses it. 'Thought you'd gone,' she says.

'Join the club,' Ferdia mutters.

'I did,' I say. 'But I missed you.'

'Smartarse!' Caxton stuffs the amulet back in her pocket.

Ferdia tosses a pinch of herbs into the brazier. 'Adonai, Tetragrammaton, Jehovah, Tetragrammaton.' There's a bit of spitting and an almost invisibly thin thread of smoke drifts up.

'Where've you been, anyway?' Caxton asks.

'Nowhere.'

'Your lot were round, asking for you . . .'

'The Society? When?'

'Couple of weeks ago. I told them I hadn't seen you, and if they found you not to send you back to me.'

'Did you put in for the new forcer?'

There used to be two forcers – forensic sorcerers – in Doughnut City: Ferdia and me. But I pissed Caxton off once too often, so she gave me the boot. Last thing she told me, she was writing to the Society of Sorcerers for a replacement. Someone who wouldn't ask awkward questions about her cases.

33

I look around. 'So where is he?'

'Sorcerers don't grow on trees.'

'A bit like sharks, then.'

Actually I'm worried about the shark. What if one of the cleaners manages to get into my robing room and comes over peckish? I need to rescue it and get it back to my place and start chopping and purifying—

And talking of chopping and purifying, Ferdia has pulled away the blue sheet covering the body.

'Bloody hell!' I mutter.

The left side of the dead boy's chest is covered with magic symbols.

It's more than a year since I bounced out of Saint Cyprian's Institute of Sorcery with instructions to go and be a forensic sorcerer; so it's not like I haven't played with quite a lot of dead bodies. But as I lean over the slab I realise that this kid's spooking me out. He's got this . . . it's hard to describe, but it's like he's radiating some sort of frozen immobility.

I've got my left hand up to my face as if I'm trying to shield my eyes from the glare of the lights, but who's kidding who? I realise that I'm scared of getting a surprise. The kid feels . . . I dunno, like some sort of trap that could spring out at me.

It takes an effort, but I manage to stop myself leaning away. 'You didn't tell me he was a sorcerer.' And even as I say it, I realise I'm being stupid. The black signs right over the kid's heart are nothing like the magical mark

34

that every licensed sorcerer bears across his chest. I can
see two concentric circles with symbols between them:
planetary signs, the usual stuff. And this big, complicated symbol at the centre of the circles that's like
nothing I've ever seen before.

'Tattoo?'

But when I run my fingers over the ice-cold skin I
realise it's not a tattoo because the marks are slightly
raised . . .

'Scarification,' says Ferdia. 'Sharp knife, maybe a
scalpel. Then they've rubbed herbs of some sort into the
incisions to prevent healing.'

Body magic. 'Have you told the Society?'

'Not yet. I want to see if I can find a cause of death
first.'

The boy is no more than a skeleton, as if someone
got under his skin and sucked all the flesh off his bones.
His hair is black, down to his shoulders. His fingernails
are like talons.

'Not often we get invited into the Hole,' says Caxton.
'People said there was something wrong—'

'In the Hole?'

She shrugs. 'Everything's relative. There were noises
from the crypt of an old church, sometimes lights. The
smell of incense. At first they thought it was haunted.
Finally they opened it up.' She turns to Mr Memory.
'Show him.'

The little man smiles and pushes himself off the

35

wall. He raises both hands and makes a gesture like the outline of a square . . .

And I'm looking through a hole that's been knocked through a stone wall, into a small chamber. The light seeping in from behind me reveals the dead boy, lying naked on his back, mouth gaping.

It's like I'm really there. More of the wall crumbles in front of me, and as the dust settles and someone tosses a burning brand into the chamber, I can see symbols drawn all over the walls and ceiling in red and black chalk.

Magic.

'What's that wrapped around his arms and legs?' I ask.

The vision vanishes. The electric lights throw a merciless glare down at the body on the slab. Mr Memory is holding several lengths of rose briar. When I raise the boy's arm, I see scratches from the thorns across the skin—

'You shouldn't be touching him,' Ferdia points out. Correctly, by the way.

The thing is, though, the boy's skin may be ice cold, but it's still firm to the touch.

'Are you sure he's dead?' I ask.

Ferdia snorts. 'Don't be stupid.'

'No signs of decomposition.'

'He's been on ice.'

I put my finger to his throat: no pulse. Ferdia sighs

and grabs a knife and puts the blade across his mouth; after a minute, there's no sign of misting.

'See?'

But when I pull the boy's eyelids back, the corneas haven't clouded over. The pupils of his brown eyes have shrunk to pinpricks, when they should be dilated.

'Look, I've no idea what's going on,' says Ferdia.

'But there's some sort of magic *in* the boy – is that what you're saying?' Caxton is pulling out her notebook. 'And that's what's keeping him from decomposing . . . ?' She sticks her glasses on her nose. I watch her leaf past page after page of block-capital notes until she finds a blank sheet. 'What do you think?' she says.

'Who cares what he thinks?' says Ferdia.

'Yeah.' It's not often that Ferdia and I agree on anything. 'I don't work for you any more, remember?'

'What are you doing here, then?' Caxton asks.

'Marvo invited me.'

'So where is she?'

'I thought she scried you.'

'Ten minutes ago. Didn't say anything, just closed the lid on me. Stupid bloody kids!' Caxton seems to be trying to draw the scarifications, but she keeps having to squint madly and push her glasses up and down her nose as she struggles to shift her focus from the boy on the slab to her notebook and back. 'Is it . . . I don't know, human sacrifice, or something?'

Unbelievably, Ferdia and I agree again: we're both shaking our heads.

We did human sacrifice when I was a novice at Saint Cyprian's. Well, didn't actually *do* it . . . got warned off. Any serious magic ritual demands some sort of offering, but demons seem perfectly happy with animals – particularly rats, which they like to swallow whole.

Ferdia parrots what the books say: 'Human sacrifice is so powerful that it can be performed with only a single aim: to summon Satan himself, who demands the heart of the victim as his fee.'

'And as you can see . . .' I point to the boy's chest, which may have scars across it, but hasn't got a gaping hole.

'I read once, in a book' – Caxton blushes and blinks down at her notebook. We all know she hasn't read anything smaller than big capital letters in years – 'about parasitic wasps. They lay their eggs in live caterpillars, which go into this kind of zombie state . . . still alive, but not moving or anything. Then when the eggs hatch out inside the body, the grubs eat their way out . . .' She takes a step back, away from the slab. 'What if the boy is the host to some – I don't know, a demon or something?'

'Nothing in the grimoires.' But I remember the sense of some hidden threat that I got off the boy's body.

Caxton's blinking furiously, labouring away at her drawing, painful to watch. I have to fight the urge to jump in and do it for her.

The Blur. Presbyopia. She's thirty-five, so even with her glasses, anything closer than a couple of yards away is pretty much a mystery to her. She's digging the tip of her pencil into the paper, trying to fix a mistake.

'You don't have to do that.' I point at Mr Memory. 'Isn't that what *he's* for . . . ?'

Caxton goes red in the face.

'Can I get on with this?' Ferdia tosses herbs into the brazier.

As they flare up, Caxton draws a decisive cross through her drawing. 'Anyway, it's nothing to do with you.'

I've done what Marvo asked: I've seen the boy. I know what the inside of a body looks like, so I don't particularly need to watch Ferdia open him up. And anyway, there's lots of boring chanting to get through before Ferdia actually digs in. I've got a dead shark that isn't getting any fresher. I head for the door.

Caxton says, 'Does the Society know you're back?' She pulls off her glasses. Without the magnifying effect of the lenses her eyes have this wavering, frightened look, like children lost in the forest.

'Dunno,' I say. 'But please, Beryl, don't tell them you saw me.'

To my amazement, she nods.

CHAPTER SIX

Summoning

Marvo dragged me over here, so she can bloody well drive me back to my place. The trouble is, I've no idea where she's got to and I can't call her: I've hidden my scryer away because I'm not sure the Society can't listen in to them.

I wander about the basement, looking for her. The kid in the ice room hasn't seen her. So I flog upstairs, rescue the shark from my robing room and hunt around until I get bored.

The shark's getting deader and heavier by the second. Outside in the yard, I stagger across to the van and ask the driver to give me a ride; but he says he isn't going anywhere except on Marvo's say-so – especially not with that bleedin' fish stinking the place out.

So I'm back inside again, peering around the lobby and getting some very funny looks, when I remember that Marvo once found her way down to the summoning room in the sub-basement. I can't imagine why she'd wander down there, but it's worth a try . . .

There's no lift from the lobby, but there's a door at the back and a narrow staircase where I have to go down sideways to avoid banging the shark's head on the brickwork. At the bottom I stumble around a maze of dim corridors.

That's when I hear a noise, like the rumble of thunder. It's coming from the summoning room.

It can't be Ferdia. He's too far post-peak to risk invoking a Presence. And anyway, it's only ten minutes since I left him standing over the Crypt Boy with a scalpel: nowhere near long enough to get a summoning going.

I turn a corner, past the lift that comes down from the autopsy room. Up ahead of me there's a set of double doors, glowing white. There's an alcove to my right, with cupboards and sinks. Whoever's messing about in the summoning room, they've left a mess behind them: knives, wands, sachets of herbs and spices, lumps of charcoal, sticks of chalk, scattered all over the place.

Someone's in a hurry.

I ditch the shark again, on the floor inside the alcove. A crash of thunder shakes the floor as I step up to the double doors. I hold out my hand. My security ring flickers. Nothing happens. I put my hand on the surface of one of the doors and I can tell at once: it's not happy. In fact, it's scared.

I've been through these doors maybe four or five

times since I started as a forcer at the mortuary. The summoning room has only one purpose: it's where you go if you want to summon a dangerous Presence. The room is buried deep beneath the mortuary and embedded in blocks of granite. There's even a thick layer of silk behind the black marble walls. Partly to contain anything that manifests. Partly to prevent the outside world getting wind of what's going on down here.

These doors have seen it all – except, apparently, whatever's going on right now. I put both hands to them. 'In the name of he by whom all things are made . . .'

The doors whimper and open.

I know I've stepped into a perfect cube, thirty yards each way, but I can't see a thing. It's pitch-dark, apart from the dim red glow of a brazier and the pinpoint flames of four flickering candles that cast no light over anything. When I look over my shoulder, it's as if an impenetrable black fog has descended, smothering the light from the corridor. I smell burned herbs and spices. I hear a voice, but I can't make out a word it's saying until it starts wheeling out names of God—

'El, Elohim, Elohi, Ehyeh.' A girl's voice. Which is odd, because, according to the Society, girls can't do magic.

My eyes are adjusting to the darkness and I can just make out a figure in a white linen robe, with a thatch of close-cropped blonde hair, standing with its back to me, arms out wide . . .

42

'Marvo?'

Here's the scary thing. Normally the summoning room has an echo that bounces back at you like a tennis ball. But right now, the space is utterly dead. My voice is sucked away like water into sand.

And I realise the hair's wrong: Marvo's bleach job is growing out. But the girl I can see dimly now – the girl in the crumpled linen robe decorated with symbols, with two knives tucked through her belt and a sword balanced across her toes . . .

It isn't Marvo, is it? It's Kazia – the girl Matthew was needling me about. The girl that the shark was supposed to help me find.

Two things about her: she's a sorcerer, and she used to be the girl of my dreams . . . until I noticed that once she'd got a wand in her hand, people tended to wind up smeared across the walls.

Right now, I don't have time to stop and ask her who's in line for a good smearing. I can hear a distant cawing, like a huge flock of birds. I've got a feeling like ants crawling all over my skin. We're minutes from a manifestation, and for all I know I'm standing in the way.

Outside, in the alcove, I tip scraps of paper and wood shavings into a small brazier. I grab a black-handled knife, a hazel wand, a piece of chalk, a box of matches. I shove sachets of herbs into my pocket. I dig a three-foot length of cord out of a drawer.

43

My hands are trembling. I stop. Breathe. I tie a loop in one end of the cord and drape it round my neck.

Back in the summoning room, I can't see a thing. Kazia is almost at the point. The candle flames have vanished into the darkness. The room stinks of sewer gas and rotting flesh.

I feel my way along the wall to my right – trying to hurry, trying not to fall over – until I hit the corner. I have to do as much of this as I can in the darkness. I can barely hear Kazia over the cawing of the birds. Once I'm standing with my back into the angle of the corner, I put the brazier on the floor behind my feet, where I can find it again, and take two paces towards the centre of the room.

Kazia still hasn't noticed me. She's too busy waving her arms and chanting away – in Lithuanian, I suppose.

I've got five minutes at most to stop whatever she's up to. I slip the loop of the cord over my ankles. I wind the other end round the chalk and draw around myself on the floor. Not a perfect circle, but close enough.

I hope.

I take another few turns of the cord around the chalk and draw a second circle, inside the first. And that's as much as I can do in the dark. I fumble behind my back until I feel the brazier.

Kazia doesn't hear the scrape of the match. There's too much noise now: not just the screaming of the birds,

44

the crash of waves breaking against a cliff-face. She doesn't notice the flames licking up from the brazier.

Peering into the gloom, I see that my circles are surprisingly regular. I scrawl symbols between them: north, south, east and west. I scrape the tip of the knife around the outer circle.

It's all crap. Nothing's been purified. I haven't washed myself or put on the proper gear. I didn't use a flint and steel to start the fire, like I'm supposed to. The symbols and herbs make no sense whatsoever. But the thing is, I don't have to do magic . . .

I just have to mess up hers.

I tip the herbs into the flames, raise my wand over my head and scream: 'Adonai, Tetragrammaton, Jehovah, Tetragrammaton, Otheos, Tetragramma-ton—'

A blinding flash of white light cuts through the darkness, and for a split second everything stands out flat like it's been cut from paper. The silver candlesticks. A wand protruding from a brass brazier, flames flickering along its length. The circle chalked on the floor—

And Kazia, spinning round at me to stare, mouth open in a perfect O.

'Athenatos, Aschyros, Agla, Pentagrammaton.' It doesn't matter which names of God I throw into the room. This isn't real counter-magic. All I'm trying to do is disrupt the magic space that Kazia has created. And it's working: the obscurity is dispersing; her candles

45

flicker as cross-currents of air cut across the room . . .

The wand projecting from the charcoal slips and falls to the floor in a shower of sparks. The flames flicker and go out—

There's a sound like the wingbeats of a thousand birds rising into the sky. The light in the room flashes repeatedly like someone's switching an electric lamp on and off – only the battery's dying because each flash is weaker than the last . . .

. . . until I'm staring around the room in the dim, flickering glow of the candles.

Kazia's cornflower-blue eyes stare back at me. She's panting for breath, her breasts rising and falling—

I manage to gasp, 'We can't go on meeting like this.'

She doesn't seem to think that's funny. To be honest, neither do I; but I'm still busy scanning the room for any sign of the manifestation.

The birds' wings fade into the distance.

Let me tell you something about Kazia: she shouldn't exist. One of the first things they taught us when I was a novice at Saint Cyprian's was that girls can't be sorcerers – they don't receive the Gift. I still can't work out if they were lying deliberately; but Kazia is living proof that they were wrong. I've been on the receiving end of her work, so I know.

It's obvious she's trying to get in and out of here fast. Her geometry, it's just two concentric circles with pentagrams at the four points of the compass. I couldn't work with that.

She's powerful.

And dangerous.

I'm still looking around, wondering if it's safe to step out of my circle. 'What are you playing at?' I ask.

'Leave me alone, Frank.' She's got this east European accent that for some reason makes me think of blackberries. Like I said, she's originally from Lithuania. When she was ten, her mother was accused of witchcraft. My boss – the guy in the cellar – was observing the trial for the Society of Sorcerers and he realised that it was Kazia who had really done the magic.

An unlicensed sorcerer can be a very useful thing to have around the place if you want to do stuff and you don't want anybody else to know about it. And if that unlicensed sorcerer is a girl . . . who'd suspect?

He let her mother go to the stake. He grabbed Kazia, brought her back to England and trained her up secretly. He was working for the intelligence services back then. Maybe she had something to do with him getting made Superior General of the Society of Sorcerers.

But it's not all sunshine and bunny rabbits. As an unlicensed sorcerer, Kazia is always in danger of winding up like her mother. As a girl with the Gift, she's liable to be dismantled, to see how she works, before the roasting.

The stuff that Matthew got her to do . . . it ended

47

with several people winding up dead. It was she who summoned Alastor to turn me inside out, take me apart and jump up and down on the pieces.

'I want to help you,' I say.

'You can't help me.'

An inky black cloud has spread across the floor, hiding her fallen instruments. She's staring back at me wide-eyed, like a cat on a wall. Hair hacked short so demons can't grab it. Clutching one of my swords.

The last time I saw her was down in the cellar with Matthew, trapped by her own demon. I got her out of trouble, but she didn't appreciate it enough to stick around and discuss our future together. Just lobbed a chair at me and ran.

The room is silent. The candles burn steadily. A thin plume of smoke rises unbroken from her brazier.

'How did you get in here?' It looks safe: I step out of my circle.

The sword rattles away across the floor, and she comes running at me. There's this ludicrous moment when I actually think maybe she's pleased to see me after all. But she just lowers her head and butts me hard in the stomach.

I make a wild grab for her. Something cuts into my fingers and I clutch at it. A moment later I'm sitting on the floor, staring stupidly at a silver disc swinging on a gold chain . . . and Kazia is just the slap of footsteps fading away along the corridor.

Demon?

No. Apart from me, the room is empty. Just the distant cry of a bird and the black cloud across the floor, retreating like an ebbing tide to reveal first the sword . . . then the wand, still giving off a thin plume of grey smoke, and finally the smudged gap in the chalk circle where she dashed out.

No Presence. No danger.

'Kazia, wait!' And I go charging after her.

CHAPTER SEVEN

Insight

I chase after her, up some steps and along a narrow side passage. I stumble round a few corners and struggle up another set of stairs. It all ends with a bang when I skid round a blind corner and trip over someone lying on the floor.

My first thought is that the dieners have been careless with a stiff. But when I pick myself up, I realise it's Marvo.

Yeah, well, that's *her* problem; I've got a chase to get on with. I pick myself up and scuttle off along the corridor to the foot of another staircase, where I take the first three steps in one leap—

And stop dead, one hand on the banister. I can just hear the faint slap of Kazia's slippers above me.

Damn Marvo! We didn't exactly hit it off first time we worked together. She's kind of touchy. Easily pissed off. But if it hadn't been for her, I could've wound up dead.

I can't hear Kazia's footsteps any more. I hold up my hand. The silver disc, a couple of inches across, dangles from the gold chain still wrapped around my fingers. The magic symbols etched into it identify it as a pentacle of Solomon – worn by a sorcerer to help compel a demon.

I stick it in my pocket, then turn and go back to kneel beside Marvo.

She's got this strange face, a bit like a bird's, with a sloping forehead and pointy nose. The first time we met – before she got stuck in with the scissors and the bottle of bleach – her hair was black and curly and a bit of a mess.

My Gift, it's just for magic. I don't really understand what makes people tick. But I suddenly realise that maybe Marvo's bleach job was so that . . . yeah, not so she could fit in with the rest of the CID, but to be blonde, like Kazia, in my eyes.

The great thing about falling for Kazia is that she wants nothing to do with me. I get all the fun, with none of the confusing consequences. Getting fallen *for* – I mean, what am I supposed to do about that?

Like I said, I really don't feel comfortable touching people – not when they're alive, anyway. But I put my fingers to Marvo's neck. Her pulse is faint and irregular; she feels cold.

'Marvo?'

She doesn't move.

51

Caxton would be helpless without a tatty like Marvo to see things up close for her. Right now, though, it's Marvo who's helpless. Crumpled up on the floor, eyes closed, breathing kind of strange . . .

A voice: 'What's going on?'

I look up at Ferdia. 'Help me move her.'

Together we haul her across the floor so she's propped up against the wall.

'So what happened?' Ferdia's pale, with beads of perspiration across his forehead. Something's shaken him up.

'No idea,' I say. 'I found her like this.' I blow into her face. 'Marvo?' She twitches but doesn't wake up. Back to Ferdia. 'Why aren't you carving?'

And he gives me this weird grin. I mean, it's not that the grin itself is anything special; it's just that Ferdia has never looked at me any way except down his nose.

'He woke up.' He makes this gesture, like cutting with a scalpel. 'The moment—'

'Told you he wasn't dead.'

The grin dies. Ferdia takes Marvo's hand. He lays his other hand across her forehead.

'Do you want me to look at him?' I say quickly. 'The boy?'

Ferdia hesitates. 'A second opinion wouldn't hurt . . .'

I'm tempted to laugh, but I can see that was painful. And I get one of those moments – rare and brief, thank God! – when I actually feel sorry for Ferdia. He's six

52

years older than me and he's always treated me like I'm an idiot.

And I sort of understand that. In the first place, I *am* an idiot. And in the second place, *any* sorcerer feels threatened by a younger one, simply because you've hardly got the hang of your Gift before it starts to fade, and by the time you're twenty-one – which is how old Ferdia is – you're post-peak and that's pretty much it.

He lays Marvo's hand in her lap and gets to his feet. 'Come on, then.'

'I'll follow you,' I say.

For a moment, I'm expecting him to pick Marvo up and throw her at me. Instead, he twitches and fishes his scryer out of his pocket. 'Yes, Chief,' he says into it.

Caxton, then. That's the trouble with scryers: only the owner can see or hear the person at the other end. A circle of reflected light dances across Ferdia's face.

'Found him.' He turns the scryer so that the mirror points at me. 'We're on our way.' He closes the lid and looks up at me. 'Let's go, then.'

'I can't just leave Marvo . . .'

'I've got to go.' It's like he's trying to talk himself into it.

'Go ahead. I'll just see she's OK,' I say. 'Ten minutes.'

'I'll bet.' He turns away, but stops. 'One thing, Sampson—'

'Yeah?'

'I didn't want to say anything in front of Caxton, because the Society hasn't yet made it public . . .'

'What?'

'The Superior General . . .'

I manage to look blank. At least, I hope I do.

'You must know he's missing,' Ferdia says.

'Since when?'

'Since around the time you ran off.'

Dodge a question by asking your own. 'So who's in charge?'

Ferdia pulls a face. 'Ignacio Gresh.'

The Society's Grand Inquisitor.

'That's nice,' I say. Actually, he's a shit.

'He thinks you might know something about it.'

'He would think that, though, wouldn't he? And I don't, by the way.'

Ferdia nods, but I don't think he believes me for a second. 'We need the Superior General.'

'I'm sure the Grand Inquisitor can run the show.'

Ferdia looks around, then whispers, 'Do you trust him?'

I shake my head. It was Gresh who lumbered me with that stupid pilgrimage to Rome.

'We need the Superior General,' Ferdia says again.

'If I bump into him, I'll be sure to mention that.' I point along the corridor. 'Beryl's waiting . . .'

Just before he disappears round the corner, I hear Ferdia mutter to himself, 'Skinny little freak!'

54

Once his footsteps have faded away, I get Marvo under the shoulders and haul her to her feet. She's a shrimp, but she's a heavy shrimp and she's not doing anything to help. I drag her dead weight along the corridor and down the stairs, and after a while I'm close to death but we've reached the alcove where I left the shark.

I sit her down and go through to the summoning room. All quiet. Just the smeared chalk marks, the scattered equipment and the lingering smell of herbs and spices.

'Hello,' I say, and my voice echoes reassuringly off the walls. I don't get the tingle of any kind of manifestation through my feet.

Back in the alcove, nobody's moving.

'Marvo!'

I get bored quickly. I could mix together some sort of wake-up potion, but there's a dead shark to hand. I bend Marvo over until her nose is almost buried in it. She wriggles and goes red and finally kicks out like a galvanised frog and sends me flying.

'What the hell are you playing at?' she hisses.

'Nothing. What's up with you?'

'I'm fine.'

'Like hell you are.'

'Leave me alone, will you?' She's clutching her head like she's afraid it's going to fall off. 'I don't feel great.' She looks around. 'Where the hell is this?'

'The mortuary.' Puzzled look. 'You know, we were in the Hole, but you wanted me to look at the Crypt Boy. I told Caxton—'

'Yeah, yeah. Christ, that thing stinks!' She glares at the shark. 'What the hell's it for, anyway?'

I kneel to wrap the sheet securely around the shark. 'I told you, I'm making—'

'No you're not. It's for a spell.'

Marvo's got her eyes screwed up like someone's shining a dazzling light into them. Mouth open; white as a sheet; one hand to her head . . . I know what's coming. And sure enough, she stares at me and whispers, 'You're looking for the girl.'

'What girl?' Hey, it's worth a try.

'Kazia.' Marvo kicks out at the shark. 'You stupid prat – you think you can use that to find her.'

Insights.

Yeah, that's the other thing tatties do. Most of the time, Marvo gets to stand around looking pale and interesting and reading the small print on the backs of tins . . . until some wild idea that nobody else could ever conceivably have thought up comes roaring in like a hurricane and knocks her for six.

Great for crossword puzzles, or for murders where there's nobody actually standing over the corpse with a bloody knife when the jacks roll up. Drag in a tatty. A bit of blinking and twitching – case solved! Everybody back to bed.

Marvo crouches down and runs a finger along the shark's snout, until she comes to one of those fleshy whiskers I told you about, growing out of the corners of its mouth. 'Sharks use these things—'

'They're called barbels.'

'Whatever. To detect prey in all the crap on the sea bed.'

'Been reading the encyclopaedia again?'

'So that's what it's for.' She gives the shark another good kick. 'To build yourself a search elemental—'

'Instantiate.'

'What?'

'You don't build a search elemental. You instantiate it.' Actually, I say 'build' all the time.

'Whatever. That's what you're gonna do.'

'You think you're pretty clever.'

'I'm clever about some things, Frank.'

She turns away from me and I see something glistening on one cheek. 'God,' she mutters. 'You couldn't make this stuff up!'

Best not to think about it, then. Best to change the subject. 'While you were asleep, anyway—'

'When was I asleep?' She pokes a finger into my chest. I'm skinny. She needs to cut her fingernails. It hurts, OK?

'The Crypt Boy,' I say. 'He isn't dead.'

CHAPTER EIGHT
Birds

'**H**e isn't doing much,' I point out.

There's a thin, dark line where Ferdia began his incision at the top of the breastbone. The boy is flat on his back on the silver slab in the autopsy room. His eyes are open, but the pupils are still like pinheads. No pulse that I can detect . . .

'Turn off the lights,' I say. And when Ferdia just gives me this flat stare, 'OK, turn off the lights, *please.*'

The switch clicks. The room goes dark except for a single candle. Mr Memory steps forward to peer over my shoulder. I pick up the candle and bring it close to the boy. I raise my other hand so that my ring throws a sliver of light across his eyes. He doesn't blink; just lies there with his arms at his sides, utterly still.

I put the candle back. 'Are you cold?'

'It's a mortuary, Sampson,' Ferdia groans. 'Remember?'

'Yeah, but it's freezing.' I pull a grey woolly hat out of my pocket and cram it on my head.

Ferdia sniggers. 'Did anyone ever tell you that you look like an idiot in that?'

I'm about to stuff it back in my pocket, but I realise I'm shivering.

Ferdia turns the lights back on. 'Where's Marvell?'

'She wasn't feeling well.'

That was just outside. I'd stuck the shark back in my robing room – I was beginning to get a bit bored with lugging it up and down staircases – and I was heading for the autopsy room when I realised I'd lost Marvo again.

I found her sitting on a bench with her head in her hands. 'I'm fine,' she grunted. 'I'll be along in a minute.'

'Is she all right?' says Ferdia.

'Dunno. I've got this cloaking spell on my studio—'

Ferdia groans and puts his hands to the sides of his head. 'I wish you hadn't told me that.'

A cloaking spell is on a specific location, but it can spill over onto anybody closely bound to that location.

'Anyway,' I say, 'I think it's hit her a bit hard. Like, she's all over the place.'

'Everyone knows she fancies you.' He pulls a face. 'God knows why!'

It's true: the more someone's emotionally bound up with the focus of a cloaking spell, the more it knocks

59

them about. But I'd rather not think about that right now. And anyway, I'm colder than ever and there's something definitely not right. I lay my hand on the boy's forehead. It's like ice – so cold that it hurts.

'Ferdia, what's going on?' I turn. My foot slides out from under me and I find myself sitting on the floor.

'Stupid idiot!' Ferdia's glaring down at me.

And you know what? He's right. I *am* an idiot. It's not just cold in the autopsy room – it's *demonically* cold.

There's two ways a demon can come for you: in fire or in ice. And given that they spend most of their existence in a place where the stoves are turned up and the windows are shut tight, they usually prefer to come in ice . . .

The autopsy room isn't just freezing any more. It's arctic. The floor has frozen over. Ice crystals are spreading across the surface of the door like a coat of white fur that gets thicker and thicker until, with a sound like glass shattering, the wood splits and collapses into a pile of splinters—

And the birds come flocking in. Thousands of them – more than the room can logically contain. About the size of sparrows, but black and white with silver beaks. I've got my hands clasped over my face, but I can see them between my fingers, swirling around like a whirlwind and flying clean through Mr Memory, who's wandering around the room with a confused smile on his face.

Ferdia's curled up in the corner with his arms wrapped around his head. I'm sliding about on the icy floor, trying to get to my feet; but the birds keep punching into me.

I'm screaming, 'Adonai, Tetragrammaton!' – the usual names of God because I can't think of anything else. Maybe it's helping. But I don't think the birds are that interested in me.

Or in Mr Memory, who's starting to fade away now.

Right in front of my eyes, one of them opens its beak, wide and black as a mineshaft . . .

And swallows another bird whole. It's happening all over the room. As they gulp each other up, the birds get bigger, fewer – and louder. They're the size of magpies now, squabbling and screaming and scrabbling and swallowing, until they form a thick, twitching mass of black and white feathers that covers the boy on the slab.

And suddenly, with a deafening squawk, there's just a single stupid-looking thing, like a giant grey chicken about five feet tall, sitting on the Crypt Boy's chest, crowing triumphantly and thumping its wings on its own chest.

It lets off a gigantic fart and dumps a huge dollop of grey shit across the boy's face.

The room smells . . . unutterable. Furniture and equipment are flying everywhere.

I stagger to my feet, but a flailing wing sends me spinning backwards across the room. My shoes skid on the ice and I make a grab for the handle of one of the drawers below the bench. It comes flying out. My head cracks on the floor and I'm happy for a while, watching flickers of light explode everywhere.

I can hear flapping and scuffling, and Ferdia moaning. The flashing lights clear and, like the curtains opening at the Vaudeville, the room's back again.

I can see clean through Mr Memory to the demon, perched on the slab. The Crypt Boy's head has fallen back over the edge, exposing his throat. The beak is poised to strike—

No time to do magic. I'm rolling around in a sea of scalpels, probes and clamps—

And a small bottle. The glass has shattered, but there are still a few drops of clear liquid at the bottom.

'*Te exorcizo,*' I yell. '*Spiritus immunde*—'

OK, not very original, but at least it's Latin. I chuck the contents of the bottle across the room.

'*In nomine et virtute Domini nostri*—'

Even in flight, I see the exorcised water freeze into tiny pellets of ice that hit the demon—

And explode.

The chicken throws back its head and screams. Feathers fall like snow, only to burn up as they hit the floor. Mangy patches of bare flesh writhe through the colours of the rainbow—

62

And it transforms. The head is still a chicken – and an ugly one at that, with a white comb and beady, bright-blue eyes. It has the body of an overweight man wearing a baggy pair of blue and white striped pyjamas, with grey feathers protruding at the neck, wrists and ankles. One leg is withered, and a good six inches shorter than the other.

It seems to have just one arm, ending in a pincer like a lobster's. Unwieldy, but enough to hoist the boy over one shoulder. It squawks deafeningly again, and shambles out of the room with the kid's arms flapping behind like a pair of trousers on a washing line.

I'm trying to get to my feet. But the ice is thicker than ever and the whole room's rocking . . .

I'm up. I'm down again. Now my arse hurts too. I bang off Ferdia and out through the door. I can hear the dragging, irregular sound of the demon's feet and a sort of wheezing, clucking noise. I go after it, along the corridor. The door of the children's ice room dissolves ahead of the demon—

I'm close behind. 'Look out!' I yell.

The diener is wheeling a trolley across the space. He looks round and goes pop-eyed. He throws himself out of the way.

But here's Marvo! Stumbling in through the door at the other end, looking like she's about to fall over . . .

Despite its malformed leg, the demon is picking up speed, lumbering straight at her. I can't see very clearly because the kid is bouncing up and down, and snow-flakes are swirling around the room; but a split second before the demon crashes into her, it looks to me like Marvo just tips over – bang! Flat on her back.

The demon tries to jump over her, but with the boy over one shoulder, it hasn't a hope. One foot catches in Marvo's coat and it crash-lands the other side of her.

The entire building judders. The Crypt Boy's on his own now, tumbling through the air, arms and legs flailing like a rag doll. He lands bang on top of the trolley, which starts to roll . . .

The demon's picking itself up off the floor. The trolley hits the wall and the Crypt Boy rolls off onto the floor. The diener has scuttled behind the desk and is gibbering into his scryer, with his wide-eyed child assistant beside him.

The demon is heading for the Crypt Boy.

'Halt!' It's Caxton to the rescue, standing behind Marvo, pulling a pistol out of her coat pocket. 'Or I'll shoot.'

We did all this at Saint Cyprian's. You can't destroy a demon by shooting at it. Not even with a silver bullet. Not even with a silver bullet made from melted-down crucifixes. Not even with a silver bullet made from melted-down crucifixes that have been personally blessed by the pope.

Have we got that straight?

Clearly, however, this particular demon didn't attend

the same lectures I did. It squeals like a pig and starts blowing clouds of black smoke from every available orifice. A violent explosion knocks everybody flat on their backs.

By the time we've all picked ourselves up, the smoke has cleared and the demon has vanished without a trace.

CHAPTER NINE
Feather

'What the hell *was* that thing?'

Caxton glares around the ice room. We all stand there, still shaking and staring back at her.

'Sampson?'

I know exactly what it was. It was the demon that I caught Kazia summoning. The one I thought I'd prevented from manifesting.

'No idea,' I say.

It somehow survived the collapse of the invocation, hopelessly malformed but dead set on fulfilling Kazia's intention. Until it finally ran out of steam.

'Someone must have sent it,' says Ferdia. 'Demons don't just show up of their own accord.'

Caxton nods. 'So whoever it was . . .'

'It mattered a lot to them.'

I'm struggling to make sense of all this. If Kazia sent the demon to nail the Crypt Boy, she must have known he wasn't dead. So it must have been her

66

who did the original body magic on him.

Caxton's bored of waiting for more suggestions, and she's gone into her thinking pose. It's strikingly like her world-famous detecting pose – one foot resting on a step, elbow on knee, forefinger to her mouth – but there's more lip-pursing involved. 'So who is he, the boy?' She looks around and whispers: 'Royalty?'

'None left,' Ferdia whispers back. The royal family were all rounded up and executed in 1918. But there have always been rumours of survivors . . .

We stand around, getting older, until Caxton announces that since the Crypt Boy isn't quite as dead as everybody thought he was, and since he's clearly in danger, she's moving him somewhere safe: one of Ferdia's amphitheatres.

To be fair, it's a good choice. The three amphitheatres in the mortuary were set up for forensic rituals like establishing time of death, so there's a lot of . . . OK, not exactly magic, but *supports* for magic, built into the fabric. If she wants to create some sort of line of protection around the boy, it's as good a place as any.

The dieners unfold the kid, lay him on a trolley and wheel him out to the lift. Then the rest of us troop up the stairs, into a circular space about twenty yards across, where the dieners have parked the kid bang in the centre of two concentric copper rings, about twelve feet in diameter, set into the cedarwood floor. We start arguing about what to do next.

Caxton wants Ferdia to get kitted up, grab a stick of chalk and mark up the circles so the kid's safe if there's another attack. Ferdia says he's up for it, but I can see him hesitating.

'No offence,' I say. 'But maybe I should do it.'

Caxton looks down her nose at me. 'Are you still here?'

'Nobody told me to go away.'

'They are now. Get lost, Sampson.' She turns to Ferdia. 'Is there a problem?'

Ferdia glances at me, and it's like I can see the little wheels turning: we both know he's not absolutely sure he can do it any more.

Peak Gift is around eighteen. It's not like you wake up on your nineteenth birthday and wave your wand and nothing happens; but it's getting more and more like hard work, and by the time you're Ferdia's age – like I said, twenty-one – every time you step into a magic circle you have to sweat your socks off. By twenty-five or so, all you're good for is elemental work, like Charlie.

I asked him about it once, and Charlie said it was like you're doing everything right, but it just isn't happening and you're afraid because you know you can't trust yourself any more.

He said he thought about doing himself in.

Ferdia hasn't quite got there yet. He looks Caxton right in the eye. 'No problem.'

But I can tell he's not happy. And he's standing far enough away from Caxton that she ought to be able to read his face. Maybe she doesn't realise what's bothering him. Maybe she just doesn't care.

'So get on with it.' She looks around the amphitheatre. Mr Memory is sitting in the gallery, looking only slightly transparent.

'Where the hell did Marvell get to?' Caxton asks.

It's a fair question. I thought Marvo followed us from the ice room, but there's no sign of her now. This 'now you see me, now you don't' lark is starting to annoy me.

I'm standing beside the trolley, leaning over the Crypt Boy. He just lies there, eyes wide open, staring blankly up at the patterns of diamonds set into the domed ceiling in the shape of the major constellations.

'Now what are you up to, Sampson?'

'Just wondering what he's thinking.'

Actually, I'm more interested in the small, dark object clenched in the boy's left fist . . . and how I can get hold of it without Caxton noticing.

'Maybe you'd like to do something useful.'

'Like get lost?' I keep my body between her and Crypt Boy as I sneak the object out of his hand.

She sighs. 'Like find Marvell for me.'

The amphitheatre doors drift shut behind me. I look along the corridor: nobody watching. I examine the object.

A single grey feather.

I duck into Ferdia's robing room and steal a small black silk square. I fold it carefully around the feather and stick it in my pocket with Kazia's pentacle.

I find Marvo, still down in the children's ice room. She's got one of the compartment doors open and she's pulled out the tray so she can examine the body lying on it: a boy with half his head blown away by a gunshot. She's got this strange look on her face, like she's not really seeing him . . .

'Marvo?'

She ignores me. Just slides the tray back and closes the door.

I can't see the uniformed diener anywhere, but the kid who helps him is standing beside me. He pulls at my jerkin. 'What's up with her?'

Marvo's got another compartment open. The tray glides out. The body is small. A boy, I think, aged maybe four or five. Hard to tell, though, because the features have been deformed beyond recognition by immersion in water.

'Marvo.'

She jumps and turns.

'What's going on?'

Her eyes fill with tears. 'I thought maybe Sean would be here . . .'

CHAPTER TEN
Baby Brother

The last I heard, Marvo's baby brother was dead and buried.

'He was run over by a Ghost,' she says.

'Yeah, I know. Last year. You told me.'

It's mid-morning and we're sitting on a stone bench in the herb garden in front of the mortuary. I get the smell of horse dung from the street outside the gate. Marvo's hauled a small tin out of her pocket and she's rolling a cigarette.

'I didn't know you smoked . . .'

'I do when I'm stressed. Just for a few days, then I give up again.'

'What've you got to be stressed about?'

'Nark off, Frank.' She pulls a few loose strands of tobacco away from the end of the cigarette. 'It didn't even stop,' she says. 'The Ghost.'

I've heard all this before. It didn't make sense then. It doesn't make sense now.

When the college wars kicked off and the university started lobbing fire and brimstone back and forth, the big money got the hell out of town. And Ghosts are what they raced off in. They're big. They're fast. They're shiny. And they don't need horses to pull them.

They're propelled by magic, with an elemental sitting in the front compartment, ready to open the passenger doors and haul the jewellery and silverware out of the luggage compartment at the back.

They cost a fortune, OK? If you can afford one, you're incredibly rich or incredibly important.

Or both, of course.

'Shits!' says Marvo, striking a match.

'Yeah, except it didn't happen.' I've found a rusty nail and I'm scratching a pentagram on a paving stone. 'Look, Marvo, I told you: the elemental driving the Ghost – there's no way it could run over anybody.'

I wait while she blows smoke out.

'Not even a member of the Marvell family.'

She punches me hard in the shoulder.

'I'm sorry, but it just can't happen.'

The bloke who invented the Ghost, William Morris . . . he did tests. He got the Society to dig out a couple of dozen cows and sheep, plus a couple of poor idiots who'd been condemned to the stake for unlicensed sorcery, and chain them all up in the middle of the road. Then he told the elemental controlling a Ghost to drive right through them. Every time, no matter how powerful

72

the directive, the elemental would happily plough through the animals, but would always brake or swerve round the humans.

After a week, there were a lot of squashed cows and sheep and two gibbering idiots. So they cooked and ate the animals. And just cooked the two idiots.

Marvo's doing her sulky face. 'You don't *want* to help me.'

'No, I said I *can't* help you.'

'There were witnesses,' she mutters through a cloud of smoke. 'They said it drove right over him.'

To cover the smell of tobacco, I get up and pull a sprig from a lavender bush. I rub the leaves between my palms and bury my face in my hands. I inhale one part of the smell of magic that I got when I stepped into the summoning room, two hours ago. I see Kazia's face . . .

'It's just like you, Frank: you promise stuff, then you don't do it. You said—'

'Who investigated?'

She just looks at me.

'The jacks who handled the case – have you talked to them?'

'Must've done.'

'Don't you remember?'

If she does, there's no sign of it. She grinds the end of the cigarette into the bench beside her. Finally she says, in this dead voice: 'He was run down by a Ghost—'

73

'These witnesses . . .'

'They said it drove right over him.' She's still smearing shreds of tobacco across the stone.

'Who were they?'

Blank look. It's like there's two people in there: one who remembers she used to have a brother called Sean who got run over, and another who knows nothing about it.

There's something not quite right here. I mean, obviously it's the cloaking spell on my studio, but the symptoms . . . they should be more specific – mostly physical, a bit like flu – and specifically tied to me and my studio.

'You've spoken to Doctor Death, right?'

She shakes her head.

'I give up!' I mutter. 'Come on, then, let's go see him. Maybe it'll shut you up.'

CHAPTER ELEVEN
Doctor Death

It used to be posh, this part of Doughnut City. Big stone houses, three and four storeys high, behind iron railings.

But then the university shredded itself and the Hole opened up, and all the money jumped into its Ghosts and raced out of town, up on to Boar's Lump and down the river to Abingdon where the Society of Sorcerers' headquarters made people feel safe.

The Hole itself, it's supposed to be an absolute. What I mean is, there's a wall round most of it, so you're either *in* or *out*. On the north side, though, it sort of seeped through and spread like mould.

The walk from the mortuary down to the jack shack ... at least the buildings are still standing and there's shops, even if the windows are all covered by heavy metal grilles. You've got a reasonable chance of getting from one end of a street to another without being mugged. And the gang of kids hanging around on the corner isn't actually lobbing bricks at us.

A large dog leaps out of a derelict house and crouches in front of us, ears flat against its head, teeth bared, eyes wild. We stop dead. From the corner of my eye, I see Marvo's hand moving towards her gun.

'That won't help.'

'Just gonna scare him off.'

'No. Let me do it.'

The dog growls dangerously as I extend my hand. It shuffles forward on its belly and sniffs at the ring on my finger. It barks, then turns and runs off.

'Search elemental,' I say. 'They can get aggressive if they can't find what they're looking for.' I let a cyclist hurtle past, then head off across the street. 'Bit like you.'

As we turn the corner, I look back. The kids are staring after us. One of them crosses himself.

The jack shack is this grim fortress of a building, down the hill in Jericho. Inside, we go up two flights of linoleum-lined steps, through another set of doors and along a narrow corridor. Through the window at the end I gaze down at a narrowboat drifting past on the canal and I get this picture in my mind of me and Kazia heading down the river towards London . . .

'What are you waiting for?' Marvo gives me a shove.

I grab a metal rail and haul myself up a narrow spiral staircase. It's dark at the top and I have to fumble around until I feel a door. Before I can knock, it opens silently and a gas light flares into life.

Doctor Death opens his eyes.

He's sitting in the corner of a windowless room, squeezed up under the slope of the eaves, behind a small, bare wooden desk: a chubby, rosy-cheeked little man wearing a brown suit. He smiles and raises his hand.

Say what you like about Doctor Death, he's always pleased to see you.

There are two simple wooden chairs facing him across the desk. There are always exactly enough for any number of visitors. Not that he gets many: most people are too scared of him.

So what's he for? Every now and then, the local jacks fall over a case that demands something more complicated than grabbing someone off the street at random and hammering a confession out of them. So they haul Charlie in to build a new instance of Mr Memory: a data elemental who trails around after the investigation and remembers anything anybody might need to know later. When the case is solved, before Mr Memory is terminated he passes everything on to Doctor Death, who's lived – sort of – in this tiny office on the top floor of the jack shack ever since it was built, and retains all the data for long-term archiving. If you want to know about any crime committed in Doughnut City over the last fifty years, talk to him.

I drop into one of the chairs. 'I need to know about Sean Marvell.'

Doctor Death closes his eyes for a moment. 'Sean Joseph Marvell. Born in Naas, County Kildare—'

Marvo's standing beside me, shaking her head, but that doesn't stop him.

'—on the nineteenth of July 1947. Currently serving a life sentence for—'

'No,' I say.

'Sean *Michael* Marvell,' says Marvo.

Doctor Death frowns and closes his eyes. They reopen after a few seconds. He beams with pleasure. 'Born in Littlemore, Oxfordshire—'

'That's him,' says Marvo.

'Eighth of March 2005. Died fourth of August 2014.'

Marvo nods.

'Cause of death?' I say.

'Traffic accident,' says Doctor Death.

'Show me.'

And it's like the walls of the room have fallen away. We're still sitting in our chairs on the wooden floor, but I see overhanging trees and a cab lying on its side in the ditch, one wheel broken. The only light is from the oil that has spilled from its lamps and traced flickering paths of fire across the road.

The horse is still attached to the shafts, eyes rolling, legs spread-eagled, struggling and threshing desperately while several men – one of them a uniformed jack – wrestle with the harness. Its hooves skid on the tarmac, then find a secure purchase—

The body of a ten-year-old boy.

I can hear Marvo screaming.

'That's enough,' I say. And the walls close in again. Doctor Death sits, smiling blandly, behind his desk. His eyes drift closed. His head falls slowly forward onto his chest.

The gas light is dying.

'Come on.' I pull at the back of Marvo's chair as I get to my feet.

The door closes behind us, leaving me fumbling for the metal rail of the spiral staircase. I lurch down a couple of steps, but I'm pretty sure I won't get far—

'Where'd he get that from?' Marvo's right behind me; her voice is still shaking. 'Was someone there with a scryer?'

'You mean, at the crash site?'

I stop and turn. It's almost pitch-dark, with just a gleam of light from below. Marvo's a couple of steps up, looming over me.

'When the jacks turned up, there'd have been a data elemental.' I'm guessing, but it seems reasonable. 'It would see everything—'

'Don't you think that's suspicious? That there was a data elemental—'

79

'Someone died. It's routine. The elemental remembered what it saw and passed it on to Doctor Death.'

'Why do you call him that?'

'What *should* I call him?'

'The archive.'

I sigh. 'Like I said, Doctor Death.' I head off down the stairs again. 'And I'm sorry about your brother, but it was just a traffic accident.'

I can hear Marvo's shoes slapping on the metal steps. Her breath on the back of my head. I pull my hat out of my pocket and put it on.

'Is this because of that girl?'

'Huh?'

'Kazia.'

We're at the bottom of the stairs, beside the window looking out over the canal.

'You'd rather run around looking for her than help me.'

I was going to ask Marvo to drop me across to the mortuary so I could pick up the shark. Maybe this isn't a good time to ask. Maybe I'm more pissed off than I realise.

'I saw Kazia.'

Marvo's eyes go wide. 'Are you mad?'

I shrug. 'No more'n usual.'

'She tried to kill us!'

She sure did. Not just me and Marvo, either: Marvo's mum as well – although that's sort of understandable.

80

'I mean—' It's like the words are all mashing them-selves up in Marvo's mouth so she can't get them out. 'Did you talk to her?'

'Didn't really get the chance.'

'But you would've. Christ, Frank, you can't still fancy her. I mean, it's stupid!'

'That's not fair.'

'Look, you did six years in that sorcery joint—'

'Saint Cyprian's. And it was seven—'

'Then a year or so holed up in that bloody monastery. What the hell do you know about anything?'

I mutter, 'I know jealousy when I see it.'

So she hits me.

'Anyway, I don't want to talk about it.'

'No.' Marvo gives me a good looking-at. And I'm still wondering why I'm so interested in the fact that her eyes are a sort of greyish-brown – not blue, like Kazia's – when she mutters, 'You're a prat, Frank.'

And she turns and walks off along the corridor towards the stairs. At the last moment she stops—

'Still cutting yourself?'

When I was at Saint Cyprian's, there was this kid who crucified himself.

OK, he was weird, even by Society of Sorcerers standards. He'd already jumped off one of the pinnacles over the chapel and the idea was that angels would appear and catch him. Only they didn't . . .

81

Luckily – or not – he fell into the branches of a tree and there was a bit of bouncing and screaming before he landed on his head in a pile of manure that the gardeners were spreading around the rose beds. He woke up in the college infirmary. But he refused to believe about the tree and the manure and insisted that God really had sent angels to save him and that he must, therefore, be the Son of God.

He got out of the infirmary after a couple of weeks . . . and promptly summoned a demon to nail him to a cross.

This time he didn't make it and they carried him out in a box. But all the novices were dead impressed, and for a while we had this craze for banging sharp objects through our hands and feet.

I got really good at it. For some of the novices, I think it was a religious thing – like they thought if they emulated Jesus no demon could touch them. Me, it was a way of focusing on all the stuff I couldn't handle. A nail through my hand – I dunno, I felt sort of clean . . . as if I could deal with everything.

Such as people telling me that because I had this Gift I was special, when I didn't feel like anything much except an arsehole.

After a while I got . . . well, embarrassed by the crucifixion bit. It was just too creepy. But I liked the cutting, so I carried on with it, mainly on my arms. A bit of blood. Enough pain to feel like I'd done something to myself. Then a quick lick of magic goo. A few words. Good as new.

I'm staring at Marvo. 'How'd you know about that?'

'People talk.'

'Charlie?'

A gas light is still burning. With the cold light flickering across her face she looks like some sort of wraith.

'Well, I'm not,' I say. That's a lie, by the way. 'And I was doing fine till you came busting in.'

'Course you were.' She runs off down the stairs and I'm just about to go after her when I hear: 'Goodbye, Frank.'

And I realise I'm not supposed to.

It seems to be my day for listening to footsteps fade away into the distance. I'm just standing there with one hand on the stair rail, thinking: OK, at least I can get out of here now . . . when I hear voices below me.

'Where've you been?' Caxton to Marvo.

'Sorry, Chief. Wasn't feeling too great.'

'But you're all right now. Good. I want you in my office. What about Sampson?' Long silence. 'Did he get lost like I told him? Good.'

'No, Chief. He's upstairs.'

CHAPTER TWELVE
A Lost Tortoise

There's been an exciting change since the last time I was in Caxton's office: a shiny new desk lamp. Still the same silver talisman, though, hanging on the wall behind the desk: an owl perched on top of an open human eye. Caxton steps over to rub her finger across it; then she tosses her coat over the back of her chair and thumps down. She plonks her glasses on her nose, opens a drawer and hauls out a clean new notebook and freshly sharpened pencil. She looks up and blinks.

'So what are you two playing at?'

I make one of my occasional stabs at an expression of innocent outrage, but I don't think I've quite mastered it yet. Caxton glares at me.

'I told you to find Marvell.'

'And here she is.' I point, just in case Caxton can't see her.

'Instead, I find her wandering around the place like a lost tortoise and you lurking in the shadows like . . .'

Apparently she can't decide exactly *what* I was lurking like; so she mutters, 'Smartarse nekkers,' and turns to Marvo. 'So what happened to you?'

Marvo just stares at her.

'Back at the mortuary . . . what happened to you?'

While Marvo puzzles over this, let me fill you in on who's here. There's me, Caxton and Marvo, obviously. Ferdia is sitting by the window, still looking shaky from wrapping the Crypt Boy in magic. And Mr Memory's beside him, leaning forward to flick specks of dirt off his shiny black patent-leather shoes.

'It's Frank's fault,' says Marvo at last.

'Thanks a lot,' I mutter.

'Stupid bloody kids.' Caxton takes off her glasses and peers at the lenses. 'What's wrong with you?'

Marvo shrugs helplessly.

'I don't employ you to fall over.'

'It won't happen again.'

'It better not.' Caxton has found a handkerchief and is polishing her glasses fiercely. Without the magnifying effect of the lenses, her eyes are small, with red rims. She looks scared of . . . well, of everything.

Until she looks up. I don't know if it's just the effort of having to struggle to focus on me, but she's got this mad look on her face like she's going to jump up and punch me.

'Hang on,' I splutter. 'You don't think *I* sent it . . .'

'One of your little friends . . . ?'

85

'I don't *have* any little friends.'

Marvo's got this wounded expression on her face. Ferdia smirks.

'There must be some way of tracing it back.' Caxton turns to Ferdia. 'Demons have to be invoked, right? So you can do contiguity . . .'

'Not on a demon.'

'Why not? If any two people or objects come into contact with each other, that creates an eternal magical link between them. A contiguity.' She looks up at me. 'And a sorcerer can detect that link, right?'

'Top of the class, Beryl.'

It's not often that Caxton smiles. When she does, it's like you've fallen asleep long enough for a completely different person to come in and take her place.

It doesn't last long. She looks from me to Ferdia. 'So what's the problem?'

'Contiguity can only exist between physical objects,' I say. 'A demon is a non-physical being—'

'Try telling that to the boy.'

'Think of it as a force, like the wind.' OK, I'm over-simplifying like hell. 'It can knock you over but there's nothing you can grab hold of.'

'No contiguity,' says Ferdia.

'A demon has a spiritual affinity with the operator who summoned it up,' I say. 'But like Ferdia says, no physical contiguity.'

Glasses on. Caxton is printing in her notebook: NO

86

CONTIGUITY. 'So neither of you has anything useful to suggest . . .'

Ferdia's shaking his head. Caxton pushes her chair back. She puts one finger to her lips, then touches the silver talisman on the wall again. 'I've notified the Society.'

'Not a good idea,' I say, catching Ferdia's eye.

Calling in the Society is *never* a good idea.

'As I understand it, summoning a demon is a lot of hard work.'

I nod.

'So this kid must be very important to somebody.' She looks over her shoulder and whispers, 'Maybe some of the royal family *did* survive . . .'

It's clouded over outside and the room has gone dark. Caxton leans forward to switch her desk lamp on. But someone forgot to change the battery and all she gets is a dim glow. 'Bugger!' The Blur. She goes red and shoves her notebook in Marvo's face. 'What does that say?'

'Short. Feathers. Male.'

'All demons are male.'

'Like sorcerers,' Marvo mutters.

Caxton glares at her. 'What's that supposed to mean?'

I say quickly, 'The only person who knows who sent the demon is probably the Crypt Boy.'

'What if they send another one?'

Right now, I'm more worried that Marvo is going to have another of her famous insights and pipe up that Kazia has to have something to do with the Crypt Boy.

It's one of the things the Society is very insistent upon: unlicensed sorcerers are a Bad Thing. Kazia's more or less responsible for three deaths that I know of. If I hadn't messed up the ritual in the summoning room, I think she'd have made that four. But I don't think she deserves to wind up screaming on top of a stack of burning wood. She's not evil, just desperate and a bit bonkers.

Like me.

You want the real truth? I figure that maybe if I can save her, she might, you know . . .

Yeah, I know. I'm a prat, like Marvo said.

Ferdia's staring out of the window.

'So what am I supposed to do?' Caxton grumbles. 'Just wait around for the next demon to turn up?' She glares across the desk at Marvo. 'What's wrong with you?' she snarls. 'I don't employ you for your policing skills. You're a tatty and I expect insights.'

Marvo's staring down at the floor. And actually, Caxton's got a point. I've seen Marvo come up with stuff nobody else could've figured out. She spotted what the shark was for, quick as a flash. I know I haven't told her about what Kazia was up to in the mortuary – at least, I don't think I did . . .

And I'm sitting there wondering why Marvo seems to be broken, and hoping she doesn't choose now to start working again—

When I hear the shuffle of horses' hooves from outside. Ferdia beckons. 'Sampson . . .'

Caxton's window overlooks the street outside the jack shack. Two riders are dismounting from their big white horses. Knights of Saint Cyprian. The Society of Sorcerers' goon squad. Bronze helmets. Black capes over silver breastplates. Swords. They look like something out of a pantomime.

Dangerous, though, when your licence is suspended – probably revoked altogether by now – and you're supposed to be on a pilgrimage to Rome.

A big shiny, grey vehicle has drawn up behind them. No horses: it's a Ghost. A figure in a black uniform steps out from the driver's compartment at the front and walks round to open one of the doors at the back. A man in a dark overcoat gets out. As he looks round, I see a fringe of tonsured silver hair and a heavily scarred face.

A split second before he looks up, I jump back out of sight. I recognised him immediately. Ignacio Gresh. The Society's Grand Inquisitor and a leading member of the Frank Sampson Appreciation Society.

I hate it when the Society pays house calls. Marvo'll have to look after herself. I've got to get out of here.

* * *

I slip out of the back door into the yard behind the jack shack. A horse shuffles in the shafts of a van, so that it can get a good look at me. I walk quietly round to the archway leading out to the street.

Nobody in sight, apart from a passing cyclist . . . and the driver of the Ghost, standing there like a statue, holding the reins of the Knights' horses.

He's an elemental. That's how Ghosts work.

I can hear a bell tolling somewhere; and the iron wheel-rims of an omnibus grinding its way along Walton Street, up at the top of the hill.

It's not that cold; but I open my satchel and pull out my woolly hat. Officially, the Society is a religious order so I'm supposed to shave my head into a tonsure, like Gresh. There are two reasons for this. It's a sign of devotion; and it's meant to stop demons being able to grab you by the hair – although I reckon that if a demon wants to grab you, it'll always find something. But whatever the point, it's not a good look. So I just shave my entire head clean every morning. Almost every morning, anyway. I was otherwise engaged today.

Having my head shaved isn't an automatic giveaway that I'm a sorcerer; but it's a reason for people to look at me. And there are a surprising number of people who, once they get a good look at you, can spot a sorcerer. I want to get back to my place in one piece. I jam my hat on and head up the hill. The driver ignores me. It's like he's been switched off.

If anyone bothered to ask him, though, he'd re-member me.

Twenty minutes later I pitch up at the mortuary and ask if I can get something from my old robing room. They tell me to get lost.

CHAPTER THIRTEEN

Affinity

I've got a termite nest to get into.

Actually, it's a monastery; and the termites are Agrippine monks: a small order set up to keep sorcerers like me safely tucked up in bed until Satan gets around to coming to gobble us up.

For once, the Anti-Sorcery Brotherhood aren't hanging around outside the front gate; but they've left a new calling-card chalked on the wall opposite: a crude drawing of a burning five-pointed star with a scrawled inscription: 'Rot in hell!'

I ring the bell. The gate opens.

Brother Thomas is my least favourite termite. 'Brother Tobias?' He gasps, and fumbles for his spectacles.

That's me, by the way. Let's stick to Frank.

I don't have to push him over; his eyes roll up in their sockets and he goes over backwards with a thump that shakes the city. I have that effect on quite a few people these days. I step over him and sneak across the cloister, past the chapel, from where I can hear the sound of frantic praying. I haven't eaten all day and I'm starving. I duck into the kitchen.

In the good old days the termites used to leave food around the place for me. Since I built my cloaking spell, that's all stopped. I hack off a few slices of bread and a lump of mouldy cheese. And while I'm at it, I grab a couple of handfuls of cinnamon and cloves for my studio – almost as far gone as the cheese, but I can work around that . . .

The termites are still howling away to themselves. I nip across the vegetable garden towards my studio, where we can stop for a moment to admire the magic that sent Brother Thomas flat on his back.

Nice work, my cloaking spell, even if I say so myself. It's kind of like an invisibility spell except that this time it's my entire studio that's disappeared. Not literally; it's misdirection. The building's still there, but people find more interesting things to look at instead. And anybody who gets really close to it . . . they just fall over.

Always backwards, for some reason.

The entire outside wall of my studio is covered with symbols drawn in red and black paint. There's all the usual stuff, and what looks like a wobbly, eight-pointed star but is actually an octopus. It took me a whole night to get it bang in the middle of the wall and draw the long, twisting arms with dozens of small circles, each containing a symbol. It's a miracle I got away with it, even with all the termites locked in the chapel. It's even more of a miracle that I didn't die of boredom or writer's cramp.

Anyway, much as I'd like to, I can't stand around here all night patting myself on the back. I close the outside door behind me. At the end of the corridor, I touch the surface of another door. For a split second, the wood twitches into the head of a wolf. It barks enthusiastically. I tickle it between the ears and the door swings open.

My studio was never much to look at: just a disused chapel with a fireplace at one end, where the altar used to be, and an iron stove at the other. One small stained-glass window, high up in the wall. A photograph of an old Japanese bloke: Pope Innocent XVII. Tiled floor: cold, but good for drawing on with chalk. Stone walls: even colder than the floor . . . and damp.

It's pretty much a tip. The last time the Society paid a visit, they left the joint looking like a tornado had hit it. One chair lived to tell the tale; I've used the others for kindling. I mended the bench, so I'd have somewhere to repair and repurify the instruments they smashed, and to prepare herbs; I screwed a couple of the shelves back onto the wall; I managed to round up most of my white rats and stick them back in the cage; and I've swept up the broken glass and cleared enough floor space to make magic. The place could be worse.

But I get tired, and some days I'd rather stay in what's left of my bed: a mattress, all slashed and oozing stuffing. I throw myself back onto the pile of dirty sheets and blankets, pull off my boots and lob them across the room.

A small dog with blue ears scampers out of nowhere with a yelp of delight and starts licking the soles enthusiastically.

I manage to raise my arm, but I'm too far gone to read my watch. I close my eyes. But I can't sleep. The dog's claws scratch on the tiles. And there's this thin, dragging whine in my ears like somebody's passed a needle clean through my head and they're pulling a long, long thread through with it . . .

I jump to my feet as a deafening crash shakes the studio. I know what it is and I know where it comes from. Strictly speaking, it isn't real. It's just in my head. Alastor reminding me that he's bored of being stuck down in the cellar with Matthew.

My heart has agreed to start beating again. Even if I could sleep, I don't have time. I haul myself across to my bench . . .

Six hours later I'm still there, holding my head and wondering how I'm going to do this.

I've spent the evening fixing and repurifing the instruments I need. Two white candles flutter. The plume of smoke rising from a brass brazier smells of the lavender and rosemary I used for the fumigations.

I've calculated and recalculated the planetary alignments. I don't normally bother with all that astrological shit – as a working forensic sorcerer you can't ask the jacks to leave the bodies lying around for a couple of weeks, until Jupiter condescends to wander into the house of Mercury or whatever. But if you want that extra punch, planets are your friend.

I've got it all worked out. The place: a magical convergence outside the city in Wytham Wood. The time: just before two o'clock in the morning, when a few planets are in the right place. The symbols and smells. The right words in roughly the right order.

But I could've done with that shark. The barbels, anyway.

It's your basic sympathetic magic, innit? I want to sniff Kazia out. I could mince up a bloodhound's nose, but a nurse shark's barbels are better. I was going to build myself a search elemental that wouldn't take no for an answer and would winkle Kazia out before she got the chance to zap it.

But of course the bloody shark's locked in the mortuary. I could hike out to Marvo's mum's place and ask Marvo to help me get it back, but I'm not in the mood to grovel, and I don't think she's that keen to help me.

And I'm tired. It's not just the whine and the explosions in my head. Any spell, it's like you feed a bit of yourself into it. I've had the cloaking spell up for nearly three weeks and I can feel it sort of nagging at me, dragging on my stomach. I wish I could just go to bed and sleep until I go post-peak and all my problems solve themselves . . .

I've had enough. I open the cabinet and start putting the cutlery away. The black-handled knife goes in a silver box lined with blue silk. I turn for the white-handled knife. I run my finger along the razor-sharp edge of the blade and get a whisker of blood. I lick it away. I told Marvo I wasn't cutting myself any more, but that's a lie. What else is a boy to do when he's shut up with only a door and a dog to keep him company.

It's at my feet, the dog, staring up at me with one paw raised, whimpering hopefully. The cut in my fingertip is still oozing tiny red beads. I lean down and offer it. The dog yelps and I feel its tongue brush across my skin.

I could give it something to get really excited about. I roll up my sleeve and lay my arm flat on the bench, palm up. The tip of the knife is sharp against my skin.

The candlelight glints along the blade . . .

Does it matter if I don't find Kazia? She doesn't seem to be missing me – she's got useful things to do like sending demons to polish the Crypt Boy off.

The thing is, though: the Society doesn't take kindly to people summoning demons without authorisation.

Ignacio Gresh will move heaven and earth to find out who sent a Presence to mash the Crypt Boy. So if I don't get to her first, Kazia has an appointment with a stack of dry wood.

Her pentacle of Solomon glints as it revolves on its gold chain. I've put the knife safely away. I've got a silk square open in front of me. Lying on it, one small, grey feather.

When Ferdia told Caxton that you can't trace who conjured up a particular demon, I kept my mouth shut. True, Ferdia couldn't have done it, even before he hit peak Gift. But I'm better than he ever was, and I reckon I *can* do it. A demon may not have a contiguity with whoever summoned it; but what it does have is an *affinity*. It's not a physical link, it's more . . . spiritual. That's why, every time you summon a demon, you have a ritual sword that you wave around to symbolically sever the affinity and stop the demon bouncing back at you next time it fancies a brain salad.

OK, so it's just a feather. But according to the magical rule of synecdoche, part of a thing can stand in for the whole. If I have the feather, I have the demon.

The demon has an affinity with Kazia. The pentacle has contiguity with her. And when I find her, maybe she'll tell me who the Crypt Boy is and why someone wants him dead . . .

Marvo'd appreciate that.

Why am I thinking about Marvo?

I spend two hours hunting through what's left of my books and scrawling symbols and equations on virgin parchment. Finally, everything's ready.

I wrap my instruments. I fold the silk square carefully around the feather. I stuff everything into my satchel, and knock back a dose of my special wake-up juice. It kicks me hard in the stomach, but it clears my head like a stiff brush down a lavatory. I bounce out of my studio, into the cold night air . . .

CHAPTER FOURTEEN
Naked Magic

At the bottom of the steps outside my studio, the whining noise in my head doesn't quite drown out the tuneless wailing from the chapel.

I take a moment to admire my handiwork, scrawled across my studio wall; then I push into the bushes, trying not to get snagged up on the thorns, and fight my way into the corner. I grab the drainpipe and stick my left foot on one of the supporting brackets. My right foot jams into a hole in the masonry, and after a bit of a struggle I find myself peering over the top of the back wall into the alley that runs behind the monastery.

I can't see anybody lurking to jump out at me, so I roll over and drop down. I look around again: all safe. I make another check through my satchel – wolfskin that I cured and tanned myself, sewn with red silk thread and fastened with silver buckles.

No, I didn't kill the wolf with my bare hands – although the *Liber Bonifacii* insists that I should've . . .

The moon is peering over the houses, pale and open-mouthed like it's upset to see me off on the rampage again. According to my watch, it's just after ten o'clock. It's freezing and I'm under-dressed, as usual; so collar up, hat pulled down . . .

I can't afford to blow money on a cab, so I walk. Halfway down the hill to Saint Clement's, I think I hear footsteps following me, but when I stop and look round, the road behind is empty. I walk on, faster, but I can't quite shake the suspicion. As soon as I turn the corner at the bottom, I sprint till I'm nearly bursting and collapse into the porch of the church, where I wait, heart pounding . . .

For nothing, apparently. When I've finished chalking a pentagram on the wall, I peek out. There's a police van rattling along the road and a couple of drunks yelling; nobody with any interest in me.

I head off over the meadows and across the Cherwell, round the north wall of the Hole, and over the Isis. I still haven't managed to throw off the idea that I'm being followed, but I can't see anything – unless you count six horses in a field who follow me along the fence, their breath forming clouds in the crystal-cold air. They probably want their noses rubbed, but I'm pushed for time, and magic and horse-slobber don't mix.

Finally, I'm at the edge of Wytham Wood. Last glance around: all clear. My satchel weighs a ton, so I swing it over the other shoulder before jumping the ditch and pushing through the undergrowth into the trees.

A sharp, cold wind springs up to fight me as I struggle uphill along a dangerously slippery path that twists and turns through the trees. I duck under an ancient holly tree, split right down the middle of the trunk, with ribbons tied to its branches. Some are recent – I can even make out the colours, red and blue in the light of the setting moon. Most have been there for years and are just tatters of loose threads fluttering in the breeze. People from the village think the ribbons will make wishes come true.

If only.

Owls screech in the branches above me as I break into an awkward trot, with my satchel bouncing against my hip. Suddenly, an abrupt clatter of wings . . .

And utter silence.

The wind dies. I step out of the trees, look around, and scuttle across open ground to a rickety wooden shed. Inside, I push a stack of timber aside and dig out a bundle wrapped in oilcloth. I stagger up to the bare top of the hill, where the ground sinks into a deep crater from whose rim three huge shapes cast long black shadows.

The stones are about twelve feet tall, one of them narrowing at the top to resemble the shoulders and head of a cowled figure. The locals call them the Weird Sisters. But then they would, wouldn't they?

I don't come here often – that final slog uphill is a killer and I'm resting with my hands on my knees, gasping for breath. But the great thing about it is that nobody's going to bother me because the place is supposed to be haunted.

My watch says it's eleven forty-five. The moon has set. The stars glisten in a cloudless sky. It's the perfect time and place to do magic. I slide down the side of the crater and feel a chill as I pass through the shadows cast by the stones. This place isn't just spooky; it's eerie. It was the Boss who first brought me here, seven years ago. He described it as a magical conjuncture, a place where natural energies reach a pitch of intensity that a skilful sorcerer can tap into.

Whatever.

I unwrap the oilcloth and lift out a small brazier, a sharp wooden stake, a mallet and a length of cord. I unpack my satchel. Wands and knives. The sheet of parchment: my crib sheet. Sachets of herbs, spices and precious stones. The silk-wrapped feather from the demon. Kazia's pentacle of Solomon . . .

I hammer the stake into the flat ground at the bottom of the crater, then use the cord and a knife to mark out a series of concentric circles in the dirt. I scratch symbols between them and drop amethysts and jasper around the place.

The wind has dropped. The owls are back in the trees, sending soft, sad calls drifting through the darkness. The brazier is glowing at the centre of the circle, next to the blue silk square where I've laid out my instruments and materials.

What I'm about to instantiate is a monster elemental, a powerful entity that'll go out there and find Kazia and won't take no for an answer.

Ready to go . . . except for one final detail. I get my kit off. Jerkin, jumper, jeans, shoes and socks, vest and underpants. I pull off my ring and park it out of harm's way, in the pocket of my jeans. Bollock-naked and shivering, I dive back into the circle and grab my knife—

'Adonai, most high, deign to bless and to consecrate this knife, that it may show the necessary virtue through thee, O most holy Adonai, whose kingdom endureth through all the ages. Amen.'

I seal the circle with my knife and manage not to scream as I pour a bottle of exorcised water over myself.

'O creature of water, cleanse me of all impurities and uncleanliness and wash away all delusion, so that no wickedness may still find place within me. Amen.'

To do magic, a sorcerer normally wears a robe decorated with symbols to assist the process, and exorcised to prevent either it or the sorcerer from contaminating the procedure.

But tonight I want an affinity.

In the bad old days, if you wanted to find somebody,

you had to give a bloodhound an item of clothing or whatever to sniff. Around 1890 they discovered how to instantiate an elemental that has a magically induced contiguity with whoever or whatever you're looking for. It's a bit like a Ghost, where the passenger's intention creates an artificial contiguity between the elemental driving the vehicle and the desired destination.

Anyway, I'm trying to explain why I'm standing around, soaking wet and freezing my arse off, stark naked in the middle of nowhere. One of the things I discovered when I was a novice at Saint Cyprian's – one of the things nobody would believe – was that desire is a force like contiguity. If you want something badly enough it's like there's an affinity with whoever or whatever you want.

With my kit off, there's nothing between my physical form and the rest of the world. Simple. OK, a bit creepy too. I open a small bottle of my own blood. I dip a quill pen into it and spend half an hour drawing symbols all over my body, using a mirror to see round the corners.

I'm shaking with cold now. And when I look at myself in the mirror . . . it doesn't bear thinking about. I put the mirror on the ground and smash it with a stone. I hang Kazia's pentacle around my neck. I unfold the silk square and run the tip of my finger along the spine of the feather, and I'm just trying to imagine that I can feel its affinity with her when I hear a voice—

'Will this help?'

A ragged white bundle unwinds as it tumbles down the side of the crater and finally spits out a four-foot nurse shark. I look up and see Marvo grinning back at me from the rim of the crater.

CHAPTER FIFTEEN

Two Elementals or
One Elemental Twice

It's like I'm outside my own body, floating in mid-air and staring down at this bald, skinny little runt who's squatting down there in the dirt, shivering like a skinned rabbit, staring wildly around . . .

I know what that little runt's thinking: should he just run for it? Is there any way he can pretend this isn't happening?

'I'm not a perv!' he yells.

Wham! I'm back on the ground and *I'm* the skinny little runt in the circle. Someone's laughing.

'I have to do it like this.' I can hear my own voice echoing back at me off the three standing stones – shrill, like a cracked trumpet.

'So get on with it.' Marvo's sitting with her legs dangling over the rim of the crater, grinning down at me. I notice that she's swapped her black trousers for a pair of jeans.

107

'Don't be stupid!' My famous sense of humour has deserted me. 'Turn round—'

'No way!' She's swinging her feet up and down so her heels bang off the ground and clods of earth run down the slope. 'Let's see some action.'

'How did you find me?'

I get my answer as this kid a few years older than me pops up beside her, waving and smirking like a gargoyle. Brother Andrew, one of the monks from the termite nest: grey habit, tonsured carrot-coloured hair, buck teeth and all. My humiliation is complete.

'He knows all the places you go,' says Marvo.

'Come on,' Andrew jeers. 'We haven't got all night!'

He's going to pay for this; but I haven't got time right now. I kneel over the shark and hack off the barbels. I ought to take an hour to purify them. I ought to chop them up. The world is largely made up of things I ought to do . . .

Marvo slides off the rim and scuttles down beside me. 'The word you're looking for is "thankyou".'

I take a moment to consider changing the spell and blasting her and Andrew back to Oxford. Later, maybe. Right now, she's staring at the sorcerer's mark across my chest. It's like a tattoo, but it isn't; it's my licence from the Society of Sorcerers to practise magic. It looks like one of my magic circles: a series of concentric blue rings with symbols in black and red . . .

'What happened there?'

I shiver and jump back as her fingertips brush across the outermost circle, where a couple of symbols have vanished, leaving a gap in the design.

'I lost my licence, remember?'

'I thought they just suspended it.'

'I guess they had second thoughts.'

Symbol by symbol, the mark is disappearing. It'll be gone in a month or so. Luckily, it doesn't affect my ability to work magic. Kazia doesn't have a licence and that doesn't hold her back. It just means that, like her, I'm toast if I'm caught at it . . .

'What are you doing here, anyway?' I ask. 'I mean—'

Marvo is down on one knee, reaching for the feather.

'Don't touch!' I slap her hand away.

She jumps up and punches me back. 'What's it for?' Her eyes widen. 'The demon in the mortuary—' Her eyes go wider still. 'Caxton'll kill you!'

'So don't tell her.'

'Christ, you've been busy.'

And Marvo gives me this look. It starts at my head, where it flickers from my eyes to my shaved skull and back again. It moves down to the pentacle and the sorcerer's mark across my chest. It darts down, just for a split second, then back to my face.

We both blush.

'Yeah.' Andrew's nineteen, but he's got a giggle like a five-year-old. 'Get on with it.'

'Out of the way, then.'

I wait while Marvo scrambles up the side of the crater and settles beside Andrew. My fingers are numb with cold, but I manage to pick up my wand with one hand and the feather with the other. This'd better work, or I'll be seriously pissed off.

I kiss the feather. 'Adonai, Tetragrammaton—'

'You gotta be joking, right?' That's Marvo's idea of being helpful.

It's an hour later and I'm shivering so badly that I can barely get my jumper over my head. 'It's your fault,' I moan.

'How?'

'Throwing this thing around the place.' I kick the shark, which is lying on the ground gathering dirt. 'What chance did I have?'

'Maybe you just made a mistake.'

'I don't—'

'—make mistakes. Yeah, we've heard that one before.'

'And it doesn't help, you and him' – I'm pointing at Andrew – 'sitting up there giggling at me.'

All the way through the ritual I had this idea that Andrew wasn't just watching me intently; he was watching a particular *part* of me intently.

'Funny's funny. Get used to it.' Marvo turns and points. 'So what about them two?'

Them two . . . they're not really what I planned. Identical twins, about three feet tall. Each with the body of a shark, only sort of squeezed up till it's almost spherical, with two stubby legs growing out of their sides and ending in scaly, clawed feet. They stomp up and down at the bottom of the crater, grinning at each other. Then they both stand on one leg, put the spare claw round each other and look up at me and chorus:

'OK, boss?'

Some monster elemental! They look totally stupid and incredibly conspicuous. Especially with the single grey feather sticking out of the top of each of their heads. I doubt if they could find their own arses, let alone Kazia.

I could blame Marvo for bouncing the shark around; or her and Andrew for staring at me. But the truth is, I messed up. It's another of those things they told us to watch out for at Saint Cyprian's. The entire ritual was overdetermined: I was all worked up and I just threw too much stuff at it. The feather. The pentacle. The shark. All tangled up.

I've got a picture in my mind where I go over to the Weird Sisters and start banging my head off them. Instead, I kneel and tip a few herbs into my hand. 'Adonai, Tetragramm—'

'What are you doing?' says Marvo.

'You said it yourself, they're a joke.'

'Yeah, but they're a cute joke.' Marvo tickles one of the elementals, just behind the protruding feather, and they both giggle. 'Give 'em a crack at it – what've you got to lose?'

'My dignity?'

'You lost that when you took your kit off.'

I look down at the two elementals. They grin back up at me: two mouthfuls of wonky teeth. 'Oh Christ!'

The grins fade. 'Boss . . . ?'

I snap, 'Don't call me that!'

Despair is always a tempting option. I want to crawl back to bed, pull the blankets over my head and pretend none of this ever happened.

The thing is, the feather from the demon went up in smoke twenty minutes ago, along with the potent bits of the shark; so unless I want to start again, right from scratch, I've got no choice. Marvo's right, as usual: I've nothing to lose.

'Oh, what the hell. I'm gonna call you Preston.'

'We'd be proud and honoured, boss.' They look at each other and murmur dreamily, 'Preston . . .'

I take off Kazia's pentacle and dangle it in front of them. They sort of sniff it, then stand there looking at each other.

'So get on with it.'

They know my intention. They both turn and start

clambering towards the crater rim. I run after them and grab one by the tail.

'You stay.'

His twin has stopped and is staring back at me.

'You go.' That's how it works: one does the searching, the other hangs around with me and jumps up and down when his twin has followed the affinity to Kazia. 'And for God's sake stay out of sight!'

'OK, boss. Whatever you say.'

I pull my jerkin on while I watch him scramble to the top of the crater and duck ostentatiously behind one of the standing stones. After a moment, his face re-appears. He looks around, one foot raised to shade his eyes. He runs across to vanish behind another stone—

'Don't overdo it.'

'Sorry, boss,' says the Preston beside me. 'Whatever you say.'

I look down at him. 'And you, heel.'

There's a voice from the distance: 'OK, boss. Whatever you say.'

Marvo mutters, 'OK, maybe you *are* wasting your time.'

Preston looks up at her. 'Hey, give us a break, willya?'

CHAPTER SIXTEEN
Power

It was a hard slog coming up through the woods. Even downhill, it's a hard slog going back. Preston keeps falling over his own feet.

'Sorry, boss.'

'Just pay attention and get on with it.' The oilcloth bundle is back in its hiding place. I've got my satchel over my shoulder. Marvo's cradling the shark, wrapped up in the sheet again.

'Listen,' I say to her. 'You didn't have to bring me that.' I nod towards the shark.

'I couldn't leave it lying around the mortuary.'

I'm still shivering. I got chilled to the bone, dancing around back there, and I don't think I'll ever warm up again.

'You're a fool, Frank,' Marvo says quietly.

I know I am; I know I'm letting her down. So I don't need Andrew sniggering, 'Well, we all knew that!'

114

'She's only interested in what she can get from you.' Marvo means Kazia, obviously.

'That's not important.'

'Yeah, yeah. I know. If the Society gets hold of her . . . blah, blah, blah . . .'

'I'm not a complete fool,' I mutter. 'I realise she's only interested in staying clear of me.'

'So why are you doing it?'

I shrug. 'It's not really about her, anyway.'

Marvo's been on her scryer, so at least there's a ride waiting for us down in the village. Some of the new vans have heaters inside – OK, just a tin box full of hot bricks – as well as pneumatic tyres. Not this one. My teeth have started to rattle almost as loudly as the wheels.

'So what *is* it about?' Marvo's sitting across from me with her nose wrinkled up. The shark has managed to wriggle its head out from the sheet and is eyeing her like she's its lunch.

I look round from drawing a pentagram in the dirt on the window. 'Huh?'

'Kazia. If it's not really about her—'

'Doesn't matter.' What it's about is that as long as I'm chasing around after Kazia, I can forget all the other stuff. How I get the Society off my back. What I do about—

'What about your boss?' Sometimes it's like Marvo can read my thoughts.

'Matthew?'

'Where is he?'

'Where d'you think?'

Marvo was there when I left Alastor to look after Matthew. And that tame sorcerer he had – the one that I was telling you about? Yeah: Kazia. And it was Matthew who told her to rub out me, Marvo and her mum.

'He'll starve.'

'I took care of that.'

'You can't just leave him there for ever. You have to talk to the Society, Frank.' And I'm just making a mental list of all the reasons this is a bad idea when— 'Jesus, this thing stinks!' Marvo elbows Andrew in the ribs. 'Open the window.'

He blinks nervously as she leans across him and pushes the front end of the shark out into the big wide world.

I grab the tail. 'Hey! I need that. There's all sorts of stuff—'

'Then look after it yourself.' She heaves the shark across to me.

'I'm sorry,' I say.

'Huh?'

'For dragging you out all over the place. This *was* good of you . . .' I pat the shark. 'I mean, I know you—'

'Know I what?'

'I dunno. Disapprove.'

'I hate her, OK?' She turns to Andrew. 'Will you shut that bloody window?' Back to me: 'I just don't want to feel I helped get her killed, that's all.'

I don't say anything. Know what I'm thinking, though? That the only reason Marvo dug the shark out of the mortuary was because she realised I'd never forgive her if she didn't help me save Kazia.

And thinking this . . . it gives me, I dunno, a sense of power. Which makes me feel dead uncomfortable.

So apparently, what happened, anyway: Marvo rolled up at the termite nest with the shark about five minutes after I went over the wall. She grabbed Andrew and they came after me. They got lucky and reached the bottom of Headington Hill just in time to see me duck into the church porch. After that, they simply had to follow me on foot—

'Hang on. You asked for me at the front door?'

'How else was I supposed to find you?' Marvo points at Andrew. 'He was on the gate. Said you'd sneaked out . . .'

'Yeah,' says Andrew. 'I saw you climb over the wall—'

'You saw me? What about my studio?'

'Clear as day.'

'What's the problem?' Marvo asks.

She asked for it. 'There's a cloaking spell on my

117

studio.' I watch her clutch her head. 'Nobody should be able—'

Marvo's rocking backwards and forwards in her seat. I put a hand under her elbow to steady her, but she just lashes out.

'I know you did something to it – I watched you.' Andrew does one of his famous graveyard chuckles. 'You looked pretty stupid dancing around in front of it.' He chuckles again. 'Almost as stupid as tonight!'

You can hide buildings with a cloaking spell – even an entire city, if you've got the time. But a significant flaw is that anyone who watches you cast it is immune.

'It's been fun watching all the brothers fall down.' Andrew's laughing like a drain now, his hand over his mouth to cover his buck teeth.

Preston joins in for a moment; then, seeing that I'm not laughing, puts on a straight face.

'So you didn't tell anyone . . . ?'

Andrew attempts a sinister smile. 'Who's to say?'

I match his sinister smile. 'I have ways of finding out.'

He blinks. 'I didn't tell anyone.'

'Good.'

'It's too much fun watching them all fall over.' He grins.

Preston chortles, his mouth a tangled mass of glistening white, razor-sharp teeth.

* * *

118

For some reason I thought that Marvo would drive off with the van, and leave me and Andrew to deal with the shark. But of course she doesn't. When I jump out, she tells the driver to get lost, and we all trail off round the back of the termite nest and stare up at the wall. All twelve feet of it.

'Where the hell are we, anyway?' says Marvo, like she's never been here before.

'I'm fine now.' I pass the shark to Andrew and lob my satchel over the wall. I turn back to Marvo. 'You can leave us to it. Andrew'll help me, yeah?'

But before Andrew can even open his mouth, Marvo says, 'But I thought you were gonna help me find out who killed Sean?'

'It's waited a year. It can wait a bit longer.'

'But you promised.'

For the record, I never promised her a thing. I've told her all along she's wasting her time. 'Gimme a break.' I worm my fingers into a crack and get my foot up to an iron peg hammered into the mortar. A push and a wriggle—

'I brought you that.' Looking down from the top of the wall, I see her punch the shark.

'Go home, Marvo.'

She looks up at me with these big disappointed eyes and I can't help wondering: does she practise in a mirror? She turns and heads dejectedly off up the alley.

'OK, Andrew,' I say.

But just as he steps up to the wall with the shark, the tinny cracked rattle of the chapel bell echoes across the inside of the termite nest.

The shark hits the ground with a squelch. Andrew's up the wall like a ferret up a trouser leg. He vaults over the top, nearly taking me with him, and lands inside with a crash—

'Sorry, Brother!' And he's a dot in the distance, scampering off towards the chapel.

Nothing else for it, then. 'Marvo!'

CHAPTER SEVENTEEN
Bat's Blood

A few minutes later, Marvo's managed to get the shark over her head. Weight-lifting isn't her sport and I can see her arms trembling, but I just manage to lean down and grab it by the tail before she lets go. The sheet falls over her head and she's stumbling around in circles like a kid dressed up as a Halloween ghost, trying to pull it off.

Suits me. I've got loads to do, and I don't need her breathing down my neck and telling me I'm a prat. She'll enjoy the walk home . . .

'Thanks. See you later.' I roll off the inside of the wall and drop into the bushes.

The chapel bell is still clanging away. At least all the termites will be safely shut away, praying like Methodists. Preston bounces and giggles. A moment later, Marvo crash-lands beside him.

'Look,' she says. 'If you think I came all this way——'
And the cloaking spell kicks in. Her eyes glaze over.

One shaking hand clutches her head . . . and she falls flat on her back at my feet.

Preston seems to be immune to the spell, which is encouraging: if my magic can't knock him out, hopefully Kazia's can't either. He tickles Marvo's cheek with one clawed foot. She groans and sneezes. Her eyes flutter open.

'Not feeling too good,' she mumbles.

I've lost the shark, but I don't think it's going anywhere so I haul Marvo to her feet. What I want to do is bundle her back over the wall and get rid of her, but I realise it isn't going to happen. I look around: all clear. I lead her out of the bushes towards my studio. For the first few yards she's at least trying to help, moving her legs like a swimmer. But then this stupid grin comes over her face and she goes limp on me, and I just have to drag her, the toes of her shoes leaving two grooves in the gravel.

I built the spell, so I know what to expect. At the foot of the steps I bend her over so she can throw up in the lavender. The grin has gone; she's dripping with sweat and shivering so violently that I can barely hold her.

'They've poisoned me,' she croaks. 'Call an ambulance.'

I haul her up the steps and manage to get the outside door open.

'C'mon, nearly there.'

No reply. I don't know what she's seeing, but I'm pretty sure it's not the stone-flagged corridor leading to my studio. I kick the outside door shut. For a moment we're in total darkness. Then I hear sharp little barking noises and a sliver of light spills across the flagstones as my inside door swings open.

'Say hello to Auntie Magdalena.' Magdalena Marvell, I ask you!

I hold her up. The wolf's head emerges from the surface of the door and gives her a long, wet lick across the cheek.

'Where am I?'

'My luxury residence.'

She's got the use of her legs back, but she has to lean on my shoulder until I can dump her in the chair.

'You need to clear this mess up,' she mumbles as my little dog races over.

'Haven't had time. And it's not that bad—'

'When'd you get the dog?'

'It's not a dog. It's an elemental.' It looks like a Jack Russell, apart from the blue ears: not deliberate, I just wasn't concentrating. As it scuttles past her, Marvo reaches down. 'What's it for?' But before she can stroke it, she's thrown up again all over the floor.

The dog hops around and starts cheerfully licking up the mess.

'That's what it's for,' I say. 'The Society pissed all over the place.'

'Ugh!'

'Smell it—'

'What?'

I kneel and hold out my hand. The dog licks it. I hold it up to Marvo. She sniffs suspiciously—

'Cinnamon!'

'It's done the job, but it's kinda cute, so I just drop something on the floor from time to time to keep it happy. You're a *big* treat.'

The pool of vomit has almost gone.

Marvo unwinds her scarf and unbuttons her coat. She fans her face with her hand as she slumps back in the chair. 'What's wrong with me?'

'Magic. I put a spell on the studio. It's invisible.'

'You made an entire building disappear . . . ?'

'Yup.'

She groans. The dog gives her shoe a sympathetic lick, then farts. The smell of cinnamon fills the room.

I say, 'I'm waiting for you to tell me how clever I am. Then I'll find something to make you feel better and you can go home.'

'Just get on with it!'

I stick a beaker of water on a tripod over a Bunsen burner – the gas is still working, thank God. I toss in a teaspoon of brown powder. 'Wait here,' I say.

Outside, Preston has grabbed the shark with one foot and is trying to hop backwards on the other. I snatch the shark off him and turn to see that Marvo's followed me out. She's right beside the door, peering closely at the brickwork. 'What are these?' She's grey in the face and shivering desperately.

'Pearls. The red stones are jaspers – don't pick at them, you'll damage the spell!'

She steps back and stares open-mouthed. 'Why an octopus?'

'Because of the way they can change colour to camouflage themselves. It's—'

'Yeah, I know. A metaphor.' She points up at a small object pinned to the lintel above the door. 'And the leaf?'

'It's not a leaf, it's *gonepteryx rhamni*, the common brimstone butterfly. Camouflage again.'

What I want is for her to move out of the way, so I can get the shark inside. Instead she just stands there, staring. Finally, she says, 'So that's how it's done.'

'Cool, eh?'

'Frank, stop trying to bully me. I'm impressed, OK?' She still hasn't moved. 'It's beautiful. Sad nobody gets to see it.'

'You can, and that's reward enough. Can I get past?'

She stands aside, waving her hand in front of her nose. 'I thought they all had the flu or something, the monks . . . and they'd given it to me.' She follows me inside and closes the door. 'You know, when I came looking for you—'

'I told you, it's misdirection,' I pant. 'It's not that you *can't* see the building, you just *don't* – your brain won't let you. But there's termites who've lived here for twenty years or more . . .' I stagger across the studio, narrowly avoiding tripping over Preston and the dog, eyeing each other up suspiciously. I drop the shark on the bench. 'The spell has to block all those memories.'

'Yeah.' Marvo nods. 'Some of them didn't even seem to know who you were!'

I turn the Bunsen off and strain the brew into a cup. 'Drink that. It will make you feel strong.'

She sniffs and pulls a face. 'What's in it?'

'Your favourite. Bat's blood.'

'Seriously?'

'Drink it.'

It's weird, this feeling that I'm in charge here: that I'm the grown-up and she's like this frightened kid. Obviously, she's still feeling the shock of the cloaking spell. But watching her hands tremble as she knocks back the concoction, I can see that she's been through it. She hasn't got any less skinny; and with the bleach job growing out, she just looks ill.

'Marvo, have you seen a healer?'

'Don't be stupid. I'm fine.'

She isn't the only one who's been through it. The shark is lying on the bench, stinking the place out. The dog is sitting underneath with its tongue out, catching drops of liquid as they fall, wagging its tail and

126

farting fit to bust. The dorsal fin has bent in half, so it's no use to me, and even the Chinese doctor at the bottom of the hill would turn his nose up at it. There's scrapes and scratches all over the shark's body and it's come dangerously close to losing one eye.

As I pull open the mouth to check the teeth I ask Marvo, 'What about your mum?'

'She's fine. Doesn't remember a thing.'

'That's good.'

Most of the teeth are present and correct, and the gills are intact.

'Blames me for the mess,' Marvo grumbles.

When a demon comes for you, things usually get a bit messy.

'Do you want to talk about it?' I ask.

'Not to you I don't.' She bangs the empty cup onto the bench beside the shark. 'What are you playing with that thing for? I thought you'd done.'

'What can I tell you? There's a lot I can do with the parts.'

I don't *have* to dismantle the shark right now. OK, so it's pretty niffy; but I've put up with worse, and I could easily steal a couple of buckets of ice from the monastery kitchen . . .

But I have this idea that if I can gross Marvo out enough, she'll go away.

CHAPTER EIGHTEEN

A Fine Line

No such luck. Two hours later, I've got the bits of the shark that I want – the eyes, the teeth, the heart and liver – in jars, covered by a simple preservative spell. The dog's still licking happily away at the tiles where Marvo's thrown up again.

She's on her feet, wandering around the studio, picking things up and sniffing them. I look up as she drops a bunch of dried hyssop and pulls her scryer out of her pocket. 'Yes, Chief,' she says into it.

Caxton, then.

Marvo listens. 'Frank's place,' she says.

'"What the hell are you hanging around with that skinny little freak for?"' I mutter. 'Right?'

Marvo turns round long enough to punch me. 'That's not fair, Chief.'

She listens. I assume Caxton's giving her some friendly advice; like wise up, go home and stay away from the idiot . . .

'I understand, Chief.' Marvo closes her scryer and turns to me.

'Understand what?'

'Caxton's handed the case over to the Society.' The scryer goes back in her pocket.

No surprise. Still a pisser, though. I glare at Preston. 'Well?'

'Sorry, boss. Nothing yet.'

I'm hunting along the bench.

'What are you looking for?' Marvo asks.

'The pentacle.' The last time I remember having it was when I waved it under Preston's nose. 'Must've dropped it.' Doesn't really matter, and what I really need to do, anyway, is sit down and think everything through . . .

Marvo has other ideas. 'My turn now. What about Sean?'

Oh, bloody hell. 'Now's not good.'

'That's typical of you, Frank! Promise stuff then let people down.'

'I told you before. I'll tell you again: Ghosts don't run people over.'

'You know your trouble?'

'Yeah, I'm stuck here with you. Haven't you got a home to go to?'

'You think you're this outlaw, right? A desperate character summoning demons without authorisation. Licence gone. People chasing you around the city. Make you feel important, does it?'

'Not particularly,' I mumble.

'But you never question any of the crap the Society taught you. Like you swallowed it when they told you girls couldn't be sorcerers.' She shoves me in the chest. 'Wrong about that, weren't you?'

'Go home.'

'Not till you help me.'

'I told you,' Marvo says. 'It wasn't an accident.'

'You sure did,' I mutter. 'Loudly and repeatedly. And I told you—'

'I'm cold, by the way.' She pulls up the collar of her coat.

'I need the rays – I've been doing a lot of magic.'

Not that I'll get much off the sun, which has barely risen over the wall of the vegetable garden. I told Preston to stay in my studio and now I'm sitting beside Marvo on the steps outside. She's rolled a cigarette and stuck it in her face. I lean back and let the smoke drift past me. My ears are so cold it's like they're about to fall off, but I can feel the warmth of the sun on my head. I run my hand across the stubble. I need to shave it. Getting sloppy, Frank.

'There were witnesses an' everything.'

'Who can't have seen anything different from what Doctor Death showed us.'

'You told me once . . . he's been around for fifty years, Doctor Death.'

'No, I said he has data going back that far. I've no idea when he was instantiated.'

'He could be, you know . . . getting stuff scrambled.'

I shake my head.

Marvo's frowning furiously. 'But you said data elementals have to be maintained.'

'That's security elementals and it's only coz they're installed by private contractors and they want to keep the money flowing; so they do a quick, dirty job then come back to fix their own mistakes. I dunno who instantiated Doctor Death, but he's solid.'

'Sez you.'

'He's too important—'

'Like that Montgolfier that crashed last week.'

'Just an accident.' Not true, by the way: airships don't blow up of their own accord. 'Same as Sean.'

Marvo puts two fingers to her lips and flicks away a shred of tobacco.

Time to change the subject. 'Can I have a drag?'

She stares at me for a moment, then passes me the fag. The paper at the end is damp with her saliva and I feel it cold between my lips. It's a bit, you know, yech!

'God, that's disgusting.' I'm coughing fit to bust and I drop the roll-up. She picks it up and blows away specks of dirt.

'Didn't you know?'

I shake my head. 'They were banned at Saint Cyprian's. The smell messes with the magic.'

131

She blows smoke past me. 'You get used to them.'

'Should you, though?'

She gets to her feet. 'Why don't you ask your boss?'

'About smoking?'

I'm taking the piss, but she doesn't get it. 'No.' She jabs her elbow into me. 'About Sean, you idiot.'

I sigh. 'What would Matthew know?'

'You don't know till you ask him.'

'Yeah, well, I don't want to ask him.'

'You've seen him, right? You gotta let him out.' She gets up and dusts the dirt off the back of her coat. 'So this is fun.'

'Huh?'

'Working together again.'

'We're not working together.'

'What *are* we doing, then?'

I walk up the steps to my outside door. 'I'll see you later.'

'There's a fine line between being a smartarse and being an arsehole,' Marvo says. 'You're a mean shit sometimes, Frank.' She heads off along the path through the vegetable garden.

'Not that way!' I call after her. 'They'll see you—'

'They're too busy praying.'

True: the termites will be locked away in the chapel, wailing and gnashing their teeth.

'And who cares, anyway?' But she turns off into the bushes, pushing the thorns out of her way. Halfway up the wall, she turns to look down at me. 'If you don't do something about Sean, I swear to God . . . I'll tell Caxton about Kazia.' She rolls out of sight, over the top, and I hear her feet hit the ground outside.

'She's right, boss.' Preston is standing in the doorway. 'You're dead mean.'

'What do you know? You're just half of an elemental and a complete waste of time.' In my mind, I'm forming an intention.

Preston goes white. 'Boss, you're not gonna—'

'Terminate you? Why not? I'm stuck in this craphole, practising magic without a licence. I've got everybody on my case and Marvo bleating on about her stupid brother. I've got you dragging round after me, getting in the way—' I don't exactly kick him. But I get my foot under him and sort of . . . bounce him off down the corridor. 'Just get inside,' I yell. 'And stay there!'

He scuttles into the studio.

The sunlight catches the pinnacle of the chapel and turns the Montgolfier trails across the sky to gold threads. The wind has sprung up. I'm cold.

And Preston's right: I'm being dead mean.

I don't know what's up with Marvo, but it's like this stuff with her brother is eating into her brain. It's been a year. She should've got over it. Took me fifteen minutes, at most, to get over my dad . . .

I've got this picture in my head of Marvo spilling

133

the beans to Caxton, soon as she gets into the jack shack. I've got enough on my plate without feeling bad about her.

But I do. Preston too. If he can't find Kazia, it isn't his fault: I built him, and a right mess I made of him.

I run into my studio. Preston looks up fearfully—

'Come on, then.' I grab my jerkin and hat.

Over the back wall, we catch up with Marvo a few streets away.

'What?' she says.

'Have you still got Sean's stuff?'

'My mum wouldn't chuck anything out . . .'

'So suppose we have a look at it . . .'

'OK.' She actually smiles, and it's like she's a different person who doesn't have this angry scowl on her face all the time. 'Thanks, Frank.'

Wow! Is it really that simple?

CHAPTER NINETEEN
A Little Angel

The fancy roof tiles on the terraced houses of the street in Littlemore are silhouetted against the sky. There's the usual array of painful-looking spikes; and finials in the shape of horned, winged figures.

Protection against witches landing on the roof.

Outside Marvo's mother's house, the broken fragments of the front gate are lying around in the bushes beside the narrow path up to the front door. We duck under the ivy covering the entire face of the house. Marvo puts her finger to her lips and pushes the door.

It doesn't open. She starts hunting through her pockets.

'I told you I could give you a spell for that,' I say.

'No thanks. You've done enough magic.'

'Ring the bell,' I suggest after a bit.

'And wake my mum up?'

'Then let me do it.'

I've said it before: doors like me. It takes a couple of

words and a few passes. The door opens without a murmur.

Marvo slips off her shoes, hangs up her coat and tiptoes along the narrow hallway. I unlace my boots and follow her up the stairs. The landing is dark. I can hear the faint sound of snoring from the bedroom at the front of the house. A sliver of light spills across the carpet from the room next to it. I figure it's Marvo's room and I can't resist it: I push the door open.

'Frank!' she hisses.

Small room. Bed. Faded curtains with kittens rolling around, playing with balls of wool. A battered chest of drawers, missing one handle. I've only got a few seconds before Marvo whacks me one, so I step quickly across. The framed photograph shows a girl of six, if my arithmetic is right, clutching a baby in her arms and beaming proudly up at the camera.

Marvo and her kid brother.

'You've no business!' And here's the punch on the arm: hard and sharp.

I've spotted something else. There's a table beside the bed. On top of it, a black cloth, folded to make a bandage. And leaning against the wall, a white stick.

I grab it. 'Practising?'

'What do you think?' Marvo pulls the stick out of my hand.

A tatty can see crystal-clear well past the age when everybody else is going Blurry. The downside? You hit about thirty and go crash-bang stone blind. Just like that. Overnight, in some cases.

I put my hand behind my back. 'How many fingers am I holding up?'

'Don't muck me about, Frank. I can't see round corners. I've got ten years—'

'More'n that—'

'Not much more. I'll be totally blind.' She leans the stick back against the wall. 'I figure maybe I should be ready for it.'

'Yeah, but it's not like you won't be able to afford a guide elemental,' I say.

'And spend the rest of my life relying on something?' Marvo mutters. 'Not much future in that. Let's get on with it!' She pushes me out along the landing and into a narrow room at the back of the house. She pulls the curtains open. I see a desk under the window and a bed at the end.

'Nice view,' I say. The sky is completely blocked off by a massive horse chestnut. Withered brown leaves have collected in soggy piles on the flat roof just below. 'Was he depressed, your brother?'

At some point the room has been painted an oppressive mustard yellow. Maybe Sean was trying to cover it over, because he pasted stuff up everywhere, from just above the chipped skirting boards almost to the ceiling – as far as a small boy could reach standing on a chair, I guess.

It's mostly faded pictures torn out of newspapers and magazines. Marvo is gazing at a crumpled, spidery drawing of a sort of black splodge perched over a couple of vaguely circular shapes that are probably supposed to be wheels. It reads, 'Hapy birthday Mad' in tottering letters before it runs out of paper.

'I chucked it out,' Marvo whispers. Her voice is shaking. 'I mean, I didn't see any point in keeping it. He found it in the bin and he was dead pissed off with me.'

'Did you do drawings as a kid?' I ask.

'Course. My mum's still got them somewhere.' It takes her a couple of seconds to ask the question she's supposed to ask: 'You?'

'Not that I remember.'

'Yeah, Frank. You an' your deprived childhood.'

'It wasn't much fun.' Didn't last long either. I was six – a year younger than the other novices – when they hauled me off to Saint Cyprian's and started shoving demons in my face.

All Marvo's interested in is her brother. 'Can we get on with this before my mum wakes up?'

I can see one obvious thing about the pictures on the walls: they're all of Ghosts. The Lord Mayor getting out of one, wearing a funny hat and a robe with bits of dead animals hung round it. Some self-important fool in military uniform staring out of the window of one.

I look round at Preston.

'Sorry, boss. Nothing yet.'

138

I unfold a huge blueprint: the side view of a Ghost, labelled with magic symbols.

'Daddy brought that home for him,' says Marvo. 'I told you he worked at the Ghost works in Cowley.' She smiles sadly. 'That's what killed him – the fumes in the paint shop . . .'

'I'm sorry. Don't you think it's funny, though? That you say Sean was killed by a Ghost and here's all this stuff.'

She blinks and sits down hard on the side of the bed. 'Oh,' she says, like it's the first time this has occurred to her.

I open the wardrobe. 'Didn't your mum throw *anything* out?' There's a school blazer and pairs of trousers on hangers. Neatly folded shirts, socks and underwear. It smells of lavender.

'For a long time she wouldn't admit he was dead,' says Marvo softly.

'She must've seen his body.' I close the wardrobe. 'Marvo?'

She looks up at me and nods. She's started crying again.

I don't know if this is fair, but anyway: 'What about you?' I ask. 'Did you see him?'

She nods.

'So was he . . . ?'

'All smashed up?' She smiles. 'No.' The tears are pouring down her face.

I find that hard to believe. Doctor Death's reconstruction of the accident . . . let's just say that it looked like a mortician would have his work cut out. And looking around the Marvell household, I don't see any sign that they could afford the magic involved.

Marvo whispers, 'He looked like a little angel.'

I've met a few angels in my time. None of them looked even remotely like the plump kid grinning out of the school photo on the desk.

I'm going through drawers. I find a camera – and boxes and boxes of photographs. I haul them out and stack them on top of the desk. I open the first . . .

Marvo's bro, he didn't just *like* Ghosts – he was *obsessed* by them. That's all there is in the boxes: picture after picture after picture. There's Ghosts in city streets and Ghosts in open country. Ghosts on straight roads and Ghosts going round corners. Ghosts moving and Ghosts parked.

'He was a Ghost-spotter,' says Marvo.

'What, like train-spotters?' The things normal kids get up to! I was busy dodging demons when I was that age. 'Wow!'

The second box contains a small red notebook, with 'Spotting' scrawled on the cover in wobbly letters. When I open it, half a dozen photographs fall out onto the desk. One of them is an out-of-focus, underexposed shot of a toad-faced, middle-aged man in a black skullcap, sitting in the back seat of a Ghost.

'Who's he?' Marvo asks.

'Dunno.'

He's some sort of cleric, with a big sparkly crucifix strung round his neck. He stares up through the open window, startled and angry, from the sheet of paper he's holding.

'He isn't wearing glasses.' Marvo looks me dead in the eye. 'Another one of the lucky ones?'

We've been here before. Marvo's noticed that there are some grown-ups who don't seem to go Blurry. The official story is that a few happy bunnies just found life's winning lottery ticket in their pockets; but Marvo's twigged that luck's got nothing to do with it. The fact is, the Society has a very special procedure – not just *any* procedure, *the* Procedure – to fix the Blur. I as much as admitted it to her once, so it's just a matter of time before she pulls her gun on me and tells me to get to work.

Meanwhile, here's the interesting thing about the man reading the document: he isn't just some ordinary priest from the parish church round the corner. Judging from the complicated black robes and the sheer *size* of that crucifix, and from the fact that he's sitting in the back of a Ghost, this is some sort of bishop or cardinal or something. An important bunny.

And the Procedure isn't just something you can organise through your friendly local apothecary. You need a demon – a particular demon – and the Church says that's messing with Satan and, all things taken into consideration, a Bad Thing.

141

So if you've got a Big Cheese in the Church and he's reading a document without glasses . . . there's something funny going on. No wonder he looks pissed off at having his picture taken.

'So what does it mean, Frank?' Marvo's grabbed the photo off me and she's staring at it; and I'm racking my brains for something clever to say—

When fate comes to my rescue. The door flies open and knocks me across the room onto the bed. Marvo loses her balance and the photographs scatter everywhere. When I look round, her mum is standing in the doorway staring at us, with her hair all over the place and her spectacles swinging on the string around her neck. She's wearing a nightdress and clutching her usual kit for greeting visitors: a kitchen knife.

'What are you doing?'

'Nothing.' Marvo starts picking up the pictures.

'Who's he?'

'Frank. You've met him—'

'I think I'd remember.'

'Don't confuse her,' I whisper to Marvo. The last time I saw Mrs Marvell I hypnotised her into forgetting me.

'She's my mum,' Marvo hisses back. 'And I'll confuse her if I want to.'

CHAPTER TWENTY
Crossed Keys

Why confuse somebody in a cold bedroom when you can do it in a warm kitchen?

There's a fire flickering in the grate. They've washed away the magic circles I chalked on the floor last time I was here, to prevent Alastor from ripping all three of us apart and juggling with the pieces. The table that got broken has been fixed, but it rocks dangerously as I drop the notebook on top.

'Burglars,' says Mrs M. 'They smashed everything.' She's grabbed an unbroken cup from the Welsh dresser and tipped out a small metal disc on a chain. A Saint Benedict amulet, with the man himself clutching a cross and an open book. And an inscription. *Vade retro Satana*: get thee behind me, Satan. As she drops it around her neck, it rattles against the lenses of her spectacles.

She may not remember who I am, but somewhere in a corner of her brain there's a little voice screaming that I'm trouble. She's not very happy about Preston, either—

'What's *that*?'

'Well?' Marvo punches me in the shoulder.

'Abyssinian truffle hound,' I say. 'And that bloody hurt!'

'Abyssinian truffle hound?'

'What am I supposed to say?'

'I like it,' Preston murmurs.

Mrs M is muttering away to herself and kissing the medal. I open Sean's notebook and spread the six photographs across the table.

Marvo's mum's spectacles go on. 'What's all this?'

'He's helping me find out what happened to Sean,' Marvo says.

'Why?'

Marvo looks a bit taken aback. 'Because I want to know.'

'What's there to know?' Mrs M grumbles.

I can feel Marvo's breath on my scalp as I shuffle through the photos.

'I said, what's there to know?' Mrs M's voice is sharp now. 'He was run over.'

'Marvo says—' I try.

'What's wrong with her given name?'

'It's stupid, for a start,' Marvo mutters.

'Magdalena was your grandmother's name.'

'And she made everybody call her Rose.'

I dive in again: 'Marvo says it was a Ghost.'

'What sort of nonsense is that?' Mrs M mutters. 'I don't believe in—'

'Ghost, as in luxury vehicle.'

Mrs M thinks for a moment. 'A cart, a van . . . I don't remember the police saying anything about a Ghost. It was late at night – God knows what he was doing out—'

'There were witnesses, Mum.'

'No there weren't.'

'There was somebody . . .'

'Who?'

I look round and see that Marvo's gone all weird on me again. Her eyes are drifting around the kitchen, like maybe somebody's written a name on a scrap of paper and hidden it in one of the cups on the dresser and she just has to guess which one.

'It was—'

'What would *you* know?' her mother says, startlingly loudly. 'You were away.'

'I know I was away.'

Thank God we can agree on that, at least.

I'm leafing through the notebook. Page after page of dates, locations . . .

'When was Sean killed, exactly?'

'August last year,' says Marvo.

'The fourth,' says her mother.

'So the last entry here is July 29th, on the Grandpont near the Red Bridge. "Crossed Keys".'

'Huh?'

'It just says, "Crossed Keys".' I point. 'He's under-lined it.'

'There's a bar called the Crossed Keys,' says Mrs M. 'Just the other side of Garsington.'

I know it. My dad drank there for a bit, when he was barred from the Brazen Head for beating the crap out of me after I knocked over his glass. That was three months or so before I killed him.

'Where's that?' Marvo is poring over a photograph of a Ghost passing through a gateway into a big, ugly building.

I recognise it. 'Saint Cyprian's.'

'But that's miles!' She looks up at her mother. 'How'd he get out there?'

'I couldn't tell him what to do.'

I've picked up the photo of the cleric sitting in the Ghost. 'Did you show these to the jacks?'

'Why?' Marvo's gone very pale. Her hands are shaking.

'Are you OK?'

'I'm fine.'

'The police were a waste of time, anyway,' says Mrs M.

'That's not fair, Mum!'

'What would you know? You're just a secretary.'

'I'm not a secretary. How many times—'

'So why didn't you do anything?' There's tears

running down her cheeks. 'May God forgive you.'

Don't look at me: I've no idea what's going on. All I know is, Marvo's pretty shaky, nobody's enjoying themselves and I'm not helping.

'I'm sorry,' I say.

Mrs M is staring at me. 'And you don't look like a policeman.'

'I'm not. I'm a sorcerer.'

Her hand flashes to the amulet around her neck. 'I want you to go now,' she whispers. 'I don't like sorcerers.'

'I'm a good sorcerer. I wouldn't hurt a fly.'

But she shivers and steps back. 'I told you to go.'

I avoid catching Marvo's eye as I nudge Preston out into the hall with my foot.

At the bottom of the stairs, the door to the front room is open. Inside, nothing's changed since the last time I was here. Same dish of sweets and jar of coloured pencils; same pair of thick glasses; same magnifying glass. Same framed photograph on the piano, with a black silk ribbon pasted across one corner. I pick it up: same plump kid, maybe eight or nine, grinning happily back at the camera.

Sean Marvell.

There's a creak behind me. Marvo's standing in the doorway.

'Now what?' I know what I want: to get back to my studio and catch up on some sleep.

'I don't want to upset Mummy.'

'So let it go.'

She shakes her head.

Even I can see there's something weird going on here. 'Then get back to me when you've worked it out between you.'

'Put that down!' Mrs M has appeared behind Marvo, holding the amulet aloft.

Preston and I look at each other, waiting to see who's going to be the first to disappear in a puff of green smoke. When I realise that neither of us has, I stick Sean's photograph back on the piano and step away.

'There's nothing wrong with my memory – is that what you've been telling him? That you've got this silly old woman at home and she doesn't even remember what happened to her own son?'

Marvo tries, 'That's not what he said—'

'It's what he meant, though.' Mrs M's face crumples, like someone's let the air out of a balloon. She stares down at the picture and wails, 'He was my baby!'

You'd laugh if it wasn't all, I dunno . . . so sad, I suppose. I mean, my mum . . . Oh, forget it! Did I come here to make trouble? I don't think so. But Marvo's got her arms round her mother's shoulders and she's giving me this 'what did you have to do that for?' look as she turns her round and leads her away.

I hear the kitchen door close, so I give Preston another nudge in the direction of the front door.

CHAPTER TWENTY-ONE
Our Beloved Boy

It's raining. Of course it's bloody raining! I've taken a shortcut across the fields and I'm thinking about my own mum and dad . . .

My old man never gave a flying fart about me. He used to watch me eat and I could see him thinking, *That's good beer money going down that skinny little freak's gullet!*

My mum's still alive, living on her own in the heap she bought out on Boar's Lump, after she won the lottery. Not that I ever see her . . .

'Frank!'

For a split second I imagine that I've actually managed to conjure my dear mother up. But of course it's Marvo, running after me.

'What?' I've had enough of the Marvell circus for one day.

She jumps a ditch and slithers to a halt beside me. 'I brought you this.'

Sean's notebook. A photograph slips out and goes face down in the mud. She shoves the notebook into my hand and stoops down.

I open the notebook and find the rest of the photographs stuffed between two pages. 'What am I supposed to do with all this?'

'Keep it dry.' She's lifted the hem of her coat, wiping the wet paper on the lining. She stops and stares down at it.

'Here.' She shoves the picture at me. It's still smeared with mud, but I can see a Ghost parked outside a swanky-looking building. 'It's the same,' she says.

'Same Ghost?' All I'm really sure about is that I'm getting wet. I look down at the photo. The figure staring back at the camera is wearing a peaked cap and a black, belted jacket. I recognise an elemental: the driver of the Ghost. There's some sort of metal badge on his peaked cap, but I can't make it out.

Marvo grabs the photo back. 'You'll spoil it.' She's pulled the notebook out of my other hand and stuffed the wet picture inside. She shoves the notebook under my jerkin. 'Keep hold of it.'

I pull my arm tight across it, so it doesn't fall out.

'Come on,' she says. 'I'm going to show you where Sean's buried.'

'Marvo, it's pissing down!' She's already on the move and I have to call after her, 'In case you hadn't noticed.'

I could run for it, but she'd just come after me and beat me up. So I trail after her, back the way I came, down the hill and over a wooden bridge across a ditch piled up with garbage – bicycles, a dead dog . . .

'You can come back later for that,' Marvo says over her shoulder.

'I'm fine, thanks.' Even by my standards, the dog is a bit far gone.

We're on a narrow path beside a line of poplars. The rain is easing off, thank God. A pale, sad rainbow rises behind the houses.

'How old's your mum?' I ask.

'Fifty-three.'

'She looks older.'

'She's had a rough time. First Daddy, then Sean.'

It was weird, listening to Marvo's mother. I mean, she's a right old bat and I'm sure she gives Marvo a hard time. But even so, it's like she cares.

I don't think my mum ever cared much about me, one way or the other. If I was in a job that actually paid money, maybe she'd think differently; but my recruitment by the Society . . . it was a one-off, a lump sum—

Quite a big lump, as it happens.

Anyway, my dad drank it away in no time at all. I think my mum got a pair of shoes out of it, and that was about all. She never forgave him. Or me.

She never told me whether she minded that I'd killed

151

him. To be fair, she never really got a chance to express an opinion: the Society had got hold of me by then.

There's a rusty sign on the wall: *Littlemore Old Cemetery*. The iron gate groans as I push it open. Inside, it's more like a wood than a graveyard, with heavy drops of water falling from rotting trees held together by shrouds of ivy.

I like cemeteries. You can turn up all sorts of useful bits in cemeteries that you wouldn't find anywhere else.

'So which way?' I ask.

I follow Marvo along a muddy path through a tangle of brambles. A rat scuttles between my feet and I look round in time to see Preston bare his teeth at it. The rat squeaks and vanishes into a pile of soggy leaves. I can see the dead now: moss-covered, broken headstones scattered among the trees, tilted by the roots, leaning against each other like a crowd of drunks trying to get each other home.

The rain has stopped and the sun is struggling to push out through the clouds. We've come to a clearing with a circular stone platform and a tall plinth supporting a statue of a woman clutching a cross. There's an inscription: 'In the vault beneath this tomb are interred . . .' The rest has worn away, except for a final paragraph: 'Her bereaved husband, in token of respect for her virtues and in grateful remembrance for so good a wife, erects this monument to perpetuate her memory.'

'So come on, Marvo,' I say. 'Where have you perpetuated Sean's memory?'

She doesn't say a word. Just leads me past a headless statue of an angel and along a path between black yew trees that block out the light, through a gap in a crumbling wall and down a flight of steps into the new burial ground. A couple of dozen sheep look round at us, then go back to grazing on the grass between neat rows of simple headstones.

'He's over here,' Marvo whispers.

She leads me towards the far corner of the cemetery, where the crosses and slabs peter out into open ground.

It's just a simple rectangular stone, a couple of feet high. There's an inscription carved into it: *Sean Michael Marvell.*

'No dates?'

And I'm still waiting for a reply when Preston comes shooting between my ankles and charges full tilt into the headstone. He falls back and rolls over.

'What was that about?' I ask.

'Sorry, boss.' I can actually see small red and yellow stars orbiting around the feather sticking out of the top of his head. 'Nothing yet.'

'Well, just concentrate, OK?'

The stars pop like soap bubbles. I look along the row of headstones . . . and here's a funny thing: all the way along, the sheep have cropped the grass close to the graves.

Except Sean's. Up to about six inches away, all around his headstone, the grass is long. I crouch down and touch the stone and I get a tingle through my fingertips. I know the buzz of residual magic when I feel it. I push the long grass aside and at the bottom I see another inscription.

I read it aloud: 'Our beloved boy.'

I can hear Marvo sobbing quietly. To be honest, I'm feeling a little teary myself. I wipe my sleeve across my eyes and stand up.

Marvo is sitting on one of the other headstones. She's gone deathly white and her cheeks are wet with tears. She's trembling, and she's clutching the corners of the stone each side of her like she's terrified it's going to rear up and throw her off.

'I can't think,' she whispers.

'Welcome to my world.'

'It's not a joke.'

No shit. In the twenty-four hours since I tripped over her in the Hole, she's been getting paler and paler. She's lost weight and she even looks smaller.

'Marvo, you need to see that healer.'

'Don't need one. I'm fine.'

'Yeah, but you don't look fine.'

'I was OK till you came back.'

Is that true? Sailors – not that I know any, but I've

read about it – they have this expression: a *Jonah*. Someone on board who brings bad luck and ends up sinking the ship. Is that what I've done to Marvo?

Closing the cemetery gate behind us, I stare back between the bars. The reason I like graveyards, well, it's not just the parts . . .

I didn't ask to be Gifted. Since I got dropped into this world, I've met dozens of Presences who've been very clear about what they'd like to spend eternity doing to me when I fall out the other end.

Just lying there, in the still, silent darkness under the trees, looks like a far better plan.

CHAPTER TWENTY-TWO

Kicking

'**S**o I was right,' says Marvo.

So far we haven't agreed about much. One thing there's no argument about, though: we're both starving. Marvo's paying for breakfast in a little café off the main road.

'About Sean,' she says through a bacon sandwich. 'It *was* a Ghost. I mean, if you got this – what did you call it? – magical residue off the headstone . . .'

'Yeah, but a Ghost—'

'Spooked *him* too.' She jerks her knife under the table, where Preston is hiding.

'Sorry, boss,' he mumbles.

'Just stay out of sight, OK?' I turn back to Marvo. 'A Ghost doesn't give off magic.'

'It works by magic.'

'Not the same thing.'

'You told me a Ghost's not supposed to be able to knock somebody down, right? So if it *did* happen—'

She's waving the knife around. I lean back. 'Don't you get it? It'd have to be something pretty weird.'

I can't argue with that, even if it doesn't make sense.

We're just round the corner from her mum's place, when Marvo stops in her tracks.

'Come on, Marvo. I'm getting wet.'

Yeah, it's raining again. A woman with a shopping basket and an umbrella brushes past her, but Marvo just stands there and when I look round I see why.

Across the road, people move aside for a man, about thirty, walking uncertainly along the pavement. He's waving one hand blindly in front of him, while the other clutches the leather harness strapped around a dog.

Only it isn't a dog; it's a guide elemental. And this isn't just any blind bloke. He used to be a tatty.

Talent gone. He's got this fixed, anxious expression plastered across his face. It's like Marvo said: when it's time for the tats to go, they don't hang about.

I take her arm and for once she doesn't whack me one. Like the dog with the blind man, I lead her down the path to her mum's house. I ring the bell. The door opens. Mrs M fishes her medal out from under her cardigan and kisses it, then we both wait for Satan to come and haul me off to hell . . .

After a while, when he still hasn't shown up, I step back so Marvo can go inside. The door slams behind her.

* * *

So I'm halfway up the wall at the back of the termite nest, soaked to the skin and looking forward to the sharp knife on my bench, when there's this whisper behind me – only it's two voices . . .

'Hey, boss.'

I look round. I've got two wet Prestons, standing side by side on one leg, sort of hugging each other.

'I've found her!' they both say together.

'Whaddya mean, found her? Found who?'

They give me this puzzled look. 'Come on, boss, don't play games.' And they turn and splash off, side by side, along the alley. I drop down and follow them, round two corners—

'How did you find her?'

Stupid question. I instantiated Preston, so if I don't know, who does?

We're at the front of the termite nest. 'Where are we going?'

They both stand there looking pleased with themselves. Then, before I can tell them to stop messing about and get on with it, they sort of shuffle up to each other and go back into the hug. I don't actually notice it happen – you never quite see it, no matter how hard you try – but next thing, there's just one Preston. Still looking pleased with himself.

He turns and points. 'There, boss.'

Kazia? Nope.

158

A dozen men standing around a glowing brazier. Thick coats to keep warm. Heavy boots to administer a good kicking.

I look down at Preston. 'Thanks a lot.'

'It's him!' one of the men yells. 'The nekker!' He's overweight, with a black birthmark bang in the middle of his forehead, wearing a priest's cassock and a whole heap of crucifixes strung around his neck. He's waving a long pole with a pointy metal cross on the end. 'Repent!'

Won't you give a big friendly welcome, please, to the boys from the ASB: the Anti-Sorcery Brotherhood. The name says it all, really: they're a brotherhood and . . . wait for it . . . they don't like sorcerers.

They move away from the brazier and form a line between me and the monastery gate. They're all wearing the ASB's emblem round their arms: a burning five-pointed star.

'OK, arseholes,' I say, trying unsuccessfully to stop my voice shaking. 'Come and get it.'

Obviously, this can only go one way. I make a vague attempt to fight back, but I keep missing and after I've taken a couple of heavy whacks I realise: (a) that this is much less fun than I thought it'd be; and (b) that I'd be much safer curled up on the ground.

The kicking settles down to a routine. They're taking it in turns, in silence, mostly aiming at my back and legs, and at my arms which I've got wrapped round my head. Then someone grabs me and turns me on my back. I try to stay curled up, but I'm getting it in the stomach and shoulders now. I can't keep my legs tucked up any more. I flop out and I'm just thinking that if I was still thinking straight, I'd be thinking what a stupid fool I am, except I'm not thinking, just hurting . . .

When it stops. Just like that.

I'm lying there, too scared even to open my eyes because I'm sure they're just taking the mickey and as soon as I move they'll start in again. But then I hear feet running away.

Silence.

A single set of footsteps coming closer. Is this the *coup de grâce*?

I'm dead impressed by this next bit and I hope you are too: I open my eyes.

And it's Kazia.

CHAPTER TWENTY-THREE
Malformed

My mum used to sing me this song about how love makes the world go round – usually when she'd had a few drinks and the bruises my dad made didn't hurt so bad any more. She was wrong, of course: any fool knows it's money that makes the world go round.

But love sure can make your head spin. My heart has decided that my blood can do its own circulating and has stopped dead. There's this magic moment where it's like the first time I ever saw Kazia . . . before she started trying to kill me.

'Hello, Frank,' she says quietly. 'Surprised to see me?'

She holds out her hand. I don't want to, but I can't stop myself: it's chillingly cold as I take it. Like an angel, she draws me to my feet.

We did love spells at Saint Cyprian's. Except that when I say 'did', I don't mean that we actually performed them: the Society wouldn't go so far as to stick you on a bonfire for doing a love spell, but it'd do several things to you that hurt.

Fact is, before the Society came along and started handing out gold stars and badges, sorcerers were a sad bunch of flea-bitten losers, hiding out in caves and cellars and desperately in need of something to cheer themselves up. And what better morale-booster than a maiden taking her clothes off? Of course, when the Society came along it wanted to convince everybody that sorcery was about serious things like comprehending the full mystery of the divine creation in all its complexity.

Girls in their underwear, they kind of give the game away, you know . . . ?

Most love spells are very silly. Scraping the gold paint off a statue of the Virgin Mary. Pulling chickens apart and throwing the bits around. Sleeping with a wax image under your pillow. Or invoking a demon to compel the victim . . . which is what got Kazia into so much trouble in the first place.

Preston is bouncing up and down. 'Told you, boss!'

I put my finger to my lips. I turn back to Kazia and croak, 'A bit surprised, yeah.'

Suspicious too.

I've lost my hat, but I realise that's good because the cold numbs the pain. Did I mention that everything hurts? Trust me: it does. I shuffle round and try to move towards the monastery gate, but my left leg is protesting that it's happy where it is.

162

Kazia steps up and puts her arm round my waist, to support me. Her clothes are wet from the rain.

'I'm fine,' I say. But I don't pull away.

'Who were they?' she asks.

'ASB.' With her help, I limp a few steps. 'Who else?' I want to ask her how much she saw – how long she watched before she stepped out from wherever she was hiding. Was she afraid they'd turn on her? Did she wait until I'd got the kicking she thought I deserved?

Questions best not asked. Try a different one. 'What are you doing here?'

'I need your help.' I can see bruises on her face and a smear of blood under her nose.

'I've heard that one before.' Specifically, a few hours before she sent Alastor to nail me.

'I made a mistake,' she says. 'I'm sorry, Frank.'

I know I'm making a mistake too; but I've got to know. 'So who wanted the boy dead?' I manage to raise my hand and ring the monastery bell. 'That demon you were summoning . . .'

For a moment, I think we're both expecting her to ask, What demon? But she just looks down at the pavement.

'It turned up,' I say. 'Malformed.'

The Society says demons are maleficent, conscious spiritual beings that a sorcerer can compel to manifest in the physical world. Sometimes the ritual's wrong, or

163

something interferes, and they turn up broken, like the pantomime chicken in the autopsy room.

The gate opens. Andrew stares out at me. 'Where've you been?'

'None of your business.' I grab the side of the gate and try to haul myself over the threshold, but he just stands in my way, giving me this reproachful look.

'Brother,' he says. 'Brother. Beware lest your sins should find you out.'

Welcome home, Frank. I'm tempted to ask him to compile a complete list, in case it ever comes to any serious repenting.

'The other Brothers—' He sniggers. 'The rest of the Brothers are in the chapel.'

'I'm pleased for them,' I groan. 'Now get out of the way.'

His eyes have opened wide like saucers. 'Brother Tobias,' he whispers. 'It's that girl again.' Yeah, Andrew's met Kazia. He doesn't know she's a sorcerer, and I'd prefer to keep it that way. 'You shouldn't be talking to her: she's a proximate occasion of sin.'

I should be so lucky. 'For Christ's sake, Brother, will you just get out of the way?'

Andrew's probably about to explain why he can't do that when another voice breaks in. 'Who's that?'

Just what I needed: Brother Thomas sticking his fat, shiny head over Andrew's shoulder. My popularity knows no bounds.

And my cloaking spell takes no prisoners: Brother Thomas is too close to see me clearly without his spectacles. He steps back, blinking furiously. He focuses.

'Just me,' I say.

He makes a noise like a lavatory flushing and tips over backwards.

Kazia's eyes widen and I realise she recognises a cloaking spell when she sees one. No time to discuss the finer points, though. I drag her inside, but Andrew's still in the way.

'I told you, she's a proximate occasion—'

'And this is a proximate occasion of pain.' I wave my fist under his nose. 'Now get lost.'

But he won't. He trails after us, out into the cloister, where I prise Kazia off my arm and sit her down on a bench.

'I did it, boss!' Preston crows.

'Yeah, now don't bother me.' I sit beside Kazia. 'It was supposed to kill the Crypt Boy, right?'

She just stares at me.

'The demon.' I'm whispering, so that Andrew can't hear. 'It was supposed to kill the boy . . .'

She shakes her head, but I don't think she's denying it. She just doesn't want to talk about it.

I do, though. 'I guess it's kind of my fault. I made you jump. But I checked the summoning room and I was sure nothing had manifested.' Yeah, should've looked more carefully. 'Which demon was it?'

165

There are several books that list all the demons a sorcerer can invoke. If you want to take a crack at it yourself, the best is Jacques Auguste Simon Collin de Plancy's *Dictionnaire infernal*. Names, appearances, special skills, unpleasant habits . . .

Kazia's eyes are this amazing cornflower blue, but there's this thing across them, the thing that's always defeated me . . . like sunlight sparkling on the surface of a pond, hiding what's lurking beneath.

'Who *is* the boy?' As I ask the question, I see something moving, deep below the surface. 'Look, he's under a spell. I mean, the marks on his body—'

Andrew's been shuffling forward, inch by inch, hoping I won't notice.

'Will you go away?' I shout.

'Make me,' he says.

Back to whispering, then. 'It was you who did the original magic, right? But why go to all that trouble? What's so important about him?' I'm getting this weird sinking feeling. I don't really understand it, but it's like I almost had something – and it's slipping away from me . . . 'Who wanted him dead?'

Of course, I realise why Kazia's here. After I messed up her summoning, she reported back to whoever told her to do it. They bashed her about a bit and now I'm starting to look like a better prospect. And while we're asking questions: why did she have to sneak into the mortuary to do the summoning?

166

She's shaking her head like it's hurting. We're putting on quite a show, and I'm thinking I could sell tickets when she says, 'I had nothing to do with it.'

'Stop lying, Kazia. Someone gave the orders—'

Her fingers tighten on my arm. I think she's drawing blood. 'You said you'd help me!' she wails.

I can wail too. 'But why should I trust you?'

She's looking at me funny, and I realise . . . that thing I thought I had . . . that I felt slipping away . . .

It's gone. I don't know what it was, but it was something important.

Andrew's shuffling again.

'So what do you want me to do?' I hiss into her ear. 'Help you get away, or help you take another crack at the Crypt Boy?'

Her eyes fill with tears. 'Please, Frank.'

Do I believe any of this? What do you think I am? Stupid? But somebody certainly hit her in the face a few times, which kind of makes my heart bleed.

Yeah, my heart's busy when she's around. But I can't help thinking: that's what she's counting on, isn't it? So sure, she probably *does* need my help — but not in the way she's saying and maybe not even in the way she's thinking . . .

'Time to go,' I say.

'I need to sleep.' She stumbles to her feet. 'Where's your lair?'

I can't help glancing towards the back of the cloister,

and before I can stop her, she's off along the passage that leads past the chapel towards the gardens and my studio.

I go after her.

'We can hide her somewhere.' Andrew's right behind me, eyes shining. 'There's an empty cell next to mine.'

She doesn't get far. Out into the open and down the steps, onto the gravel path, where she collapses.

I grab her hand to pull her up, but she gives this almighty wrench and drags me down beside her. Her arms go round my neck. I can feel her tears on my cheek. Andrew's dead right: she's an incredibly proximate occasion of sin.

'You must have somewhere I'll be safe.' Her whispered breath is hot on my cheek.

Despite appearances, I'm not a complete fool. I realise what's going on here. She recognised the cloaking spell when Brother Thomas went over backwards. And the quickest way to break a cloaking spell is to get whoever cast it to drag you through it.

And of course she's got magic of her own: the spell she cast over me the moment I first set eyes on her. I've got voices screaming at me:

Don't be an arsehole, Sampson.

You've been dreaming about this moment.

Take her back to the studio – help her off with those wet clothes . . .

For someone whose immortal soul is in peril,

Andrew is suspiciously happy to help me haul her to her feet. He's a bit slow sometimes; he lets me drag her a couple of steps towards the cloister before he cops on—

'Where are you taking her?'

'Outside. She'll be fine.'

'Brother, you can't!'

'You said it yourself: she's a proximate—'

'No.'

He steps away and I'm left standing there with Kazia's dead weight hanging onto me. Her eyes open. She's staring at Andrew so hard that he goes red.

I'm beginning to feel jealous. 'Come on.'

Brother Thomas is back on his feet, stumbling around the cloister. He stares glassily at Kazia. 'How did she get in?' He crosses himself.

'She's just leaving,' I say, and Brother Thomas collapses in the same heap he just got up from.

'Brother.' Andrew plants himself in front of me, one hand raised like a jack directing traffic. 'This is wrong.'

All wrong. I barge past him and manage to get Kazia as far as the gate. It creaks open.

'Please, Frank – he'll kill me.'

'Who will?'

And when she doesn't reply I say, 'Let's see if he does.' And push her outside.

There's nobody waiting for her. She's just standing there weeping in the drifting veil of rain. Her hands fall open, like the statue of the Virgin Mary in the monastery chapel.

'Please, Frank.'

I'm closing the gate, telling myself that she's a great little actress. A split second before the bolt clicks home, I hear her say, 'All right then. Have it your own way.'

I've got this sinking feeling. I let it sink for a while, as I walk back across the cloister. Then I go back and open the gate.

She's gone. Just my woolly hat, lying on the pavement, a couple of feet away. As I scoop it up, Preston whispers proudly: 'I found her.'

How do you explain to a search elemental that it's found the person it was built to find – even if that person hasn't stayed found – and that it's time to go?

It usually starts as just a feeling, that there is somehow *less* of the elemental. Give it a bit longer and you can actually see through it. I've seen it take as long as forty-eight hours; but once a search elemental has done its job, it just fades away.

'I found her.' Preston can't get over how clever he is.

'Yeah,' I say. 'Great work.'

CHAPTER TWENTY-FOUR
Gift Object

I spend the afternoon helping the dog clean up my studio. I've still got Alastor buzzing and banging away in my head, but I curl up on the mattress and manage to fall asleep, and I wake up feeling a bit less wrecked. I light a lamp and spend an hour scrawling symbols on a piece of paper. Then I sneak into the monastery stables and steal a horse.

I'm wearing my jerkin with a scarf across my face and my woolly hat jammed down over my eyes. It's five o'clock in the morning. What better time to get rid of the remains of a dead shark?

There's an incinerator at the mortuary. OK, so last time I tried to get in, they stopped me at the door and told me to get lost. This time, once I've tied the horse up round the back, I mutter a few invocations, make a couple of passes over the piece of paper that I prepared, and pin it to the front of my jerkin. Now you see me . . . now you don't! I stroll into the mortuary with the shark wrapped in its sheet under my arm.

Of course there's a weakness to an invisibility spell. It doesn't hide the smell. As I pass the desk, the night receptionist stares around blankly and mutters, 'What the hell's that?'

Down in the utility area, the diener on duty . . . I've had run-ins with him before and he's an arsehole. He runs one bony finger down a greasy ledger—

'So when was this item purchased?'

'Last week,' I lie.

'I don't see no shark.' He shakes his head. 'God, it stinks.'

'So chuck it in the incinerator.'

He makes a face like he's sucked on a lemon. 'More'n my job's worth . . .'

I hoick the shark up under my arm and press the other hand against the door to the children's ice room. It sighs and opens.

A single gas fitting throws a cold, dim glow across the empty room.

The ledger is on the desk. I park the shark on the floor, and take the ledger over to the light. As far as I can see, compartment sixty-seven, up at the end of the room, hasn't been reassigned since the Crypt Boy was carted off to the amphitheatre.

I open the silver door. The tray is empty. I toss the shark in and close up. I'll come back tonight, when everybody's gone home, and rescue it. OK, so the smell's a bit of a giveaway. But it isn't exactly fragrant in here anyway, and if anybody finds the shark, what are they going to do except toss it in the incinerator . . . ?

'But Charlie, you don't get it—'

I'm sitting on a rickety chair, clutching a murderously strong cup of coffee, in a big, high-ceilinged room with a window taking up most of the end wall. Half the panes are patched with cardboard where the glass is broken, but through the others I can see a Montgolfier drifting across a grey sky.

'Sure I do.' My pal Charlie's on his knees, pulling a battered leather case out from under his bed. 'The girl's a menace.'

'But it's not her fault!'

'Try telling that to the boy in the mortuary.' He opens the case and pulls out a paper package.

'Is he still in the amphitheatre?'

Charlie nods. 'The Society's sending somebody in to reinforce Ferdia's protective spell.' He unwraps the package and pulls out what looks like a mouldy parsnip, with withered branches resembling arms and legs. Mandrake. 'And obviously they're looking for an unlicensed sorcerer who conjured up a demon without authorisation.' He tosses the mandrake to me. 'I think your name came up . . .'

I put the mandrake to my nose and get this stale, mouldy, slightly sulphuric smell.

173

'Not very fresh,' says Charlie. 'But at least the beetles didn't get to it.'

The mandrake beetle crawled out of nowhere about six years back and chewed its way through most of the crop. Not a real beetle, by the way; nobody really knows what it is. Some people think it's some sort of demonic emanation, whatever that might be.

'Thanks, Charlie.' It's not even remotely fresh; but it's better than nothing. I put it down on the bed.

'My advice, Frank: turn her in. She's killed people, right? She tried to kill you. I know I didn't see this demon' – he crosses himself – 'but it's obvious she doesn't know what she's doing.' He pats my knee. 'She doesn't give a damn about you, Frank. You're just a pair of eyes she can pull the wool over.'

I don't like that. Because I know it's true.

Preston's wandered over to sniff the mandrake. He sneezes and rolls over on his back, then kicks desperately to get himself right end up. I don't know what's going on inside him – actually, there shouldn't be *anything* going on inside him any more. He found Kazia. It's not his fault I couldn't hang on to her. Job done. He keeps giving me these . . . I dunno, it's hard to read the expression on the face of a beach ball with fins and a feather sticking out of the top, but it's kind of like a cat that knows it's got a one-way appointment with the vet . . .

I jump at the sound of an explosion. Through the window I see a momentary ball of fire glow behind the Montgolfier. The airship judders and goes into a turn as a second rocket explodes, further away.

'Never fly over the Hole.' Charlie picks up Sean's notebook from the table beside me. 'So what's this?'

'It's not important.'

'Why'd you leave it where I was bound to pick it up, then?'

'It's Marvo's brother's stuff. He was a Ghost-spotter.'

While Charlie leafs through the notebook, I sip my coffee and look around. Bare floorboards. Damp patches down the walls. A bucket to catch waste water from the sink.

'Charlie, why do you live in this craphole?'

He doesn't even look up. We both know the answer. Elemental work pays peanuts, but it gives him a last fingerhold on the only thing that ever mattered to him: his few years as a sorcerer. Which is what the jacks count on.

It's not difficult, by the way, instantiating basic elementals. You don't need a huge Gift – in fact, you need very little at all. The forces are out there and they're up for it. But you do need the skills acquired during training as a sorcerer. And when the Gift fades, those skills remain.

I sometimes wonder what I'll do when my time comes. But I prefer not to wonder about it for very long at any one time . . .

I'm looking up at a small cupboard in the corner to the right of the window. It's got glass doors and inside there's just a single object: a small, crudely carved wooden horse with chipped black paint and one leg missing.

Charlie's Gift object.

It's one of those weird things. It's not like it's official or anything; in fact, as far as I know the Society never even talks about it. Nobody ever said anything to me, not even Matthew.

But all sorcerers have one. It's something or other: usually a childhood toy, as far as I can make out. I dunno, it's like you've got this superstitious idea that your Gift sort of lives in this object and that keeping it safe will stop you going post-peak. Bollocks, of course: every sorcerer goes post-peak. But we all like to imagine we're different . . .

Even Matthew had a Gift object. It took me a long time to find it, but one day when I was in his office I spotted a small wooden box on the top shelf of his bookcase. So next time he left me alone there, I got up on a chair and took it down and opened it.

Just a small, cloudy, white glass marble. I managed to put it back and get down off the chair a split second before he came back.

Have I got a Gift object? You bet. Buried for safety in a tin, down by the river outside Abingdon.

Will it save me? Not if I leave it there.

CHAPTER TWENTY-FIVE
The Procedure

'**Y**ou know who this is, don't you?' Charlie's holding up one of Sean's photographs: the toad-faced cleric stares out from the back of the Ghost. 'Bruno Vannutelli.'

'Who's he?'

'Come on, Frank, pay attention at the back. He was a Dominican friar, then Bishop of Cremona. He's the papal legate to the Society.'

'Yeah, so . . . ?'

Charlie sighs. 'He's that cardinal who wants to close the Society down.'

'Oh, him.'

I know the story. Vannutelli popped out of the woodwork when I was a novice at Saint Cyprian's. He preached this sermon about how the Society was an agent of Satan and that it ought to be dissolved and its money and estates confiscated.

The bit about the money and estates went down

particularly well. The pope liked the idea and Vannutelli got the job. When he was my Master, Matthew used to mutter about these meetings he was having with him. He didn't reveal much detail, but I could tell he thought Vannutelli was a puffed-up, sanctimonious shit. Although obviously he put it differently.

I point to the photograph. 'No glasses . . .'

Charlie nods. 'Must've had the Procedure.'

'Wonder how much *that* cost him . . .'

'Come on, Frank, think about it: Vannutelli wants to excommunicate the Society for treating with demons . . .'

'Yeah, yeah. I get it.'

Every novice who survives his first year at Saint Cyprian's undergoes the Procedure. It's an elaborate ritual that lasts all night and involves kissing the back end of a Presence called Buer, a Great President of hell with fifty demons at his command and the power to fix the Blur.

If Vannutelli doesn't have to wear glasses, he must have puckered up for a demon. The cardinal who wants to close the Society down for doing exactly that.

'So if Marvo's bro took a photograph of him like that . . .'

'It'd be a reason to run him over.'

I scratch my head. 'Except a Ghost can't run *anybody* over.'

'What does Doctor Death say?'

178

'That it was an accident,' I say. 'A horse stepped on him.'

Charlie shrugs. 'If anybody knows, Doctor Death should.'

'So where did Marvo get this stupid idea from? Coz it sure doesn't add up.' Doesn't square with what her mother says, either.

'Maybe she just misses him,' Charlie suggests. 'Maybe it's some fantasy she dreamed up so she doesn't have to think about, you know . . . going blind. Strange kid . . . sweet, though.'

'All right, Charlie. I get it.'

'I don't think you do. My advice? If you really want to save someone, stick to Marvo.' He grins. 'Or yourself.'

'I like Marvo . . .'

'There you go, then.'

'But it's not like that.' I grab the photograph. 'I can see this stuff upsets her like hell and I really want to help her, even if she *is* a pain in the neck. I mean, tatties get a raw deal—'

'Yeah, and you could get Buer in to fix it for her.' Charlie puts his hand on my knee for a moment. 'Don't, though.'

Good advice: it'd get me in even deeper shit with the Society.

'I know you don't want to believe Marvo fancies you.' Charlie opens his tobacco tin. 'Because you don't

179

know how to deal with it. That's fair enough – you're only a kid and you've led—'

'Yeah, yeah. A sheltered existence.'

'Will you shut up for once, Frank? The thing about Kazia is, it feels safe saying she's the only girl for you and you've got to save her, because you know she's lying . . .'

Ouch.

'So you don't really have to deal with her.'

Preston's found a new way of amusing himself. He stands on one leg, then leans sideways – if you can really say he's got sides – until he falls over. He bounces back up like a ball and giggles every time.

'If you've found her,' says Charlie, 'what do you need *him* for?'

Preston does this thing . . . I think it's supposed to be an appealing smile, but he's got too many teeth to get away with it, and they're all in the wrong place.

Charlie's rolling a cigarette. 'How did you get dragged into this Crypt Boy malarkey, anyway?'

'Marvo.'

'See what I mean? Inseparable, you two.'

'Yeah, but she doesn't seem that interested.'

'That's not how it looks.' He grins and licks the edge of the cigarette paper. He's enjoying winding me up.

'In the Crypt Boy, I mean.' I jump at the sound of a sharp bang.

Charlie drops his cigarette on the table and goes across to open the door, and it turns out that the thing doing the banging is a metal hook, and that the bloke attached to the other end of it is Dinny.

CHAPTER TWENTY-SIX
A Clever Duck

The thing about Dinny, he has this particular way of coming into a room. He takes one look at me—

'*Salaud!*' That's French for shithead. Dinny flies in like he's on springs and pins me to the wall with the sharpened tip of one hook pricking my throat. 'I look for you.'

'That's nice.'

'Don't be clever duck—'

'Dick, Dinny. Clever Dick.'

The hook bites deeper. I may never breathe again.

'You 'ave money that belong to me. One 'undred twenty pounds.'

'For what?'

One of the reasons I like Dinny, even though he's a total nutter: he never stays mad at you for long. He looks at me reproachfully. '*Mais, pour le requin.*'

I know what he's talking about, but why make it

182

easy? I look blank. He waves his other hook around desperately, his face creased with concentration. Finally, the light goes on—

'For the shark!'

'What shark?' I've got one finger round the hook, trying to lever it out of my throat. 'I mean, we talked about it, Dinny, but I don't remember a deal.'

'But still, you 'ave the shark—'

'Last I saw, it was still lying on the floor back in the Hole.' Hey, it's worth a try.

'Fronk, Fronk.' The sharp tip of the hook glides across my throat. 'I speak to your friend Carter . . .'

'I wouldn't exactly call him a friend, Dinny. Just a jack I know to say hello to.'

'He say, you and your girlfriend—'

Now I know who he means, but suddenly it's like part of my brain's grabbed the lamp and gone wandering off on its own, leaving me standing there in the dark waiting to catch up with myself. After a while it strolls back, and of course the picture it's holding up is . . .

Kazia.

Yeah, bonkers. But just for a moment, I imagine Dinny's looking at me with some sort of respect, and it's like I'm not just this sad case – I'm this kid who's got a girlfriend.

Even if she does keep trying to kill me.

'—what her name?' Dinny's face brightens. 'Marvell!'

183

Charlie's trying not to laugh.

'She's not my girlfriend.'

'If you say. But Carter tell me you take it away together, you and Marvell. So you 'ave the shark, and I do not 'ave one 'undred twenty pounds.' He glares round at Charlie. '*Est-ce juste?*'

Fair? Not really.

'Tell you what, Dinny.' Charlie opens a drawer and pulls out a roll of banknotes secured with an elastic band. 'Sixty quid. Call it quits.'

Dinny frowns.

I say, 'Charlie, that's not fair on you.' But I don't say it very loudly.

'Just till you're sorted.' He turns back to Dinny. 'OK?'

Dinny shrugs and steps away. I check my throat for holes while I watch him open his coat with one hook and pull the inside pocket open with the other. Charlie drops the notes in.

'You understand, Fronk,' says Dinny. 'Business.'

'Sorry, Dinny. Things have been a bit desperate, you know?'

'That is what I 'ear.'

'All right, Frank. Time to go.' Charlie grabs the mandrake and tosses it over to me. 'Just do what the Society wants, for once. Go on the bloody pilgrimage like they ordered you to – you look like you need the fresh air.'

'It's not that simple,' I whine.

'Look, even if you *have* found the girl . . . now what?'

'Yeah, yeah.' I stick the mandrake in the pocket of my jerkin. I'm not a complete fool and I know I'm kidding myself. Kazia keeps kicking me in the teeth; but never hard enough to knock me right out and stop me picking myself up and sticking my chin out again.

Charlie grabs me by the arm and leads me over to the window. He murmurs, 'If it was her who did the magic on the Crypt Boy—'

'Yeah, I know: Matthew.'

Whatever Kazia did to the Crypt Boy, she must have done it long before I dumped the Boss in the cellar.

While he was still giving her orders.

'So talk to him,' Charlie says.

I glance round at Dinny, who's kneeling down, scratching Preston's back with one hook. 'Not that simple.'

'I know he's missing, and it sounds like you've got an idea what happened to him. Frank, the Society know you didn't go to Rome – and what I hear is, they think you know where Matthew is.'

'They won't find him.'

'For Christ's sake—'

'He's not dead. Just . . . somewhere they won't find him.'

At least, I hope not.

'Don't tell me where.' Charlie's got his hands over his ears.

I grab his arms and pull them away. 'Charlie, I'm screwed. It's like I built this thing and now I'm stuck on top of it and it's rigged to explode. I can't get off it. Can't defuse it.'

Charlie whispers, 'If she's a sorcerer . . .'

'Who is sorcerer?'

'Shut up, Dinny. Make coffee.'

''Ow?' Dinny waves his hooks.

Charlie turns back to me. 'The Society won't burn her, if that's what you're afraid of.'

'Wanna bet? They'll take her apart to see how she works. Then burn the bits.'

The Society spent centuries trying to work out why some kids are Gifted. Originally, they thought it was a gift from God. But in 1867 this guy called Walter Beckford started conducting autopsies on the bodies of members of the Society. And he claimed to have discovered characteristics of sorcerers' brains that were different from those of the rest of the population.

His conclusions have always been controversial. But Saint Cyprian's has a whole room full of sections of sorcerers' brains, preserved in formaldehyde and sand-wiched between sheets of glass.

As far as the Society's concerned, Kazia would be a novelty. If they got their hands on her, I figure they'd get slicing. And I know for a fact that some of the research has been done on live subjects.

'A girl with the Gift.' Charlie shakes his head. 'Who'd've thought it?'

'Makes you wonder what else they've been lying about.'

'Wonder all you like, Frank. I don't care any more. Now clear out. Me and Dinny, we've got things to discuss.'

Preston rolls away from Dinny and follows me to the door. I stop with my hand on the knob. 'One thing, Dinny. You know most of what goes on in the Hole.'

He nods proudly.

'Marvell,' I say. 'She had a brother, aged nine. Got knocked down by a Ghost—'

Dinny shakes his head. 'Is not possible.'

'OK, a van or a cab. Ring any bells? It'd be about a year ago—'

'Young boy?'

'Nine.'

'I hear story.' Dinny glances at Charlie. 'The man who tell me, *c'est un connard*—'

'An arsehole.' Charlie grins. 'Like you, Frank.'

I pull a ten-pound note out of my pocket. 'Tell me.'

'So you 'ave money . . .' Dinny gets one hook into my jerkin and pulls it open. When he's checked that my pocket is empty now, he says, 'Not friend to you. This priest—'

187

'Can't imagine you knowing a priest, Dinny.'

'He tell me, anyways, this does not 'appen in the city; it is outside, in the country . . .'

'What was he doing there?'

Dinny watches me tuck the banknote into his pocket. 'He don't say. I don't ask. This is when you say: a year ago. He see lights on the road. A Ghost come slower and slower and stop. He hide and watch. He tell me some men get out. They go round—' Dinny makes circular movements with both hooks. 'Back of Ghost – *le coffre.*'

'The luggage compartment?'

'Yes, they open, and pull out young boy.'

'So then what?'

Dinny just does his famous French shrug.

'This priest, can I talk to him?'

Dinny smiles. 'Charlie is very good friend to you, but you owe me fifty pounds still.'

We both know I keep cash in my studio. In an emergency you can hold a demon off for a few vital seconds by tossing it coins or by burning banknotes.

'OK?' Dinny taps my forehead with one hook. 'I know 'ow you make money.'

I turn lead pipes into gold and sell it. If the Society knew, it would have my hands off.

'Just don't go telling people. OK, Dinny?'

'Of course. I like you, Fronk, *même quand tu me fais chier.*'

'Really, Dinny? I piss you off?'

'This priest: he must not know you are sorcerer.'

'He's ASB, Frank,' says Charlie.

That's handy. 'Can you take me to him?'

Dinny looks round at Charlie, who just shrugs. 'The coffee'll keep.' He gives me this look. 'Just don't go messing about, Frank.'

CHAPTER TWENTY-SEVEN

Automaton

I know I get into trouble every time I set foot in the Hole; but I feel, I dunno, at home here.

I've followed Dinny round mud and raw sewage, dodging rats and mad idiots looking for someone smaller than themselves to jump up and down on. It's pissing rain – there's a surprise. It's like the Hole has its own special weather system, squatting right on top of it.

And by the way, yes: you *can* change the weather by magic. The trouble is, one man's refreshing shower of rain is another man's scorching drought or howling tempest. That's another one that was covered by the First Geneva Convention of 1864: don't fiddle with the weather.

The place Dinny's brought me: hundreds of makeshift shelters straggle down the old castle mound towards the high wall separating the Hole from a branch of the river and the real world. The castle's long gone, except for a crumbling tower overshadowing a sea of mud where people from the Hole put themselves out as casual labourers on crap jobs around Doughnut City, or in the orchards out to the west.

There's a wooden caravan; but the wheels have gone and it's propped up on blocks. The front hinges down to reveal a counter and a small kitchen, so you can get a drink or a rat sandwich. There's a kid inside, gazing vacantly off into space. And a single customer, with a huge gut, face-down in an earthenware tankard.

'There.' Dinny points with one hook.

Over in the shelter of the tower, there's a long pole sticking into the ground, with a metal cross attached to the top. A fat priest stands facing it, with his back to me and his arms held wide. He's got a congregation of sorts: about half a dozen of them, kneeling in the mud, huddled together in the smoke from a brazier.

'You are angry?' says Dinny.

It takes me a moment to get there: 'Hungry, no.'

'Me, yes.'

As Dinny reaches the caravan, the existing customer pushes himself off the counter and lumbers in my direction.

'Try to look like a dog,' I whisper to Preston.

'Who's kidding who?' I get the smell of beer as the bloke jerks his thumb at the worshippers. My heart sinks: I know that voice . . . that seaweed-like crop of curly grey hair, that gleaming red nose—

Norrie Padstowe. Used to drink with my dad, when my dad was still alive enough to drink.

The priest's hard at it. 'Almighty and most merciful Father, we have erred and strayed from thy ways like lost sheep . . .'

'He's cute.' I think Norrie means Preston, not the priest. 'What is he?'

'Abyssinian truffle hound.'

'Any good?'

'What at?'

'Finding truffles.'

'Not really. There aren't any truffles in Abyssinia.' You do realise I'm making this up, right? 'So the breed's nearly extinct.'

Meanwhile, according to the priest, 'We have done those things which we ought not to have done, and there is no health in us.'

Norrie's still staring at Preston. 'He's a funny-looking thing.'

'Have *you* looked in a mirror lately?' Preston mutters.

'What'd he say?'

'C'mon, Norrie. He's a dog.' I give Preston a surreptitious kick.

'Do I know you?' Norrie pulls my scarf away. He blinks – 'Nekker!' – and stumbles back, crossing himself with one hand while he fumbles in his pocket with the other.

'Grow up, will you?' I'm kicking myself. Once an

192

arsehole, always an arsehole. I mean Norrie, not me. For once.

He turns to the idiots under the tower. 'Nekker!' he yells. He's hauled a string of beads out of his pocket and he's waving them around desperately.

'Piss off, Norrie, will you?'

Most of the worshippers try to ignore us and concentrate on inhaling the smoke from the brazier. But the priest has turned round. He yanks the cross out of the ground—

'He's Joe Sampson's kid,' Norrie gibbers. Even his nose has gone white.

The worshippers part like the Red Sea, then fall in behind the priest as he advances through the mud with the cross held high. And there's something about its shape that's worryingly familiar—

'You!'

And as I spot the birthmark on his forehead I realise I have a problem. Like Dinny said, this arse is with the ASB and it's only twenty-four hours since he tried to brain me with the cross, outside the termite nest.

A voice: 'Silas!'

I look round and see Dinny wading back through the mud towards us. The priest is gabbling away in Latin, his eyes burning like live coals. His followers are back on their knees in the mud, crossing themselves madly.

Dinny again: 'Silas! *Arrête tes bêtises!*'

Roughly translated, 'Stop pissing about.'

OK, so the priest's name's Silas and he's holding the cross high in the air, ready to swipe. Just to be sure I know what I'm up against, he's switched to English—

'I beheld Satan, as lightning, fall from heaven. Behold, I give unto you power to tread on serpents and scorpions, and over all the power of the enemy—'

There's this angry bellow and Dinny comes charging past me. Silas falters and stumbles back, towards the tower. Not fast enough. With a metallic crash, Dinny's upraised hooks hit the cross.

They lock together, both red in the face. Dinny gets one hook round the shaft of the cross. He pulls. The hook slides up the shaft until it catches on the cross-piece. He gives it a final, violent yank. The cross tears out of Silas's hands and goes flying past my head to smash crockery inside the caravan.

Dinny's lost his English with his temper. The worshippers scramble for safety as he shoves Silas backwards through the mud and up against the stonework of the tower. Silas is making mewing noises through the hands clasped across his face.

'Dinny.' I put my hand on his shoulder. 'That's enough.'

For a nasty moment I think he's going to turn on me. But then he blinks and smiles—

'Sorry, Fronk.' Stepping back, he hooks Silas's cassock and pulls him upright. 'See what you make me do?'

* * *

Inside the tower there's a tiny chapel. It's maybe fifteen feet square, with dirty white paint peeling off the stones and a mouldy painting of Saint George with a lance, poking a fairly harmless-looking dragon in the eye.

I don't think Silas is seeing anything much except stars. His legs are shaking and the only reason he hasn't fallen over is because Dinny's still supporting him.

'Let him sit down,' I say.

As we park him in a rickety chair, he manages to raise one trembling finger and point to a small cupboard in the wall behind the altar. I open it and find a corkscrew and a dozen bottles of communion wine; at least I assume it's communion wine because it's got the pope's coat of arms moulded on the bottle, just above the label. I grab the oldest – 1952, because that's got to be the crappiest, right? – and I'm halfway through filling a battered silver chalice when I stop dead to give that coat of arms a second look.

'Fronk?' says Dinny.

I'm just standing there, staring at the bottle. The moulded bit, anyway. The coat of arms: a papal tiara over a pair of crossed keys . . .

I'm still blinking stupidly at it when Silas grabs the chalice out of my hand and gets stuck in. Dinny gets the bottle between his hooks and peers at the label. His eyes light up. *'Châteauneuf du pape!'* He tips it back.

'It doesn't keep.' Silas has perked up no end. 'So we

might as well finish it.' He jumps up, grabs the bottle back off Dinny and refills the chalice. It's like magic, how fast that wine disappears . . .

Leaving me clutching the empty bottle. I used to have to gargle wine when they said mass at Saint Cyprian's; and the termites still drag me into the monastery chapel and administer a medicinal dose every now and then. I run my fingers over the coat of arms.

Crossed keys . . .

I haul Sean's notebook out of my inside pocket.

'I went to Saint Cyprian's.' A tear runs down Silas's face. 'But I renounced Satan's gift. I opened my heart to God and resolved to do his work.'

I'm reading Sean's spidery writing again. July 29th. The Grandpont near the Red Bridge. 'Crossed Keys.'

The photograph of the Ghost driver has still got smears of dried mud from when Marvo dropped it. I rub it across the seat of my jeans and peer at the badge on the driver's peaked cap.

'Do you see?' I shove the photograph at Silas.

He pushes it aside. 'I see only the promise of salvation and the threat of eternal damnation.'

'The badge, though – it's the same as the bottle. Crossed keys.'

Silas is hitting his stride. 'Hell yawns at your feet!'

'Yeah, but that's the pope's coat of arms. So this driver' – I'm pointing at the badge – 'the guy he's driving for . . .' It takes a bit of juggling, but I hold out the photograph of Vannutelli, the papal legate, reading without his glasses.

Silas knocks it out of my hands. 'The only thing you need to worry about is that unless you repent of your evil ways—'

'Gimme a break, will you?' I'm kneeling on the floor, gathering the scattered photographs. 'I lost my licence—'

'But did you repent?'

'Sure.' This is all beginning to make sense. I just need to get out of here in one piece. 'Where do I sign?'

Dinny has pulled another bottle out of the cupboard. He sticks it between his thighs and levers the cork out. Wine splashes into the chalice. 'Silas,' he says, 'a year ago you tell me a story . . .'

'What story?'

I've got a sudden sinking feeling that maybe we're going a bottle too far.

'*Il s'agit d'un garçon*—' Dinny stretches out one hook, about four feet off the floor. 'A boy. You tell me you see him . . . some men pull him out from a Ghost—'

Silas just looks blank.

'Don't you remember?' I ask. 'Out in the country somewhere. Right, Dinny?'

Dinny nods. Silas stares glassily at me.

'Without repentance,' he announces, 'there can be no salvation.'

197

'This is a year ago,' says Dinny.

Silas twitches like a string's been pulled. His eyes snap shut . . . then drift open. 'Oh yes.' He's got this empty look on his face. 'But it wasn't out there . . .'

I realise what that blank look reminds me of: the way Marvo's been acting. I wait for him to say more, but he falls back into the chair and just sits there looking dazed.

Finally, I get bored. 'So where was it?'

'In the city.'

'Where exactly?' I figure that's the obvious question.

'Somewhere.' That's nice and specific. 'I remember telling you, Dinny . . . but the boy was run over by a van.'

Have you ever seen an automaton? Nobody makes them any more, because of elementals, but there's a few still lying around in museums and the Society has a couple. These were machines, OK? Clockwork, pipes, metal, leather, paint . . . They looked like a human being or an animal and you wound them up and the cheap ones could do simple stuff like bang a drum or play a tin whistle, but the expensive ones could write letters and make tea.

My point is: Silas reminds me of an automaton. The way he tells the story, it's like I can hear the cogs turning.

'He was killed instantly,' he says.

'Are you sure?'

198

'Quite sure.'

'Did the jacks come? The police—'

The cogs take a bit longer to turn. 'He was run over by a van.'

'Yes, but—'

'Stolen. Two boys, joy-riding.'

'Are you sure it was a van?'

'They had to shoot the horse . . .'

'Are you sure it wasn't a Ghost?'

The cogs jam. Silas just stops moving. The chalice falls out of his hand and rolls away across the floor. His mouth drops open and he sits there, dribbling wine down his cassock. His face has gone white.

I'm still thinking that this kind of reminds me of how Marvo's been carrying on, when Dinny taps his shoulder. 'Silas?'

It's like someone's pulled a lever. Silas twitches and topples out of the chair.

So I slip the photos back into Sean's notebook and stick it back inside my jerkin. I grab Silas by the knees while Dinny gets him under the arms and we haul him up a narrow staircase into a smelly, low-ceilinged chamber.

'That is not what he tell me,' Dinny says as we drop him onto a narrow bed.

I'm looking around at hundreds of crucifixes: wood and metal, hanging from the walls and piled up in boxes. 'So what's going on?'

Dinny smiles. 'Not my problem, Frank.'

'Some sort of spell?'

'I think he just drink too much.'

I don't. I smell a rat: a huge bloody rat about the size of the horse that Silas said got put down.

Downstairs, I grab one of the empty bottles. Outside, Dinny steps on Preston who squeals, 'Abyssinian truffle hound!'

CHAPTER TWENTY-EIGHT

Mouse

It's half-past one and we're halfway up the hill towards Saint Martin's church. I'm clutching the bottle in one hand and the photograph in the other. I've given up on thinking. It's turned into a bad habit.

All I want to do is ditch Dinny. Unfortunately, he has a different priority: he's got his hook in my collar and he's reminding me, very forcibly, about the fifty quid I still owe him—

When we find ourselves surrounded by jacks, all waving guns.

Five minutes later nobody's buying my suggestion that Preston is an Abyssinian truffle hound. Not that they care. They grab Dinny and handcuff him.

Marvo jumps down from a van. She's got her shoulders up around her ears, and she's doing her angry face. 'You knew we wanted to talk to Dinny. Why didn't you tell me—'

'Because he's got nothing to do with any of this.'

Dinny's screaming over his shoulder, 'I get you for this, Fronk!'

'Not my fault,' I yell as the jacks toss him into the van.

'Are you pissed?' Marvo grabs the bottle. She's clever: she can read. '*Châteauneuf du pape?*'

'Yeah, but look—'

She tosses the bottle back to me. I fumble and it smashes on the ground.

'Prat.' Marvo jumps into the van, which rattles off round the corner with Dinny still screaming threats at me.

Ever since I spotted Charlie's Gift object, I've been worrying about my own. It's not very deeply buried, so an animal could dig it up. Maybe the lid isn't completely watertight . . .

It's too far to walk, so I pull my woolly hat down hard over my ears, to hide my shaved head, and jump on an omnibus. I kick Preston into the luggage compartment under the stairs and get bounced along the lower deck as the driver whips up the horses.

Dinny took all the cash I had on me, so when the conductor looms over me I close my hand tight – and when I open it again, a white mouse is scurrying around my palm. The conductor pockets it happily.

I look around the deck. Nobody has noticed . . .

. . . except this little girl, five or six I guess. She's

pulling her mother's sleeve. 'Mummy, he gave him a mouse.'

'Don't be silly.'

The mother glances round at me. Does she suspect? Does she even want to think about it? The kid does—

'But it was a mouse.'

'Be quiet, Evadne.'

What sort of sadist calls a child Evadne?

'But Mummy—'

'That's enough!'

The child's mother glares at me. I smile and try to look like someone who wouldn't hurt a fly or produce a white mouse from up his sleeve.

The bus rattles out along the Grandpont and turns into the Kennington Road. I'd feel more comfortable if I could draw a pentagram on the window, but a big bloke with cropped grey hair is staring at me over what looks like a book of poetry.

We did one poem when I was at Saint Cyprian's, only it wasn't really a poem. Just an incantation to summon an army of angels, written in rhyming couplets. Matthew said it didn't work. I tried it out – natch; all I got was a shower of rose petals and the smell of tar.

As we come into Radley, Evadne's mother hoists her out of her seat and pushes her into the aisle. She catches the conductor's eye and he rings the bell. She's got Evadne by the arm and she's pushing her towards the platform at the back.

As she passes, Evadne stares at me suspiciously. I know I shouldn't . . . but I can't resist it. I hold out my hand, fist closed.

'Do you want one?' I whisper.

She glances up. Her mother is busy clutching the back of a seat, to stop herself being thrown down the bus. Evadne turns back to me and nods.

I open my fist. The mouse is pink this time. Evadne makes a grab for it, as if she suspects it isn't long for this world.

Her mother drags her off the bus and along the pavement. An old man is still struggling down the stairs from the upper deck, so the bus hasn't moved. The mother is talking; I can't hear, but I figure it's, 'What have you got there?'

Reluctantly, Evadne opens her hand. It's empty. As her mother drags her off she sniffs at her palm and stares back at me with wide blue eyes that make me think of Kazia.

The conductor rings the bell. The bus jerks into motion. Evadne is trailing after her mother, down a side street of small wooden cottages.

I wonder if she'll remember me, ten . . . fifteen years from now. A boy on a bus. Maybe just a conjuror; but maybe a real sorcerer. By then I'll be post-peak and pissing about with elementals, like Charlie.

For a moment I'm close to crying.

* * *

The Black Bridge is along the railway tracks, about a mile from Radley station.

I wander around at the foot of the embankment, looking for the right tree. I've got quite a few to choose from, but I finally find it and start scrabbling in the earth at its foot. A couple of broken fingernails later, I pull out a small, rusting tin.

Preston backs away nervously. 'What's that, boss?'

'Nothing to worry about.'

I stick the tin in my pocket, then I shoo Preston up the embankment. The bridge has been under repair for years, so I sit down on a pile of broken sleepers and hug my knees while I wait for a slow train to come along.

I'm thinking about the Crypt Boy, lying in the mortuary with those symbols cut into his body. When I was at Saint Cyprian's, they taught us that any human sacrifice can only be to Satan himself, and you'd only take that risk in order to secure something rather more important than women in their underwear or a luxury flat in Woodstock. Something like vast earthly power, infinite knowledge, or immortality.

The masters warned us off, so naturally I looked it up. The ritual involved slicing into the victim's body to create the symbols from their own flowing blood. Then cutting their heart out and offering it.

The week before they kicked us out into the big wide world, the masters got all the final year together for this big talk. There was a lot of stuff about faith and responsibility and how much we owed the Society. And then they gave us these three cardinal rules:

Don't get a girl up the duff.

Never wear brown shoes with a blue suit.

Don't mess with Satan.

Ever since I realised Kazia was doing magic and that people were winding up dead as a result, I've told myself that she had a rough childhood, what with her mum getting burned as a witch and all, and that she was being exploited by Matthew. Now, though, it seems like she's just the girl you call in if you want somebody rubbed out. And the messier the better.

Marvo always said she was trouble. That's Marvo's problem: she has this nasty habit of being right.

An hour later, a goods train slows down to a crawl as it crosses the bridge. I kick Preston aboard one of the flat wagons and we don't roll off until we're coming into Doughnut City.

CHAPTER TWENTY-NINE

Butterflies

Perched on top of the wall at the back of the termite nest, I gaze across at rags of dirty pink cloud tearing across the sun as it disappears behind the chapel roof.

I'm starving. Nobody in sight. I drop down and head off across the vegetable garden towards the kitchen.

The beds are beginning to look neglected, with leaves gathering in drifts and weeds poking through the black earth. My fault: the cloaking spell has the termites tripping over their own spades.

I tell Preston to wait, and slip through a door, down a dark passage and into the monastery kitchen. I have the place to myself. There's some stale bread in a wooden bin, and a few slices of ham in the ice box . . .

It's creepy this evening, this place. Utterly silent. Not a bump, not a cough, not a fart. It's as if all the termites got drawn up into heaven like Enoch or Elijah . . .

Anyway, at least I'm not hungry any more; and hopefully the sharp pain in my stomach is due to wolfing the grub down too fast, and not food poisoning. Out in the passage, I push open a few doors into the cells. They're all the same: bed, chair, table, crucifix, Bible.

And still not a termite in sight.

I step out into the cloister and hear this strange noise. It's like the rustling of bare tree branches and it's definitely creepy.

I open the chapel door silently and sneak in. Up at the front, the termites are flat on their faces on the floor, in a semi-circle round a statue of their patron, Saint Cornelius Agrippa. He's looking down at them like, what the hell is this? Arms out wide, habits spread out: twenty grey butterflies. They're making this sinister muttering noise that sounds less like praying than . . . I dunno, but they sound really angry.

I know I'm wrecked, but I'm in a very weird mood, even by my standards. I tiptoe towards the front and kneel silently, then lie out flat. Arms wide. The stone floor cold against my cheek.

What am I after? Do I want God to forgive me? Do I expect the saint to step down from the plinth, pat me on the shoulder and tell me it's all right? Do I need to be part of something, even if it's just the termites feeling pissed off with life? Yeah, that sounds about right.

I find myself praying. I'm asking God to give Marvo a break and make it so her brother isn't really dead after all. I'm asking him to save Kazia from whatever she's involved in. I'm asking him to tell me what to do about Matthew . . .

Who am I kidding? It's not like the man upstairs gives a monkey's. I mean, I know the termites say he made the world, but is that really true? Maybe he just tripped over it, like a kid lost in the woods falling over an ants' nest. And now maybe he's having fun poking it with a stick and seeing what scuttles out.

That happened to a crowd of us novices in my first year at Saint Cyprian's. Woods. Ants' nest. After a bit we got bored and just piled twigs over it and set them on fire.

The muttering noise echoes around the chapel, and makes me think of the wind rustling through the tattered clothes of a dead man hanging from a gibbet. There's a waft of incense that smells of rotting flesh. The light outside is fading fast. It's cold in here . . .

So I know I'm asleep because I'm having this dream. I'm in the autopsy room in the mortuary, and it's my dad lying on the slab with a black cardinal's skullcap on his head. He's dead – except his eyes are open so he can watch me. There's a river flowing through the room too, with barges drifting along it. I know where they're going: downstream, to London.

I'm all dressed up in my sorcerer's party outfit – hat, robe, belt, slippers and all the instruments – and I'm doing this spell to bring my dad back from the dead. I've got the incantation written on a piece of paper, but I've come over all Blurry, I can't find my glasses, and I can't read what I've written.

But I think I can remember some of it. I say, 'Marvo,' but nothing happens.

So I say it again and still nothing happens.

I say it again: 'Marvo . . .'

And I'm awake, flat on my face on the cold floor of the monastery chapel.

I sit up. The termites are just lying there, silent, not moving. I get this panic that they've all gone and died on me. So I reach across to the one next to me and shake his shoulder.

Brother Thomas rolls over and his eyes flutter wide, wide open. His face is as white as a shroud and he's staring right up at me . . . but he isn't seeing me.

He starts to shake. Correction: judder.

They're all juddering, like herbs sizzling on charcoal. Their sandals drum on the stone.

A voice: 'Brother!'

I almost jump out of my skin. Brother Andrew is standing over me with this angry look on his face.

I'm on my feet. 'Yeah, I know.'

It's brilliant work, my cloaking spell, even if I say so myself. But it isn't fair. As Andrew closes the door silently behind us, the angry muttering has started up again.

* * *

'That other girl,' says Andrew.

'Marvo?'

'She's waiting in your studio.'

'OK. Thanks.'

I wait for him to go away, but he doesn't.

'How do you do it, Brother?' he says.

'Do what?'

'You know, girls.'

I shrug. 'I guess I'm a sucker for proximate occasions of sin.'

He does this sharp intake of breath. 'Do you want to go to hell?'

'Can't be worse than this.'

He gives me this reproachful look.

'Sorry,' I say.

I let him trail after me and Preston, across the garden and into my studio, where we find Marvo sitting in my surviving chair, beside the unlit fire. She's still doing the black look: beret, coat, trousers and shoes. In the gloom, all I can see is her face, pale like the moon.

'Visitors always welcome.' I pull the tin out of my pocket and break the wax seal round the lid.

'What's that?' says Marvo.

'Guess.'

I hand her the tin. As she brushes her fingers across the lid, a few fragments of dirt fall away. 'It's been buried.' She closes her eyes. '*You* buried it . . . when you made like you'd left town.'

211

'Is that the best you can do?'

'So open it,' says Andrew.

I grab the tin and prise the lid off. In the dim light filtering in through the window, I can just make out a piece of paper, rolled up inside. I stick in a finger and rustle the edges.

'It's money,' says Andrew. But he's cheating because he's leaning over my shoulder.

Marvo's got her face screwed up tight, like she's in pain. 'More to it than that . . .'

'No.' Andrew makes a grab for it. 'Just a ten-pound note.'

'Something that matters to you,' Marvo says, as I shove Andrew away. 'Can I see?'

'Sorry.'

I grab the lid, close the tin and put it up on a shelf.

CHAPTER THIRTY
Falling Off a Log

Preston is perched on the back of the chair, a foot away, watching me. I'm not sure, but in the candle-light I think I detect a hint of transparency.

'What's wrong, boss?'

Why do I get so attached to elementals? I want to cry; so it's actually a relief when Marvo grumbles, 'So what are we summoning?'

'A minor demon.'

'From hell?' Andrew's voice is shaking.

'Do you see anything hidden up my sleeves? Of course, from hell.'

'I didn't think you believed in it,' says Marvo.

'If you'd been paying attention, you'd have heard me say I *won't* believe in hell. But what do I know?'

'It's there all right,' says Andrew. 'And we're all going.'

'Says who?' says Marvo.

'Says the Bible. We're all sinners.'

'Even you?'

'Especially me.' He blushes a deep, dark red.

'You don't have to stay,' I point out. He just stands there, staring unhappily down at his feet. 'Well?' I ask.

'I'll stay,' Andrew mumbles. 'I want to see what we're all in for.'

'Don't get your hopes up.' I pull off my ring and drop it on the bench. 'Like I said, just a minor demon.'

'What's the difference, anyway?' says Marvo. 'You know, major, minor . . .'

'Think of it like the army – you know, hierarchical. Actually, think of it like the Church. There's Satan at the top—'

'Like the pope?'

'That's blasphemy,' Andrew whispers.

'Yeah, but if we're all heading for hell like you say,' Marvo points out, 'who cares?'

Andrew crosses himself.

'So there's Satan at the top,' I say. 'Then half a dozen serious headbangers like Beelzebub, Belial, Mammon, Mulciber and Moloch.'

'That's only five,' says Marvo.

'Then a whole crowd of nutters you wouldn't want to bump into down a dark alley, like my old pal Alastor.'

'So is this gonna take all night?'

'Look, I could get in a lot of trouble.'

'Why're you doin' it, then? Nobody's twisting your arm.'

214

'Oh yeah?'

'I just wanted you to ask about a bit.' Marvo waves her arm around the studio. 'Never said nothin' about this crap.'

'This crap' is the usual fancy dress and razor-sharp cutlery. The inner circle has a copper brazier on a tripod, a small table and a nervous-looking rat in a cage. There's another concentric circle outside with crossed keys chalked at the north, south, east and west, to focus my intention. Outside that, a couple of squares; pentagrams and crosses all over the place; red candles; an outer circle to hold the whole mess; and, beyond that, two equilateral triangles with empty circles inside. Even for a minor demon, you've got to put in the work.

'You don't half look a prat,' Marvo giggles.

Luckily, I can't see myself: apart from my scryer, which is buried at the back of my cabinet, I'm the proud owner of just one mirror, for shaving my head; and since mirrors interfere with magic I've got that safely wrapped in silk, under the mattress.

'I can stop now, if you want.'

There's the four of them: Marvo, Andrew, Preston and the dog. I can handle the herb-throwing myself so I've stuck them all in a single circle, out of harm's way.

'Nah,' says Marvo. 'You might as well get on with it.'

Andrew's been looking nervous from the word go. 'Are we safe in here?'

215

'Perfectly safe. What I was trying to explain to you, the demon I'm going to summon, he's just a pimple on Satan's bum – couldn't hurt a fly—'

'Why can't you just get an elemental?' That's Marvo.

'Coz an elemental can't exercise compulsion.'

'Even on another elemental?'

'Especially on another elemental. Look, I don't have time for this.'

'So if he couldn't hurt a fly, how can he compel—?'

'Trust me. He can.'

I look around the studio. This ritual, it's like falling off a log. But there are a lot of dead sorcerers who thought they were just falling off a log. I've got the herbs and spices in half a dozen dishes on the table beside me. I've got the cutlery: two knives, a silver scalpel, a sword. I've got a silver pentacle hanging on a chain around my neck and a long silver pin stuck through the lapel of my coat.

Most important: I've got Sean's photograph of the Ghost driver with his crossed keys badge.

And Marvo's clutching the framed picture of her brother from her bedroom: I sent her all the way home to fetch it.

'No more interruptions.' I pull a wand out of my belt. 'O Lord God Almighty, full of compassion, aid us in this work which we are about to perform—'

* * *

216

I told Marvo and Andrew they were perfectly safe. But I would, wouldn't I?

The trouble with summoning even the most pathetic of minor demons is that you're opening a gate and you've got to be dead careful about what comes through it. The sorcerer's intention envisages an opening that's the right shape and size and in exactly the right place.

I mean, I don't believe in hell, right? Not literally, anyway. But just suppose all those paintings in churches are even partly accurate. You've got this deep, dark pit that's all spouting volcanoes and bolts of lightning and lakes of fire. You stuff it full of all these mad demons with claws and talons and razor-sharp teeth, bristling with weapons and as pissed off . . . well, as pissed off as hell.

Then I come along and knock a hole in the wall.

Casting a spell is as much about excluding possibilities as it is about making things happen. I want a minor demon, just some little chap who's powerful enough to do what I want, but not so powerful that I have to jump through hoops.

What I particularly don't want is his mean big brother.

It's mainly about my intention: I'm concentrating hard on what I want. But there's also the herbs and spices, which I'm throwing around the place—

'I conjure thee by the living and true God. I invoke thee by all the names of God: Adonai, El, Elohim,

217

Elohi, Ehyeh, Asher, Zabaoth, Elion, Iah, Tetragrammaton.'

You can't have too many names of God. They establish who's in charge around here.

That's me, by the way. In case you hadn't noticed.

We've come to the magic moment. There's a thick cloud of smoke hanging over me. I can feel a tingle of anticipation through my slippers. I risk a quick glance round at the audience.

Marvo's watching intently. Preston's managed to turn himself upside down so he can get his feet over his eyes. Andrew has pulled a wooden crucifix out from under his robe and is muttering furiously to himself.

'Will you put that bloody thing away!' I hiss.

He stares at me, utterly outraged.

'And don't give me that "Brother" shit. If you don't want to wind up as a pile of ashes—'

The crucifix disappears beneath Andrew's habit. I raise the wand over my head and take a deep breath.

'I exorcise thee and do powerfully command thee, that thou dost forthwith appear before me in a fair human shape, without noise, deformity or any companion. Come forthwith, from any part of the world wherever thou mayest be. Come thou peaceably, visibly, affably and without delay, manifesting that which I shall desire. Thou art conjured by the name of the living and true God . . .'

I'm getting the usual effects. The sound of the room

218

has gone dead, like someone's hung thick blankets over everything. The candles burn steadily, but cast no light. Marvo, Andrew and Preston are just dim shapes.

I put the silver disc to my lips, then hold it up.

'Behold the pentacle of Solomon which I have brought into thy presence. I compel thee by order of the great God, Adonai, Tetragrammaton, Jehovah. Come at once, without wile or falsehood, in the name of our Saviour Jesus Christ!'

And we have company in one of the triangles.

CHAPTER THIRTY-ONE
Any Excuse

All demons smell. There's usually a bit of sulphur and, as I've said before, they tend to fart a lot. But this little fellow comes in a blast of lily of the valley.

'Bloody hell,' says Marvo, wrinkling her nose. 'What's his name?'

'Minor demons don't have names.'

'So how do you know you've got the one you want?'

'I'm summoning attributes, not an individual. It's what he can do, not who he is.'

'He looks like a total prat.'

'Watch who you're calling a prat,' the demon growls.

The trouble is, that's exactly what he *does* look like. He's small, for a start – only about two feet tall – like a lizard standing on his hind legs with a head that's far too big for him and a tail that's twice as long as he is but comes in useful for stopping him falling over backwards. He's bright red, with glittering silver eyes, a thick, baggy hide like a rhinoceros, and horns like a goat.

So, a dangerous-looking prat.

I hold up the photograph of the driver. 'Go to wher- ever this being dwells—'

I'd say 'lives', but elementals don't exactly live.

'—and compel him, under pain of immediate dissolution, to come to me. I compel thee in the name of Adonai the most high, in the name of Jehovah the most holy . . .'

Can a demon understand a photograph? He doesn't have to: I understand it and he responds to my in- tention.

Any excuse to self-harm. I roll up my left sleeve, pick up the silver scalpel and slice into my forearm. I let the blood drip onto the photograph, then drop it into the brazier. It curls up. My blood sizzles and I feel a burning pain, all the way up my arm. The photograph turns brown and a rush of flames consumes it. For a moment the pain lances into my heart, so intensely that I think I'm going to pass out. Then it passes in a blinding flash of golden light.

The triangle is empty.

'You OK?' says Marvo.

'I'll live.' I'm binding the incision in my arm with a silk bandage.

'So now what?'

'We wait.'

* * *

After half an hour, Marvo announces that she's bored.

After another forty-five minutes she mutters, 'What's the problem?'

'He has to get here.'

'What? Can't he just—?'

'A demon can manifest . . . well, pretty much instantaneously. Once he's here, he travels at a speed of exactly two hundred and forty-seven miles an hour. The Society measured it, years ago. But the speed of the return journey is entirely determined by the subject.'

'Can't they get a cab?' Andrew sniggers.

'Only on the initiative of the subject. And by definition the subject *has* no initiative. They walk.'

'So if you wanted someone from America—'

'You'd be stuffed. There *is* a spell to have somebody knocked out and shipped in a box, but it's as complicated as hell and you've got to stay in the circle until they get delivered – and when they do, they're usually dead.'

'So you can't do everything with magic.'

'Did I say you could? Shut up now—'

Because we've got some action.

There's no fanfare or anything, just another tingle through my slippers. When I look round, the demon is glowering up at me from one triangle, and the driver is standing in the other.

He doesn't look surprised or upset or anything. That's one of the things I like about elementals: unlike

222

me, say, they accept whatever gets thrown at them. He just stands here with his hands behind his back and a willing smile on his face.

'Can I go now?' the demon growls.

'No. Sit down and shut up.' I pull the silver pin out of my lapel. 'In the name of Adonai the most high. In the name of Jehovah the most holy.' I push the pin deep into the heart of the brazier. The demon sits down with a bump and an almighty fart. His eyes droop and close.

Andrew does his graveyard chuckle. The driver blinks.

I turn to Marvo. 'The picture.'

She holds up the photograph of Sean.

'Do you recognise him?' I ask the driver.

Here's more stuff I like about elementals. They have total recall. And they can't lie.

He nods.

'Show me.'

CHAPTER THIRTY-TWO
Kill Him!

It's a bit like the kinema – except it's like it's really happening. I'm there: I can see, hear and feel everything as if I'm the driver . . .

Night. Through the glass of the windscreen, the Ghost's headlights glisten on the wet surface of a narrow road. The trees slip past. My gloved hands turn the steering wheel. There's just the faintest whisper of the tyres on the tarmac. And the sound of voices through the glass separating me from the passenger compartment.

'You promised me that the Society would be exculpated from any accusation of heresy—'

'And that's what I have recommended to his Holiness.' A thick, oily voice with an Italian accent. 'But I cannot force him—'

'He listens to you. I told you what I want: a papal bull reiterating the terms of the Concordat and acknowledging sorcery as a valid tribute to God and an expression of the divine will.'

'Which will take time.'

'You must see my problem, though. Thanks to my sorcerer, you can see perfectly. But I am still waiting . . .'

'Patience is a virtue. Your reward will be in heaven.'

There's a sound: a muffled sneeze.

'What's that?' The Italian. 'Stop!'

My boots crunch on loose stones as I slide out of the driver's compartment and walk round to the back of the Ghost. I hear water dripping from the leaves of the overhanging trees; and the occasional sharper impact of a droplet on my cap. A bird calls. There's a momentary flash of lightning. Thunder rumbles in the distance.

From the back, the Ghost is just a dark silhouette against the light spilling from its headlamps. My gloves are red in the tail lights as I touch the lid of the luggage compartment.

It opens with a faint hydraulic hiss.

The boy is staring up at me. Even in the darkness, his face is white with fear.

'Don't hurt me,' he says. And sneezes again . . .

I need to be clear about what's going on here. At the kinema you sit back and watch stuff happen on a giant scryer. Here, it's like it's really happening. When I reach in and grab the boy's jumper, I can feel the texture of the knitted wool through my gloves. When I drag him out, I struggle with his weight.

So it's kind of like I'm the driver, actually doing all this. But it's me, Frank Sampson, standing in a magic circle in his studio in Oxford, who recognises Sean Marvell from the photograph his big sister is holding up. It's me, Frank Sampson, who feels sorry for him as he tumbles out onto the road.

'I didn't hear nothing,' he whimpers.

It's me, Frank Sampson, who hears Marvo gasp. I wave my hand for her to shut up.

It's me who recognises the two men getting out of the Ghost. The one with the face like a toad is Bruno Vannutelli, the papal legate to the English branch of the Society of Sorcerers.

The other one has tonsured grey hair and a neatly trimmed beard. His left hand is missing the little finger. I already recognised his voice: the Superior General of the Society, Matthew Le Geyt.

My Master.

It's the driver who feels Vannutelli's hand against his chest, pushing him aside.

Vannutelli stares at Sean. 'I know this boy. He is the one who took the photograph.'

'Reading without your glasses. That was careless—'

Vannutelli makes a little dancing run and kicks Sean savagely in the ribs.

'—and stupid,' Matthew adds.

Vannutelli is standing on Sean's hand. 'What did you hear?' he yells.

226

'I told you,' Sean screams. 'Nothing!'

Vannutelli turns back to Matthew. 'I don't believe him.'

Matthew smiles. 'Why would you?'

'Kill him!'

I hear a cry. A crash. Something bangs into me and I'm thrown out of the vision and back into my studio, where Marvo's got me by the arm and she's screaming at me—

'Stop them, stop them!'

I don't have time to explain that I can't stop events that have already occurred. We've got enough problems in the here and now—

Because magic circles have a dual purpose.

The geometry – the particular combination of shapes and symbols – works with the sounds of the incantations, the smells of the herbs and spices and all the rest of it in order to focus the operator's will and make stuff happen.

If you like, circles break space, creating that gate I was talking about that allows non-physical beings to manifest in physical form.

But once you've got a demon bouncing around the place, you've got to stop him bouncing out of control and getting at your liver. So the geometry also *marks out* space. You summon the demon into a shape that confines him. And you work from an inner circle that he can't get into.

You see the problem: if Marvo's got me by the arm, she's no longer in the protective circle where I parked her. And by busting into mine, she's basically scrambled everything.

The space is open. The gloves are off.

As far as demons are concerned, size is a fluid concept. Our little pal . . . the only reason he manifested as little was because I expected a minor demon to be little.

Now he's bored with being the size I'd expect a minor demon to be, and he's growing. In all directions. And he's changing shape. He's sprouting tusks. Hundreds – no, thousands – of them, until he looks like a giant grey porcupine with a lizard's head and a long, scaly tail that curls and thrashes and smashes things up.

It's around this point that the driver shrivels up and disappears.

The demon's tail sweeps across the studio and right through my circle. Marvo jumps, but I go flat on my back. I see Andrew making a dash for the door.

I yell, 'Let him out!'

The door barks and opens into the room, bang into Andrew, who goes down like a skittle with blood spurting from his nose. Next thing, there's a long blue tongue wrapped around him.

I've no idea what to do.

Marvo does, though. She pulls out her gun and

starts shooting. Six ear-splitting bangs later, Andrew is still being dragged backwards across the floor. Marvo grabs one of my knives and dashes across to stab madly at the demon's tongue.

Andrew's on his feet and out of the door.

Marvo hesitates with the knife in mid-air. Should she go after Andrew or scuttle back to me?

Too late. She's kicking and yelling and trying to pull free, but the tongue has wrapped itself round her head, covering her face, and she's being dragged backwards across the floor into a maelstrom of swirling black water that's disappearing down the demon's throat.

'Adonai, Eloim, Ariel, Jehovah!' I shove my wand into the brazier. The demon starts to give off clouds of thick smoke. There's all these popping noises, like small guns going off, and the tusks are flying across the studio, shattering against the walls and ceiling. I duck as one whistles past my head.

A large ball rolls across the floor, towards the demon. It sprouts legs and a mouthful of splayed, razor-sharp teeth and Preston takes a chunk out of the demon.

This is making less and less sense.

Marvo's out of trouble, but the demon's tail is swinging round again. At the very last moment, Preston tucks himself back up into a ball. The tail hits him bang on and bats him clean off the ground. He bounces off the wall like he's made of rubber.

I grab Marvo's arm and haul her back with me. But

before I can regain control, I have to re-establish the integrity of the circle.

'Don't move!'

I fix the gap where she scraped the chalk marks and scrawl more symbols around the place. My wand's burning up and I don't have time to get to the spare in my belt—

'I charge thee to return whence thou camest, without noise or disturbance—'

Yeah, right! Preston cannons across the floor – and the demon jumps on him. It's like an elephant on a circus ball, front legs waving for balance, back legs paddling madly, tongue and tail lashing.

Preston is screaming.

I'm yelling: 'Begone in the names of Adonai and Eloim. Begone in the names of Ariel and Jehovah—'

Time for the rat. I grab it out of the cage and toss it across the studio. It's a high, wild throw—

The demon goes up for it like a footballer for a header.

I grab my sword.

The demon's still in mid-air. His jaws close on the rat.

I sweep the sword down.

But before I can scream, 'Begone!' for the third time, the demon lands on Preston and squashes him flat. A split second later he explodes, releasing an over-powering stench of sulphur and rotting vegetation.

The candles flare up again. There's chunks of lizard everywhere: skin, flesh and bone, sizzling on the walls and floor. I drop the sword, grab the knife from Marvo and cut the circle.

Preston has popped back into shape and for a second, as I dash across, I think he's going to make it. But he's fading fast and the only reason I can see him so clearly is that blood is pouring down his body, then disappearing as it splashes onto the floor.

'Sorry, boss,' he croaks.

'It's all right,' I whisper. But of course it isn't.

I can still feel his forehead when I stroke it. 'Thanks for finding her.'

He giggles. 'Hey, that tickles, boss!'

And then he just isn't there any more and there's just a small, grey feather lying on the cold floor.

'So,' says Marvo. 'Couldn't hurt a fly.'

I look round at her. 'Just get out of here.'

'Sorry,' she mumbles. 'At least let me help you clear up.'

'Shut up a minute.' I've got a fire burning in the grate. 'In the name of he who died on the tree.' I break my unused spare wand into three, and drop it into the flames.

As the pain in my heart subsides, I look around the joint. To the dog's disappointment, the fragments of demon have fizzled away, leaving a smell of grilled flesh and brimstone. Otherwise there's amazingly little damage: some broken glass, scattered herbs and spices . . .

'At least you know what happened to Sean now,' I tell Marvo.

'Frank, I'm sorry about Preston. I know you were fond of him.'

At least that stupid picture of the pope has fallen off the wall and smashed. I get a dustpan and brush and start sweeping up the pieces.

'You know your trouble, Frank?'

'No, but I'm waiting for you to tell me.'

'You get more upset about a bloody elemental than you do about real people.'

'That's not true. He was just an elemental. I can easily build another one if I want to.'

But I'm not sure that I do want to. Maybe it really is time to chuck it all in and get out of town. 'Are you going, or do I have to give you the same treatment?'

'Frank, you gotta stop fighting me. I'm on your side.'

That's when I chuck the brush at her.

She ducks and says, 'You told me an elemental can't harm a human being.'

'The driver of a Ghost can't.'

'Look, I know you don't want to talk to your boss. But you gotta.'

And that's when I throw the brazier at her.

CHAPTER THIRTY-THREE
Backbone

It's dark and deserted on the riverbank. A faint blue phosphorescence flickers along the bars of the wrought-iron gate. The security elemental steps silently out of the darkness.

I raise my hand. The gate opens.

'Welcome to the Bishop's Palace, Mr Sampson,' the elemental whispers. 'Detective Constable Marvell . . .'

'Thank you. We'll be about an hour.'

'Whatever suits you, sir.'

'Arselicker!' Marvo mutters.

We go across the lawn and up the steps to the terrace. A touch and a whisper. The French windows into the library swing open.

'What's that?' Marvo whispers.

Out of the darkness the door in the corner mutters: 'You again, is it?'

I push Marvo in ahead of me, pull the French windows shut and drag the curtains across. The door is still muttering away, promising all the pains of hell. I decide to risk a little light. I fumble my way over to the centre of the room . . .

'Careful,' says Marvo, a split second before I bang into the desk.

'Serves you right,' the door chuckles. 'Skinny little freak!'

Marvo sniggers.

I feel around the desktop and find the lamp. The battery's almost flat, but there's just enough of a glimmer to see.

The door is in the corner, to the right of the fireplace. It's narrow and comes to a pointed arch. It's still complaining: 'Miserable little shit!'

The wood is covered in symbols that go back hundreds of years to when the door was first instantiated to conceal the sorcerer's lair beneath the palace of the Bishop of Oxford.

Yeah, what does that tell you about bishops?

The original symbols were carved into the wood. Beautiful work. They keep the door invisible to anyone who doesn't know it's there, so palace staff don't go wandering down and getting dismantled.

There are some later additions crudely scratched into the surface; then there's chalk, paint—

'Is that blood?' says Marvo.

Yeah, where Kazia's tried to get in. And she'd have made it if I hadn't kept plastering the door

234

with dozens more symbols.

I place my hands flat against the surface of the door, and close my eyes. I can hear a sound in the distance, like waves breaking on rocks. The door quivers. For a moment it's cold and smooth, like glass.

'Adonai, Tetragrammaton . . .'

The door growls wickedly . . . but swings open.

'Go on.'

Marvo's eyeing the door nervously. 'Are you sure it's safe?'

'Have you got the pentacle?'

She shows me the golden chain wrapped round one hand, with the silver disc hanging from it.

'Then you're fine.'

She runs a finger down the surface of the door, and puts it to her nose. It hisses back at her. I give her a push and she stumbles off down the stone stairs.

'So how's it going down there?' I ask the door as I slip past after her.

'Get lost!' It closes behind us, leaving us in pitch darkness. 'Skinny little freak.'

We fumble our way down the spiral stairs. I can hear something moving around down there. Chains rattle. The crash of something breaking.

'Stay behind me.' I squeeze past Marvo as we reach the bottom. 'Anything could happen—'

And it does. The welcoming committee is on its way.

Alastor hasn't got any smaller over the last few days.

Still seven feet tall. Still armed to the razor-sharp, yellow teeth. He lets off a scream like a locomotive going off a viaduct. The chains of his scourge whistle through the air towards me.

Not unreasonably, I step back up the stairs and sit down hard on Marvo as the hooks at the ends of the chains carve deep, bloody gouges out of mid-air. Lumps of flesh sizzle on the tiled floor. The smell of scorched meat elbows its way into the general stench.

A deafening bang rattles my teeth. The whole building seems to shake and tilt on its foundations. It's like there's this thick glass wall across the bottom of the stairs and Alastor has managed to get his axe embedded in it. He's wrestling with it now, trying to get it out. His face is black with the effort and smoke is pouring out of his ears and nostrils.

The axe comes free and he disappears backwards into the gloom of the chamber. There's the sound of splintering wood.

'Get off!' Marvo kicks me.

I feel a momentary tug of resistance as I fly off the bottom step, like passing through invisible strands of silk. I look round: the protective symbols I scrawled down the entrance to the staircase, to contain Alastor, are undisturbed.

I wouldn't still be breathing if they weren't.

And he's doing railway engines again, coming at me like the 8.45 to Paddington, axe in one hand, scourge

236

in the other – smoke, flames, the works.

I hold up my pentacle.

It worked last time, so why not now? I turn my head away and clap my free hand over my eyes. I'm shaking all over and dripping with sweat and I'm squeezing the pentacle so tight it's in danger of just flying out of my hand . . .

Screeching noises. Then silence. OK, I still seem to be here, so after a couple of seconds I risk peeking through my fingers.

Alastor's standing just a yard away, both weapons raised to strike. He's gone even blacker in the face and he's trembling. He opens his mouth wider than the gates of hell and vomits up a stream of fire.

I can tell he's pleased to see me.

The pentacle glows, dazzling white, and goes as cold as ice in my fingers. The flames roll around me.

I'm shivering.

The fire dies away. Alastor reels back, eyes rolling. The axe and scourge rattle on the floor.

'Well, Frank.' The Boss's voice is a dry rasp. 'That was all good knockabout stuff.' He doesn't look any better than the last time I was here. More ragged. Hands trembling. And he's got this wild look in his eyes like the world has ended and he got to watch. He coughs like he's dredging garbage out of a stagnant pond, then he closes his eyes and sways on his feet. His eyes flicker open. Controlled again. 'I was wondering if you'd have the backbone to come back.'

'Are you all right?' I ask.

'Do I look all right?'

I don't really understand what happens next. But it's like he's pulled the stopper out of the bottle and there's this flood of stuff pouring out of me.

'It's not my fault!'

I fall on my knees, which hurts like hell. And I bang my head on a pillar, which hurts even more. And it's like there's part of me that's play-acting . . . and a part of me that's sitting back watching the performance . . . but there's *another* part of me that really needs this.

So I'm dribbling snot, and for all I know Alastor is creeping up behind me, but I can't stop myself—

'It wasn't my fault! I mean, I didn't know what—'

'Frank!'

The Boss is staring over my shoulder with this startled look on his face. I roll and turn, expecting Alastor—

Marvo's got her gun clutched in both hands. It's not pointing at Alastor – that'd be a waste of time, anyway – but at Matthew.

I jump up and step between them.

'Get out of the way, Frank.' She sounds like she means business.

'What's the plan, Marvo?' At least I've stopped snivelling. 'Take out the entire Society of Sorcerers, starting at the top?'

'Just him.' Her voice is dull, like she's half asleep. The pentacle catches the candlelight as it swings on its chain beside the trigger. 'He killed Sean.'

I glance round at Matthew. 'You've met my pal Marvo before . . .'

'Detective Constable Marvell. Yes, I believe I've had that pleasure.'

'She's not in a great mood right now.'

'So I see.' He's trying to sound calm, but he's got that look in his eyes like he could lose it any second. 'Who *is* this Sean I killed?'

'Don't pretend you don't know.' Marvo's hands are shaking. Sometimes the gun points at Matthew. Sometimes it's pointing at me. Even Alastor is beginning to look a bit nervous.

'August last year,' she says. 'You were driving in a Ghost with . . .' She turns to me. 'What was the bastard's name?'

'His eminence the Bishop of Cremona, Cardinal Bruno Vannutelli.'

'Right. Sean was in the luggage compartment—'

'Who's Sean?' Matthew screams.

'Her brother.' I take a deep breath. 'I don't know *how* he got there, but he was a Ghost-spotter and he took this photograph.' I pull it out of my pocket and unfold it: the image of Vannutelli stares up angrily from the document he's reading. 'Sean noticed there was something wrong—'

'No glasses,' Marvo points out.

'I think maybe he started trying to follow Vannutelli. Maybe he saw the Ghost parked at the side of the road or something, and he got carried away and decided it'd be nice to go for a ride—'

'He always wanted to ride in a Ghost,' says Marvo.

'A worthy ambition for any young man.' The Boss sounds . . . I dunno, amused and pissed off at the same time. The worrying bit is, he still looks like shit but he's got this air about him, like he knows what's going on now and he's in control. 'Although I can't imagine what it has to do with me.'

'He was my brother,' says Marvo.

'I got that. And he told you this . . . story?'

'He can't. He's dead.'

'But naturally, being a tatty, you can communicate with the dead.' I think Matthew's trying to do some sort of smile, but it's more of a grimace, like it hurts him to move his face.

'I summoned the driver,' I say. 'He told us—'

'He *showed* us.' Marvo's voice is dead flat. The gun, alarmingly, is still aimed at me. 'Frank, I swear to God—'

I flap a hand at her. 'Will you point that thing somewhere else?' I turn back to Matthew. 'Vannutelli's driver showed us how he found Sean hiding in the luggage compartment. Vannutelli told you to kill him.'

Matthew is stroking his beard. 'As I recall, an

240

elemental's evidence is inadmissible in a court of law.' He turns to Marvo. 'Detective Constable Marvell, I think there's one thing you should be aware of . . .'

He has advanced to the edge of his circle so that he's just a couple of feet from her. She steps back uncertainly, the gun shaking in her hands.

'Marvo!' I say. 'The pentacle!'

I'm trying to help, but I just make it worse. Marvo looks round and sees Alastor right behind her. She's still clutching the gun in both hands, with the chain of the pentacle wrapped round her fingers. When she tries to take one hand off the gun to wave the pentacle, the chain gets tangled up in the trigger, and she's backing away from Alastor, trying to tug the pentacle free, when Matthew says, clearly and distinctly:

'Your brother's alive.'

CHAPTER THIRTY-FOUR

The Pariah Spell

And I finally realise what's wrong with Marvo.

I thought it was just my cloaking spell that kept whacking her over the back of the head. But there's something else – some other magic. There's no other way to explain it. Her knees fold. Her head hits the tiled floor. Her arms fall wide. The gun rattles one way, the pentacle the other.

Alastor's making a dive for her, with his axe raised and this triumphant grin plastered all over his gob. I'm just realising that I can't get to her in time—

When Alastor stops dead, staring at something behind me. I spin round and see this kid come trotting out from the stairs.

He's an elemental. I should know, because I instantiated him after I ditched Matthew in the cellar. He's wearing a grey school uniform: jacket, shorts, long socks, blue cap and tie. He's got a brown leather satchel over his shoulder, and he's carrying a bucket with a lid.

'Oh, shit and hell,' Alastor groans. 'Not now!'

I built the kid so that Alastor can't get at him. As he steps off the bottom of the staircase there's a sound like a small bell ringing, and he's enveloped in a ball of dazzling golden light. Alastor squeals and puts his hands over his eyes and reels back; and I've got enough time to jump in front of Marvo, waving my pentacle, before the golden ball dissolves and the kid steps out into the circle beside the Boss.

The bucket rattles emptily as he drops it on the floor beside the one that's already there. He unbuckles his satchel and pulls out a small paper-wrapped package and a glass bottle.

I've scooped up Marvo's pentacle and stuck it back in her hand. But Alastor has done a scoop of his own: he's got her gun.

'Stop him!' Matthew gasps.

I can't think of anything better to do than wave my pentacle around. Alastor is turning blue now, starting from his feet. He's pointing the gun at each of us in turn and jerking it wildly—

But my magic is holding: he can't actually pull the trigger. As the blue colour spreads through his torso and neck, rising up his head like water filling a glass tank, he spins round and looses off shot after shot into the walls. The bullets whine and ricochet. Anyone who's not a demon or an elemental is on the floor.

243

Clicking noises. Alastor pulls futilely at the trigger. Finally, he eats the gun.

Marvo's eyes are open. I pull her to her feet. 'Damn it, Marvo! This is getting boring . . .'

She's looking around. 'Where's my gun?'

There's the sound of a brief, precise fart and a waft of sulphur. An empty cartridge case rattles across the floor behind Alastor.

'Too late,' I say.

'I'm still gonna kill him.' She's looking at Matthew.

The kid has opened a neat stack of sandwiches. He takes the lid off the old bucket and drops the paper wrapping inside. Matthew stands there, staring down at him. He's got both hands to his head, like he's trying to stop it bursting apart.

'Oh God!' he says.

Look, I try not to do . . . you know, deep stuff. Because it doesn't really get anybody anywhere and it just makes me feel bad. But the Boss . . . well, he looks like hell, even if he hasn't actually been dragged off there yet. It's like his whole face has sagged.

He's been down here for three weeks, remember. And it's my fault.

I watch the kid throw his empty satchel back over his shoulder and pick up the bucket. He may be an elemental, but he struggles with the weight in the split second before he steps out of the circle and is transformed again into a ball of light. Alastor holds his

244

hands over his eyes until the kid has disappeared up the stairs.

Another fart. Another empty cartridge case rattles across the floor behind Alastor.

'This cardinal – Vannutelli. Who is he, anyway?'

'C'mon, Marvo, I told you—'

'Yeah, but what do *you* know?' She points at Matthew. '*You* tell me.'

Matthew sighs. 'He's a papal legate – a diplomat, if you like. He came to Oxford last year to negotiate an agreement between the Society of Sorcerers and the Vatican.' He turns to me. 'You've got to let me go, Frank. This is more important than . . . some fantasy about a stupid child. It's about the future of the Society—'

That goes down well with Marvo. 'I don't care about the future of the Society,' she says in her dull voice.

'Then maybe you should!' Matthew snaps. 'What do you know about the Concordat?'

Notebooks out for a history lesson.

The Society of Sorcerers was founded in 1513. Fifty years later, Pope Pius IV issued a papal bull, *Regimini artis magicae ecclesiae*, recognising the Society and authorising it to develop the Craft in the service of God and the Church.

On 15 September 1590 a cardinal called Giovanni Castagna was elected pope and took the name Urban VII. He had two bees in his bonnet. One was tobacco:

he announced that anyone caught smoking in a church would be excommunicated. The other was sorcery: he set up a commission to close down the Society of Sorcerers.

Twelve days after his election he was ambushed at the high altar of Saint Peter's, in front of a screaming congregation, and hauled off to hell by a crowd of demons.

Over the next few centuries, the Society got into the habit of hauling demons up out of hell to make things explode. The Church couldn't stop it, but it never quite let go of the idea that this wasn't really what God had in mind.

Things got sticky again towards the end of the nineteenth century, and the Society sent in a flock of demons to pull the dome off Saint Peter's and drop it in the river Tiber. The Church didn't see the joke and excommunicated the Society. A week later, on his Easter appearance to bless pilgrims, the pope turned into a piano and started rattling out a selection of popular waltzes.

Everyone agreed that this was getting silly. So in 1908 they finally signed the Concordat, a document the size of an encyclopaedia agreeing what they could and could not do to each other.

Matthew's Gift is long gone. He's standing in a magic circle with a stack of sandwiches, a bottle of water and a bucket. But I've noticed it before: he's got this other gift, the ability . . . I dunno, just to take charge of a situation. Doesn't matter what sort of shit he's in.

'All I know is what Frank's told me,' Marvo says. 'Sounds like a stitch-up to me.'

Matthew smiles wearily. 'But a stitch-up that has kept the Church and the Society from turning on each other . . . until Vannutelli came along.' He turns to me. 'He was a member of the Society, of course.'

Of course he was.

'He was in my year at Saint Cyprian's. A marginal Gift. He left after two terms.'

'So what does he want?' Marvo asks.

'To close the Society down.'

Yeah, the Church hierarchy is stuffed with these guys who studied sorcery but didn't have enough of a Gift to go all the way. Most of them get over it and settle for doing cheap card tricks and throwing their weight around. But you always get a few of them who really resent the Society for messing with their heads and decide that it's time someone took it down a peg or two. The ASB is packed with them.

'He truly believes that sorcery is Satan's work,' says Matthew. 'He has a lot of support in the College of Cardinals. And he has ambitions to be the next pope.'

'So what?' I say. 'I mean, if he tries anything, the Society can have him turned inside out and folded along the dotted lines.'

Matthew looks up at me. 'Have you heard of the Congregation for the Defence of the Holy See?'

'Nope. Sounds fun, though.'

'The Vatican has its own team of sorcerers—'

'You couldn't make this shit up, could you?' Marvo mutters.

'With a single purpose: to defend the Church against any magical assault by the Society of Sorcerers.'

'So these guys,' I say. 'They're just hiding out on top of a mountain or something . . . ?'

'The papal palace at Castel Gandolfo, actually.'

'Sniffing the air for trouble and keeping a mob of demons ready to jump out?'

'They say angels.' Matthew smiles bleakly. 'I'd be surprised, though. Anyway . . .' He smooths his hair back. 'Let's talk about your friend's brother. Do you know what a pariah spell is?'

'What is this?' I say. 'A quiz?'

'Shut up and listen, Sampson. You might learn something.' Matthew turns to Marvo. 'It isn't taught at Saint Cyprian's. In fact, as far as I know, the only copy of the actual spell is in the Closed Archive.'

'What's that?' she says.

'An archive of documents to which only the Superior General has access.'

I'm beginning to get it: 'Pariah as in . . . outcast . . . ?'

'The immediate effect of the spell is to put the victim into a coma. In the only documented case of its enactment, in Paris in the mid-seventeenth century, the victim lay in an apartment, alive but unconscious, for more than fifty years—'

'Didn't anybody find him?' says Marvo.

'That's the "pariah" part.' Matthew smiles proudly. 'The other tenants of the building unconsciously conspired to forget that the apartment was even there.'

I get it. Like a cloaking spell, but done *on* somebody, rather than *by* somebody.

'His family, all his friends,' says Matthew. 'Everyone who knew him thought he was dead. They even thought they'd attended a funeral.'

'So Vannutelli told you to kill Sean,' I say. 'But you didn't—'

'It would have been wrong.'

I manage not to laugh.

'Vannutelli wanted him dead,' Matthew says. 'And in retrospect that would have been the cleanest solution. But it seemed . . . I don't know . . . just wrong to me. I remembered the pariah spell and dug it out of the Closed Archive.' He grins and I notice that his gums have receded in the time he's been here; his teeth are like fangs now. 'I had a sorcerer at my disposal—'

'Kazia.'

'Exceptionally talented and not known to the Society.

249

I retrieved the pariah spell from the archive. It took us several days to disentangle it and assemble the necessary materials—'

I look around at the tiled floor with its chalked traces of magic. And I'm about to ask whether they enacted the spell down here, when the answer just pops into my mind—

Of course: Matthew and Kazia took him to a ruined church in the Hole.

Sean Marvell: the Crypt Boy.

Matthew smiles. 'It all worked. Better than I had expected—'

'But not well enough.'

'With hindsight, I realise why the spell was originally banished to the archive. Any pariah spell is doomed to failure by its own internal contradictions.' He gestures in Marvo's direction. 'As you can see, in this case it persuaded your colleague to believe that her brother was dead. But it contained no mechanism to deal with her obsessive need to resolve the illusory mystery of who killed him. It was therefore doomed to unwind sooner or later . . .'

'What are you two goin' on about?' Marvo really doesn't look well.

'Sean.' I've had about enough of this now. Or maybe I'm just testing. 'He's still alive.'

Yup, it's a pariah spell. It stopped Marvo from ever entering the same room as the Crypt Boy, in case she recognised him. Now it stops her from even thinking about him. Her eyes roll up in the sockets and I just manage to grab her under the arm before she tips over.

'C'mon,' I say. 'Let's get you out of here.'

'You're going?' Matthew's holding out one hand and he looks . . . I dunno, like an abandoned child, or something. I know the look: I caught my reflection in a window, the day they dragged me off to Saint Cyprian's. 'Frank, you can't!'

But the hand he's holding out . . . it's his left hand, and I know it's deliberate. He's even holding it palm up, slightly turned out, to show where he sacrificed the little finger to save my life.

I'm a sucker for a lot of things, but there are limits. 'I got what I came for.' I can't tell you how good it feels, saying that. And I realise just how angry I am with Matthew.

'You have to let me out,' he says. 'What about the Society?'

I don't care about the Society: let Vannutelli close it down. I see no reason to tell Matthew that Sean has been found. I feel in control—

And that worries me. I step back to check the symbols keeping Alastor in. Looking over my shoulder, I see the demon sitting on the floor, his back against one of the columns, with one blade of his dagger up his nose, working away.

Matthew has folded his arms. 'I *shall* get out of here, one way or another.'

251

Alastor glances up and grins. 'Happy to help.'

I push Marvo through the door at the top of the stairs. It slams behind me, nearly catching my fingers.

'I'll get you for this, you bugger!' it hisses.

Charming.

CHAPTER THIRTY-FIVE
Shock Treatment

Out on the riverbank, the sun's just up and not looking very cheerful about it. I turn to Marvo. 'Got your scryer? OK, call Charlie. Ask him to meet you at the goods entrance of the mortuary.'

'Why?'

'Just do what I tell you.'

'Why can't *you* do it?'

In the few days since I tripped over her in the Hole, she's been getting paler and paler. She's lost weight and she even looks smaller.

'I told you, the Society listens in to scryers—'

I'm not entirely sure about that, but would *you* trust them? I watch Marvo haul out her scryer. She looks round at me—

'Why?'

'Why what?'

'Why are we going to the mortuary?'

It's a good spell, a pariah spell.

'You'll see when we get there. Outside, remember—'

'I ought to call Caxton.'

'And tell her what? Just call Charlie, will you?'

By the time we've walked up to the mortuary, I still don't know if this stunt is going to convince Marvo that her brother's alive. And even if it does, I'm damned if I know how to fix him. Kazia did the dirty work, maybe she can undo it . . . except that I've got to find her and talk her out of trying to do me in again. And I have to find some way to straighten things out with the Society – not the easiest thing to do when you've got the Superior General locked in a cellar with a demon.

And even if I sort Marvo out, I still have to find a way to explain to Caxton how Sean got into this state, without blowing the whistle on Vannutelli, Matthew . . . and Kazia.

Charlie's waiting outside the open door at the back of the mortuary. Marvo's wobbling like hell, so I prop her up against the wall and take him aside and explain what we've got to do. Which is actually very simple.

We just grab Marvo and push her inside. At first she's confused. Then she gets scared and starts to struggle. We drag her along corridors and round corners. Finally, I shove her through the door into the amphitheatre.

The Crypt Boy is still lying on the floor, at the centre

of Ferdia's protective circle. Pale as death. Black marks scored across his protruding ribs. Mouth gaping. Eyes open, but every bit as unconscious as he was before. I'm getting that feeling again, that it could be me lying there . . .

Ferdia stares. Caxton's spectacles fly off and rattle on the floor as she spins round.

'Bloody hell, Beryl, do you live here?'

'OK, so he's got under my skin. What's *your* story?' She's on her knees, fumbling around for her specs.

'I need Marvo to see something.'

Ferdia has walked over to her. He puts his hand to her forehead and gives me this angry look. 'She's running a fever.' He turns back to Marvo. 'You should be in bed.'

She just stands there, inside the door, staring around. Her voice shakes. 'What's goin' on?'

'Sean.' I point helpfully. 'There.'

'It's not funny, Frank.'

'C'mon, Marvo.' I'm still pointing. I can see her eyes darting across the floor, not seeing what I want her to see.

Ferdia has her by the hand. 'Let's get you out of here.'

I yell, 'For Christ's sake, Marvo! Will you just *look*?'

She stares at me, totally bewildered. 'Look at what?'

I'm pointing again. I can't think of anything better to do. 'Sean.'

Caxton's found her glasses. 'What are you playing at, Sampson?'

'It's her brother.'

'Where?'

Why stop pointing now? 'There!'

Caxton stares down at the kid on the floor. 'Her brother's dead.'

'That's what they wanted you to think.'

'Who?'

And it's time to shut up. If I mention Matthew, Caxton's bound to talk to the Society and they'll remember that Matthew's missing and that they'd quite like a word with me. OK, so they're already on my case and I can go back to hiding out in my studio, but sooner or later someone's going to realise that if Marvo came through the door with me tonight, she must be able to answer their questions . . .

And I don't think Marvo's in any state to know what not to say.

Shock treatment. I push Ferdia out of the way, grab Marvo by the arm and drag her into the circle. Candles and herbs go flying—

'Are you mad?' Ferdia's heading in my direction, but Charlie gets in his way.

I force Marvo down onto her knees. But it suddenly reminds me of when I was a nipper and I came home with this puppy, and the first thing it did was shit on the floor; and my dad just grabbed it by the scruff of the neck and rubbed its nose in the mess.

It didn't last long, the puppy.

Me neither. Last try—

'Marvo, it's Sean – can't you see?'

But the thing is, she *won't* see.

I hold her there for a moment, gazing down at the pathetic figure on the floor and trying to square it with the plump little boy in the photograph in Marvo's mum's front room. I see no resemblance.

Marvo's whimpering and trembling. I let go of her. She crawls out of the circle and scuttles over to the wall. Then she curls up in a ball and just lies there with her shoulders shaking.

'Nice work,' says Caxton, picking up a candlestick. 'Now, do you want to explain what you think you're doing?'

Under the circumstances, I decide that the best thing to do is just run for it.

CHAPTER THIRTY-SIX
A Plan

Since I'm here in the mortuary anyway, what about what's left of the shark?

The diener on duty, when I get down to the utility area . . . he isn't exactly a pal, but he's prepared to go off on a fag break while I fetch something to toss into the incinerator.

The door of the children's ice room closes behind me. The gas light is burning low and I can barely make out the wall of doors concealing the dead kids.

I check my watch and it's not late; there should be somebody on duty. And I'm about to yell out when I hear something. I don't know why it spooks me. It's just a bit of rustling and scratching, coming from right up at the far end of the room. I put my hand against the wall on my left, opposite the compartments, and tiptoe along the room. There's a distinct smell of decomposing shark.

I almost jump out of my skin as a black shape appears from behind the desk. The kid – the assistant – stretches up to clap his hand across my mouth. He pulls me down and whispers, 'Don't make a sound.'

I pull his hand away and whisper back, 'What is it?'

He points round the desk. I creep forward on my hands and knees.

The line of silver doors along the wall opposite is broken, right at the end, by a black gap, like a missing tooth, where one of the compartments is open. And there's a dark shape beside it, the size of a human being . . .

I know at once what it is. I turn to the kid. 'Come with me.'

In my old robing room, I drag a linen robe on over my jerkin, get rid of my ring and grab a pile of gear. Paper hat and red silk scarf. Wand, knives, sword. Brazier and charcoal. Herbs and spices.

The kid helps me carry everything back to the ice room. 'Can I do it?' he whispers.

'Just stay behind the desk.' The brazier is glowing. I've tied the silk scarf around my waist and stuck the sword and knives through it. I'm holding the wand between my teeth. I crawl out, pushing the brazier in front of me, the smoke stinging my eyes . . .

I never thought I'd say this, but it's a sad sight, the demon.

259

The blue and white pyjamas are grimy and torn, with ragged, grey feathers drooping out through the rips. His comb has collapsed and fallen across one side of his head so he can only see out of one eye, which has gone a milky white, with a trail of pus running from the corner.

He only notices me when the brazier scrapes on the stone floor. I toss in a handful of herbs and as they flare up, I recite, 'O Lord God Almighty, full of compassion, aid me in this work which I am about to perform.'

The demon stiffens and turns his head, until he can see me out of his one working eye. He has dragged out the tray where I ditched the dead shark, and has pulled away lumps of meat with his one lobster-like pincer.

'I command thee, O Spirit, by all the names of God: Adonai, El, Elohim, Elohi, Ehyeh, Asher, Zabaoth, Elion, Iah, Tetragrammaton . . .'

And we're off. The demon just stands there, chewing steadily. Finally, I get to the real business—

'I do exorcise thee and do powerfully command thee, that thou dost forthwith reveal unto me—'

Something tugs at my sleeve. I look down and see the kid.

'I thought I told you—'

'*Can't* I do it?'

'Do what?' says the demon, in Kazia's voice.

I've never been freaked by this trick before: a demon speaking in the voice of his summoner. But there's a first time for everything . . . I'm working wild: no circle to protect me. And, as my wand rattles on the floor, no instrument to control the demon. He drops the shark on the tray, clamps his pincer round the kid's head and lifts him clean off the ground.

I grab the silver disc hanging round my neck. Kiss it. Hold it up—

'Behold thy confusion if thou refusest to obey me! Behold the pentacle of Solomon which I have brought into thy presence! Behold him who is armed by God and without fear—'

That's me, OK? Although right now I'm on the floor, fumbling for my wand. The kid's kicking and screaming while the demon shakes him like a rag doll.

'Prepare to be obedient unto thy master.' I'm still on the floor, sticking my hat back on my head and thrusting the tip of the wand into the brazier. 'In the name of the Lord!'

The demon raises his head and howls. The kid hits the floor with a thud. I kick him in the arse and he scuttles away.

I pull the wand out of the charcoal and blow out the flame. 'Look, I'm tired.' I give the pentacle another peck and hold it up again. 'Now I've got this thing, so will you just stop messing me about and tell me your name?'

'Archasis,' the demon whimpers.

'Thank you.' I've never heard of him, but if a demon

261

has a name, knowing it helps you control him. And I see no reason not to be polite. 'So what's going on?'

'I was hungry.' He tears off another strip of meat.

And I think I get it. Kazia conjured Archasis up to nail the Crypt Boy. He failed, and with the kid safe inside Ferdia's protective circle he's . . . well, kind of lost. He's malformed and probably in pain – actually, I've never seen a demon look so pathetic and scared. But Kazia's intention has drawn him to the compartment where the Crypt Boy was originally stored . . . and where, because it was empty, I hid the shark.

Interesting. But back to work. Because I've suddenly had an idea.

'By the pentacle of Solomon have I mastered thee. Now I compel thee by order of the great God, Adonai, Tetragrammaton, Jehovah—' I've got my wand over my head, drawing shapes in the air. 'Reveal unto me she whom I seek!'

It's a plan, see? Archasis may be a catastrophe, but Kazia summoned him, so he still has an affinity with her. He must know where she is. Actually, if you sat him down with a sharp knife and fork and asked what he would most like served up on the plate in front of him, the answer wouldn't be a dead shark.

It would be Kazia.

So if I can get Archasis to take me to her, maybe I can persuade her to take the pariah spell off Sean. Then maybe she'll be so grateful to me for making her do the

262

right thing, she'll run off with me. Or something.

OK, there's a few holes. I'm not so sure that I want to run off with Kazia any more. In fact I've no idea what I'll do if I find her.

But a plan's a plan.

As I follow Archasis out of the ice room, I hear a whisper from the shadows: 'Wow! I *really* wish I was a nekker.'

At least the mortuary is handy for the Hole. Twenty minutes later, I've ditched the robe and the paper hat, and I'm following Archasis past the ruins of Saint Giles' church and across a sea of rubble. He doesn't look round: I think he's got enough trouble staying on his feet and holding up his pyjamas.

There isn't much left of the old north gate, but he stops to lean against the pile of crumbling stones anyway. I wait a couple of yards off, sword in one hand, pentacle in the other.

Five minutes later, Archasis hasn't moved and I'm passing the time by imagining this conversation with Kazia . . .

'I want you to fix Marvo's little brother,' I'll say.

'Why should I?'

'Coz it's the right thing to do.'

It's my fantasy, but that doesn't seem to bother her. 'Have I ever done the right thing so far?'

'Well, no. But I love you.' Why did I say that?

'Yes, but you're an arsehole, Frank. And I don't love you.'

'Marvo, then. You owe it to her.'

'Don't be stupid, Frank.'

Back in the real world, Archasis still hasn't moved, and I consider strolling over and giving him a prod with my sword. I'm cold, the rats around here are more friendly than I like and the shallow ditch where I'm standing . . . let's just say that there's more than water in it. I shuffle along a bit and go back to the picture of Kazia in my head . . .

For some reason I seem to be unbuttoning her blouse. I'm tempted to go with that – very tempted. But Marvo's standing behind me hissing, 'Are you out of your bloody mind?' So I blink and it all goes a bit misty like a scryer, and when it clears Kazia's buttons are neatly done up and Marvo's standing next to her and they've both got these smug grins on their faces, like they see right through me.

'Go away,' I mutter, and Marvo's gone. I take Kazia's hand. 'You can fix him, yeah? Her brother.'

She smiles. 'Why don't you unbutton my blouse again . . . ?'

I'm about to do just that, when Archasis pushes himself away from the stonework and lumbers off. I bang my fist off the side of my head and go after him.

We're heading through what passes, in the Hole, for a street market: basically, rotting meat and a lot of flies.

Nobody minds the sword, and I get a few nods because I come here occasionally when I need a dead animal and it doesn't have to be too fresh. Up ahead, people scream and scatter from Archasis. One guy considers picking a fight, then takes a closer look and jumps away like he's been stung.

We head past what's left of Saint Martin's church and down the hill to the south gate, where a bunch of students from Christ Church have decided to add some excitement to their lives by putting up a checkpoint. There is, of course, such a thing as too much excitement. When Archasis just crashes through their wooden pole they jump back, out of harm's way, and I slip through as he disappears round a corner into a big stone building.

I know it. The old Dominican priory.

I close the door behind me and stare around the entrance hall. No windows. Stone floor, a couple of chairs, black wooden table with a three-branched candelabrum holding – wait for it! – three candles. There's a big ugly painting splattered across one wall showing a crowd of idiots with tonsures and black and white robes, waving their hands in the air and looking pleased with themselves.

Archasis isn't hanging about now. He's heading off up the stairs and I'm about to follow when I hear a bang behind me and feel an icy draught on the back of my neck. I spin round.

The outside door has been thrown open. The big man standing there is wearing a bronze helmet and a black cape over a silver breastplate. The door slams shut behind him. He pulls out a sword.

But here's the thing: he doesn't clank. In fact, he doesn't make a sound and I realise that this isn't a Knight of Saint Cyprian, sent to nail me. It's a search elemental.

Three days ago, Caxton dragged the Society in, and the Grand Inquisitor added an unauthorised demon to his long list of things he wanted to put a stop to.

All I had to work with was a feather. The Society had the Crypt Boy – and a whole building full of sorcerers to throw at the problem. Ignacio Gresh got them to instantiate an elemental to find Archasis . . . and nail the sorcerer responsible.

Any second now, elemental meets demon. I'm not sure what happens, but an almighty bang seems more likely than a gentlemanly handshake. Either way, the elemental's twin, back at the Society's headquarters, turns to Gresh and tells him where to look.

I have to get there first. I dash up to Archasis and try to force the pentacle of Solomon over his head. The chain is too small to fall around his neck; it sticks on his comb. He makes an anxious clucking noise.

'Adonai, Eloim, Ariel, Jehovah! I charge thee to return whence thou camest, without noise or disturb-ance—'

As I always say when I dismiss a demon: who's kidding who? I've got my sword over my head. I'm making this up as I go along, but I sweep it down.

Archasis's head splits like an egg—

And dozens of birds come swirling out, screaming and flapping. Black and white feathers. Silver beaks that open like trapdoors and vomit out more and more birds, smaller and smaller, more and more . . . until the hall and stairs are a tornado of spinning feathers.

The steps have turned to ice. I slip and fall, taking the elemental with me. And when I pick myself up, at the bottom of the stairs, the birds have gone and there's just me and the elemental, stumbling to his feet.

He finds his sword and sticks it in its sheath. He picks up his helmet and straightens it on his head. He looks around, utterly confused.

'That way.' I point.

But he never gets to the door. He was built to find a demon. That demon has gone. One step, and the elemental is fading. Two, and he's just a shadow. He never even finishes the third step.

A moment later I hear the rush of feet. I catch a momentary glimpse of black and white monastic habits before bodies pile on top of me and everything goes dark.

CHAPTER THIRTY-SEVEN
Tumbling

Time drags when you're tied up with a sack over your head, and you can't see anything and all you can smell is . . . actually, I'm not quite sure *what* it is, but it's not fresh. Still, I've got other things to worry about, starting with how I'm supposed to breathe through the weave of the sack. Sweat pours down my face and I'm trying desperately to blink hessian dust out of my eyes.

Actually, I'm thinking that maybe I should just give up on this breathing lark altogether, when I hear a door bang open. Things can only get better.

I get picked up and bounced around. Just as I'm about to be sick, I get dropped hard on the ground. I can feel the rope being untied from the neck of the sack. Then I get tipped out, arse over end, as they pull the bottom of the sack out from underneath me.

I've never been in this joint before, but it's a proper Dominican priory, complete with two proper

Dominicans, who exit with the sack, locking the door behind them.

That's interesting: Vannutelli's a Dominican . . .

It's nearly dark outside, but there's a couple of candles burning in brackets on the wall. The room looks like some sort of refectory, but the benches and tables where the monks usually stuff their faces have been stacked against the wall, except for two tables in the middle, pushed together and piled up with everything a renegade sorcerer needs: knives, swords, scales, bottles and jars, braziers and candlesticks.

I smell vulnerary herbs: lavender, comfrey . . . I open a paper sachet and tip out a handful of withered yellow flowers. Agrimony. Also known as church steeples or sticklewort. Effective against diarrhoea and bed-wetting, neither of which are particularly bothering me right now – although that could change. Agrimony also stops wounds bleeding . . . except it's so mouldy it would infect any wound it got within spitting distance of.

I'm beginning to realise why I'm still alive. There's still more magic to be done, and this isn't the gear to do it with. I sniff suspiciously at a jar of comfrey salve that's grown a white mould. A pot of myrrh that's so ancient it's probably a left-over from the Nativity . . .

And heavier than I realised. The outside of the pot is all slimy: it slips and lands on my foot. I'm still hopping around the room making noises when the door opens and Kazia steps in.

I'll say one thing for her: she comes straight to the point. 'The boy in the mortuary—'

'The Crypt Boy.'

'They want me to kill him.'

I smile. 'No better girl for the job.'

'But I don't want to.'

'Don't worry. You couldn't make a kitten blink with this pile of crap.' I've wondered why Kazia had to sneak into the mortuary to summon the demon to mash the Crypt Boy; and here's the answer. All the materials scattered across the tables are hopelessly contaminated. Kazia stiffens as I pick up a couple of the knives. It's the standard set: one with a white wooden handle, the other with a black handle made of sheep's horn. I knock the blades together and raise my eyes to heaven. 'Where did you get it all?'

'The prior had it.'

'Wow!'

The Dominicans used to be down on sorcery – back in 1486 it was a couple of their blokes, Heinrich Krämer and Jacob Sprenger, who wrote the *Malleus Maleficarum*, 'The Hammer of Witches', all about how evil witchcraft and sorcery are. But the story around the Hole is that the only way the priory survived the college wars was by barring the doors and summoning Lucifuge Rofocale and a legion of heavily armed demons. So I guess even the Dominicans have moved with the times.

It's not that the knives are wrong. The handles are

right; the blades have the correct symbols engraved along them. But they've seen better days.

You do a ritual with knives, a sword and the rest of the gear. Contact with a demon, it's like it contaminates the instruments. So after you've dismissed the Presence, you have to repurify everything and wrap it in silk to keep it that way.

Time passes. Dust settles. Moths get at the silk. Mice wee over everything . . .

Then there are all the magical processes that go into an instrument's creation: forging, tempering, attaching the handle . . . Over time, these decay. An instrument has a half-life of about five years: that is to say, after five years a sorcerer has to work twice as hard to get the same effects from it. After ten years that's four times. And so on.

As far as I can see, the crap on the table is only good for melting down and starting again. I'm still sorting through it, trying to find anything that could actually do something useful, when the door opens and the monks step back in.

'Can you do it?' One of them has a long, sharp face like a hatchet, and no eyebrows.

'Kill the boy? Sure.' What else am I going to say?

'Tonight.' This second monk, he isn't exactly fat . . . more *lumpy*, like he's got pillows stuffed up under his habit.

I shake my head. 'The planets are all wrong and the moon's past full.'

271

This is all bollocks, of course. Like I said, if sorcerers still had to wait for planetary alignments and full moons, nothing would ever get done. I'm hoping that the monk doesn't know that.

Wrong again. Hatchet Face gestures. Lumpy knocks me over and bounces up and down on me a few times.

'Tonight.'

I pick myself up. Lumpy looks pleased with himself. Kazia is staring down at her feet.

'I need something that has contiguity with the boy.'

Another gesture. Another bouncing.

'Now get on with it,' says Hatchet Face.

The door closes. I look at Kazia.

She pulls this strange face. I think it's meant to be a smile but what I mainly get is fear. 'We can escape,' she says.

As plans go, it's pretty crap. We'll get all the ceremonial robes and tie them together to make a sort of rope. We'll lock the door and start a fire; then, while everybody's trying to get into the refectory to put it out, we can climb through the window and down to the ground.

OK, just because a plan's crap doesn't mean it won't work. But why would I be stupid enough to trust her? I'm still puzzling over that when she grabs my hand.

'Frank, I didn't want it like this.'

I'm tempted to ask, So why did you do it? Seems like, you know, a reasonable question. But my hand has

272

a life of its own. It's turned over to close its fingers on hers. I feel the soft warmth of her skin, the beat of her pulse. I may fall over.

In my head, I'm going over the list of all the reasons why this isn't a good idea. It's a long list so I won't bore you with all of it, just tick off a couple of items:

This girl has killed several people that I know of, and turned Marvo's baby brother into a clockwork toy with no key.

The last time I trusted her, she sent a demon after me.

That ought to be enough to settle it. But I can feel her breath, warm on my neck, as she whispers, 'Frank, I don't want to be me.'

I could say, me neither. I turn my face towards her, imagining my lips against her skin. But before they can get there, her fingers have slipped away and she's fallen back into a chair and buried her face in her hands.

'I made a mistake.' She runs her hand across her cropped blonde hair – hard, like she's trying to squeeze some sort of sense out of her own thoughts. 'I made a lot of mistakes.'

Confession is good for the soul. Right now, though, what we need is a better plan. I'm at the table rooting through the instruments. There's a sword; but when I pick it up by the hilt, the blade falls off.

'I've never had a friend,' says Kazia.

'I'm not surprised, if you keep feeding them to

273

demons.' We've got knives; two sickles; brass braziers to throw; cord to tie people up with if it ever gets that far . . .

'Anyone I ever trusted, they betrayed me.' Kazia looks up at me with a sad smile. 'I thought you would too.'

She jumps out of the chair and makes another grab for my hand. I've still got a knife and I try to pull away, but again my hand has a mind of its own. When I was at Saint Cyprian's they used to go on about the weakness of the flesh. They should've warned me about its strength. I can't stop my hand going willingly with hers. The tip of the knife touches her throat.

'He'll kill me anyway,' she says.

I'm trying to think, who does she mean? Matthew? Vannutelli? Someone I haven't even met . . . ?

But she's got both hands wrapped around mine. I'm shaking. The tip of the knife zigzags across her skin, leaving a thin red track. If I pushed, this would all be over . . .

'Please.' I manage to wrench my hand away. The knife rattles across the floor.

So I'm leaning against the table, panting for breath and wondering if other boys have this sort of fun with girls. She's beside me, tying the sleeves of two robes together to make a sort of rope.

'It won't work,' I point out.

'Have you got a better idea?'

I guess I haven't. I open the window and look out over the priory cloister. It's a beautiful evening, if I could be bothered to stop and admire it. The sky is clear, the stars are sharp and bright. There's a sloping roof just below the window, then a drop that looks further than I'd want to fall without somebody to land on.

I'm standing there, shivering despite my jerkin, when I feel the heat of Kazia's body against my back.

'There's a gate.' Her breath tickles my ear as she points over my shoulder, to the far corner of the cloister.

I'm sold.

I hunt through the pile of rusting crap that the monks left us, and I find two things that actually work. A flint and steel.

Sparks. Fire. At least everything's dry and blazes away merrily. Smoke fills the room and billows out of the windows.

Hammering on the door. Yelling and screaming.

I'm out of the window, sliding down the sloping roof, coughing fit to bust. To my relief, my feet hit a low parapet. I lie flat on my stomach and grab Kazia round the waist as she slides down alongside me.

I tie one leg of a pair of linen trousers around a stone pinnacle and toss our escape route over the edge. It stops at least ten feet clear of the ground.

There's risks either way. If she goes first, I'm not there to catch her. If she goes second, the rope is closer to giving way.

'You first,' I decide.

As she lowers herself, I can see the seams of the trousers starting to pull apart.

'Hurry up!'

She lets go and drops.

My turn. The smoke is pouring out of the window and rolling down around me. Coughing desperately, I slide over the parapet. I'm halfway down when the trousers rip apart and I tumble the rest of the way.

CHAPTER THIRTY-EIGHT

Swimming

'Where are we going?' Kazia pants. 'Your lair?'

'My lair?' I manage not to giggle. 'No. We're not safe there.'

'Then where *is* safe?'

'I dunno. But everybody knows about my place, even if they can't get past the cloaking spell. We'd just be trapped there—'

She smiles. 'Would that be so bad, Frank?'

We're out of the priory and along the riverbank, at the foot of the high wall sealing off the Hole, zigzagging through a stinking sea of rubbish and rubble. My ankle hurts where I twisted it, but I'm mainly amazed I didn't break my neck falling out of the priory. Looking round, I see the lights of a barge drifting towards us in midstream—

'We can get to London!' I point. 'See the ladder at the back? We can climb up and hide—'

'And then what?'

'If we don't do it now, we'll never do it.' I wade out into the water and it's bloody freezing.

'Don't be stupid, Frank!'

'Yeah, but—'

'I'm not going.'

'Why not? There's nothing here.'

'If we get to your lair—'

'Don't call it a lair. It's a studio.'

'Studio, then. But if we get there—'

'We'll be trapped.'

She's not budging, is she? The barge is abreast us, maybe ten or fifteen yards out. I figure that if I go for it, she'll have to follow me. I throw myself at the water.

Did I ever mention that I can't swim? But how difficult can it be? I mean, fish can do it, and how bright are they?

Brighter than me, apparently. I tumble down into the cold water. The current grabs me and turns me over. My jerkin wraps itself round my head. There's a roaring sound in my ears.

I should be feeling spiritually cleansed, because running water purifies as effectively as exorcised water. But I'm too busy drowning to appreciate that fact. I'm flapping and kicking, trying to get myself the right way up. I'm stirring up all sorts of crap, then swallowing it. My eardrums are bursting. I'm spinning helplessly. Which way's up, anyway?

I break the surface, spouting like a whale. I can't see

278

Kazia anywhere, and before I've managed to get any air I'm under again, my lungs empty of anything useful, fighting the stupid instinct to breathe water.

I can't keep my mouth shut – could I ever? The water's pouring in, choking me—

I'm panicking, but I keep thrashing away. My hand grasps something and I find myself on the surface, miraculously clutching the ladder at the back of the barge. I get the other hand to the ladder and drag myself half out of the water. I look around . . .

No sign of Kazia.

Oh Christ! I'm looking around desperately, scanning the black water for any sign of her. I throw myself back into the river and realise, as I flail around beneath the surface, that of course I'm an idiot.

By the time I crawl ashore, I'm half drowned. I feel I've made progress with this swimming lark, but I'm a hundred yards downstream and shivering uncontrollably. I don't even bother going back to look for Kazia. Pretty damned obvious, isn't it? Once she realised that I wasn't going to take her back to my studio, she left me to make a fool of myself and she's heading there on her own.

It's amazing how cold you can get when you put your mind to it. I'm soaked to the skin. My stomach has tied itself in knots and my head feels like it's going to explode.

I'm trying to run, but I'm shaking so badly that I keep falling over. My hands are raw. My knees are screaming at me to stop.

And I don't get it. Sure, Kazia can ditch me and head for the termite nest. Maybe she can talk her way through the gate; or maybe she knows the way in over the back wall ... But once she's inside, the cloaking spell kicks in. There's no way she can actually get inside my studio.

It's a two-mile run: round the outside of the Hole, over the wall, across the Cherwell Bridge and along the London road past the old non-conformist burial ground. Then another half-mile uphill to the termite nest. I'm nearly dead by the time I stagger round the last corner—

Right into the reception committee. There's six of them kneeling in the road outside the gate. Heavy over-coats. Scarves wrapped around their faces. ASB emblems on their sleeves.

I see a couple of sticks lying on the cobblestones beside them. And a long, heavy log; I guess, to batter down the gate. But none of them stay on the ground for long—

Because there's a seventh arsehole, clutching a metal cross on a pole, one hand raised to heaven. Silas spots me and leaps to his feet. He has a message from God:

'Get him!'

I've got a new plan: run like hell and get over the back wall before they see where I've gone. But I'm barely round the first corner, scampering through the pool of light cast by a street lamp, looking over my shoulder to see whether I've got enough of a head start to make it . . . when I hear the sound of hooves.

Up ahead, four men on horseback are trotting down the street towards me. Moonlight gleams on bronze helmets.

Knights of Saint Cyprian. Real ones, this time.

Why tonight, of all nights?

Can't go back.

Across the street to my right, just the flat, high wall of the monastery chapel.

On my left, a line of terraced houses. For a moment I consider throwing myself in through a window and begging for sanctuary. But the terrace ends a few houses ahead, at a dark alleyway. I keep running.

A couple of seconds later, I collapse against the side wall of the end house, gasping and thanking my lucky stars. The hoof beats haven't accelerated, so the Knights didn't spot me. I stick my nose round the corner of the house.

One way, the ASB are just standing there, scratching their heads.

The other way, the Knights rein in their horses.

OK, so this is interesting. The ASB hate the Society and anyone who works for it, while the Knights are always up for a bit of head-splitting . . .

I'm just trying to work out how I can make it all kick

off, when something gets me by the collar and yanks me round.

'Fronk!' A face looms out of the darkness. '*Quel plaisir inexprimable de vous revoir.*'

Oh hell. Dinny. Grinning like a tiger in a pet shop. His hook rips through my jerkin. He sticks his face into mine and I nearly throw up as the stink of alcohol hits me.

'Jesus, Dinny!'

'They let me go.'

'The jacks? That's great.'

OK, so he's been celebrating his release the traditional way. He's swaying on his feet. 'But you are rest—' He shakes his head. 'Respon—' He's never too clear at the best of times. Tonight he's all over the place. 'Your fault!' he spits.

'My fault?'

'That they arrest me.'

'How do you make that out?'

'The money.' He's tearing at my wet clothes with his hooks. 'Where is it?'

'I told you, Dinny, don't you remember? I'll get it for you.'

This isn't fair. He had enough cash on him to get totally arseholed. Why's he on my case?

He drags me towards the open street. 'We go in your place. You have books, no? I can sell—'

'Jesus, Dinny. This really isn't a good time.'

'That what you always say!' He gets me round the

282

throat by one hook and you know what? It bloody hurts. The other hook is dangerously close to my eye. I'm just appreciating how incredibly sharp and pointy it is when Dinny hisses, 'I kill you!'

I get a stabbing pain in my throat. For a second I really think I'm done for. Then I hear the sound of breaking glass and the pain stops as Dinny collapses in a heap. I look round and see Charlie clutching the neck of a broken bottle.

'Bloody hell, Charlie! I mean, is *everybody* here?'

'Haven't seen your mum.'

'So far.' I look around nervously. 'So what's your excuse?'

'Just wanted to warn you that Dinny was coming after you.'

'You could've been quicker.'

'Yeah, but I thought he had a point. You can't go messing people around like that.'

Dinny hasn't moved.

'Jesus, Charlie, you haven't killed him, have you?'

I can hear shouting from the street. I risk peering round the corner of the house. To my left, the Knights have pulled up abreast of each other.

To my right, the ASB mob are standing in a group with Silas at the front, holding his cross aloft.

'Nekkers!' the guy behind him yells.

That's a bit unfair. The Knights are failed sorcerers, same as a lot of the ASB.

One of the Knights draws his sword. Another hauls out his scryer.

'Now what?' Charlie whispers.

'Let's them and them fight.' I pick up a couple of stones and bung one towards the Knights. A horse rears up.

While the Knights are still blinking, I lob the second stone at the ASB and drag Charlie off down the alley. I hear screaming and yelling behind me and for a nasty moment I'm afraid they've spotted us.

But when I turn and look back, from the other end of the alley, I see one of the Knights tumbling to the ground as Silas's cross bangs off his helmet.

CHAPTER THIRTY-NINE
Scrying

Charlie drops down beside me, inside the back wall. He was in here a couple of times after I worked the cloaking spell, so he's immune.

But Kazia isn't. The corridor leading to my studio smells of vomit. In the moonlight, seeping in through the door behind me, I can see a dark shape sprawled on the floor. Amazed and impressed that she got this far, I step towards her and crash into Andrew.

'Watch where you're going, Brother!' he whines.

I shove him out of the way and hear a satisfying thud as the back of his head hits the wall. I get Kazia under the armpits and haul her to her feet. She's heavier than Marvo and it's a bit of a struggle.

'I don't get it.' Charlie's staring at her. 'How did she get in?'

I've got one free hand. I point it at Andrew.

'That's not fair,' Andrew protests, rubbing his head. 'She got inside the monastery the other day. The cloaking spell kicked in and knocked her over . . .'

I look into Kazia's eyes and actually see the blinds come down.

'Yeah, you spotted it at once, and you realised that that if Andrew was awake enough to help me carry you outside, he must be immune to the spell.' I remember her staring intently at him as the penny dropped.

I turn back to Andrew. 'She just turned up at the front gate and smiled at you, right? And you walked her through it.'

He stares down at my feet. 'I didn't realise.'

'No reason why you should. Anyway, who cares? She's just leaving.'

'Brother.' Andrew plants himself in front of me, one hand raised like a jack directing traffic. 'I can save her from sin.'

'Another time, eh?'

'Frank, you can't.' That's Charlie. 'You said it yourself: she's a sorcerer—'

Andrew squeals and shrinks back against the wall.

'Didn't you know?'

'But she's a girl!' He hauls the cross out from under his habit and clasps it to his lips.

'The ASB and the Knights are both out there,' Charlie says. 'Do you really want her dead?'

I guess not. I kick the outside door shut behind us. After a moment of pitch darkness, my studio door opens. I wrap both arms round Kazia and drag her inside, where the whisper of moonlight through the window is enough to get her across the studio without falling over anything. I drop her on the mattress and straighten up.

My ankle still hurts and I think I've dislocated my spine. I get some lamps lit. Kazia just lies there, sprawled backwards like all my fantasies come true – if it wasn't for the fact that she's thrown up on the sheet. At least the dog's happy.

She opens her eyes and gazes up at me. 'Where are we?'

Like she doesn't know . . .

Opinions vary on what I should do next.

'Let me see what's going on outside,' says Charlie. 'If the coast's clear, you pack up and you get her out of here—'

'What if she doesn't want to go?' I whisper back.

Kazia is wandering around the studio, pulling out drawers and turning over cutlery. She catches my eye and opens her arms to indicate the entire studio. 'This is wonderful,' she says.

She's looking pretty damned wonderful herself. She frowns and runs a fingertip across the skin of her forehead, where I fixed the dent she made when she fell over. That was a bit of a treat for me.

'Once you get her outside,' says Charlie, 'you ditch her. Get to London. You can hide there—'

'What about the Hole?'

'No.' He hesitates. 'The Hole isn't safe any more.'

I'm about to ask him what that means, when he nudges me. 'She's up to something . . .'

I look round and see that she's found the tin on the shelf.

'Think I don't know that?' I whisper.

I know she wants to be here. I realise she wants something. Maybe if I let her get it, things will start to make sense.

But there are limits. That tin I dug up – she's opened it and pulled out a crumpled banknote. The fat, ugly mug of the Lord Protector scowls back at her.

She holds the note up to the lamp. I can see the colours: yellow, blue . . . and black along one edge where it's been in a fire.

I snatch it away from her. 'My escape fund.'

I put it to my nose and still get the faint whiff of smoke. It's all that's left of the wad of cash my dad got for selling me to the Society of Sorcerers. I never knew exactly how much, but it was a lot. One corner has been torn away, where I snatched the note out of my dad's fingers after I set him on fire. The rest of the money went up in flames with him.

Kazia frowns. 'That won't take you far.'

Ten quid. But the amount doesn't matter because I'll never spend it. Just hang on to it and hope it stops me going post-peak.

My Gift object. As long as I still have it, I'm OK. After all, look what Charlie's Gift object did for him . . . The trick, obviously, is to keep it safe. I fold the note in half and stick it in my pocket, out of harm's way.

Andrew's off in a world of his own. He's up at the east end, where the altar used to be while this was still a chapel. He's on his knees, clutching his crucifix, muttering under his breath and watching Kazia like a hawk. A hawk with dove's eyes. It's just a matter of time before he starts dribbling.

Kazia's got one of my books and she's flicking through the pages. She looks up and smiles at me, and it's like she lights up the room and everything's going to be all right.

'We can do anything we want,' she says. The smile dies. Her finger brushes across her forehead again.

'It's fine,' I say. 'Just leave it alone.'

But she pulls her scryer out of her pocket. She opens it and peers at herself in the mirror.

'Frank!' That's Charlie. 'Can you get rid of that idiot?' He means Andrew, who's lying flat on his face, banging his head on the floor.

I fiddle with my watch. 'Andrew.' I walk across. 'Shouldn't you be in the chapel?'

He looks up, red in the face. 'What time is it?'

I turn my arm so he can see the face of my watch: a couple of minutes before nine, when compline begins.

'Oh, sodding hell!' He's on his feet.

Kazia has turned away. Is she whispering into her scryer?

Andrew bounces off me on his way to the door. 'Hey, open it!' he yells.

The case of Kazia's scryer snaps shut as I make the pass and my door opens. Andrew vanishes and, as the outside door slams shut, I reset my watch to show the correct time. The scryer is back in Kazia's pocket. The dog is still licking cheerfully away at the bedsheets. She leans down to scratch it between the ears and it does its trick with the cinnamon smell.

'Anyway,' I say, 'shall we get going?'

'What's the hurry?'

I realise that I'm scratching my head. With just stubble, that leaves unattractive red marks; so I stop. The hurry is that if I don't go now I'll run out of steam.

'No hurry. I just want to get it over with.'

'Don't you need things?'

She waves her hand around the studio. Yeah, I can see it all: books, equipment, the equations scrawled across my blackboard . . .

'It doesn't matter,' I say, even though it does.

'All your things, though: will they be safe?'

'Charlie'll look after them.' I turn to him. 'Won't you.'

There's books in my broom cupboard – that's the

invisible part of my studio, where I keep the *really* dangerous stuff – that I know I'll never be able to replace. This is a totally stupid idea and obviously Kazia realises it; she's standing there, still looking doubtfully around the studio.

'Forgotten something?' I can see what's going on here. Cold feet. If I were her, I wouldn't be running off with me . . .

And I'm still waiting for her to stop dithering when I hear a voice from my cabinet—

'Frank.' Marvo's voice, from my scryer.

I ignore it. I've got my satchel and I'm stuffing my escape kit into it. Herbs and spices, a change of underwear—

'Frank!'

Kazia can't hear her, but she can see that something's up. 'Are you all right?' she asks.

'Nothing. My scryer.' I turn to Charlie. 'Just Marvo.'

Kazia isn't giving up. 'So why don't you answer her?'

I can think of all sorts of reasons. 'Can we just get out of here?' I tell my door to open.

'Frank.' Kazia grabs my arm. 'She's your friend.'

'She's right, Frank,' says Charlie. 'You've got to talk to her.'

I'm still wondering why Kazia cares, when Marvo screams, 'Frank, please!'

Oh hell. No good can come of this, but I dive for my cabinet and dig the scryer out from the back. I open it and touch the five tips of the diagram etched into the base. I blow on the surface of the mirror inside the lid and when the mist clears I can see Marvo's face.

She looks scared. So does her mum. Behind them I can see the Welsh dresser in their kitchen.

'What's the matter?' I snarl.

'Frank, I dunno what's going on but—'

'Yeah, I can see him.' Leering over Marvo's shoulder. A face like a toad. 'What does he want?'

It's Marvo's scryer, so all Cardinal Bruno Vannutelli can see is his own ugly mug in the mirror. Marvo turns to him and repeats my question.

'Brother Tobias,' he says. 'You have something that belongs to me.'

'I thought you disapproved of sorcerers.'

Marvo passes it on. Vannutelli's face splits into a wide grin. 'True. But she is useful to me.'

'I'll bet.'

'So you believe me when I promise I will do much to find her.'

'Such as?'

As Marvo relays the message, he puts an arm round her shoulder. She tries to pull away, but he locks his elbow round her neck. 'Your friend—'

'I don't have any friends.' It's worth a try.

And I get this strange feeling, like I wish I could say

that without getting . . . I dunno, it's a sort of tug and I remember what my dad told me when I was little: too little to be a sorcerer; too little to set him alight yet. He told me I was a skinny little freak and I'd never amount to anything, never have any friends . . .

Good of him to warn me. A loving parent can set you up to deal with everything life throws at you.

'Yes, you have friend.' Vannutelli pulls Marvo closer and kisses her hair. 'You come here. We talk.'

And I'm left looking at my reflection in the mirror. After a moment I close the scryer. 'He's got Marvo. He wants to exchange her for you.'

Kazia shakes her head.

'So what am I supposed to do?'

'Talk to him. He couldn't see me in the scryer, so tell him . . . tell him we had a fight and I've gone.'

'He's not going to believe that.'

'He's not a monster. He won't kill your friend if you talk to him.'

I can't say that I like this. That's the thing with friends: you can't trust them not to mess you about. At best they'll let you down. At worst they'll turn on you. And somewhere in between, they'll get themselves stuck up to their necks in shit and they'll stare up at you with these big doggy eyes and you know you've got to take a big breath, hold your nose and jump in after them.

CHAPTER FORTY

A Rat

My feet hit the ground outside the back of the termite nest. Charlie's knee buckles as he lands beside me, and he grabs my arm for support.

'Sorry,' he says.

'Do you smell a rat?'

He nods. 'Dunno what colour, but definitely a rat. The idiot—'

'Andrew's not an idiot. Just a termite.'

'Clever of her to use him to get through your cloaking spell.'

I nod. 'And she's still up to something. She scried someone – didn't you see that? Probably Vannutelli.'

There's a place somewhere, where this all makes sense. I just haven't got there yet.

'Charlie, there's some herbs I need. Moonwort, asafoetida, Judas's heart . . .' I'm scribbling on a scrap of paper. 'I'll meet you back here . . . say an hour and a half.'

Forty minutes later, I peer round the corner at Marvo's mum's place. The street is empty as I scuttle along in the shadow of a high fence. I creep up the path to the house and duck under the ivy. No lights that I can see. Silence inside. I hesitate with my hand on the bell-pull. I touch the door and it opens.

I nearly jump out of my socks as Mrs Marvell appears like a ghost out of the front room, knife in hand—

'They've gone.' She drops the knife on the hall table and pulls out her amulet. 'And you can go too. You're not welcome here.'

'What about Marvo?'

'They made her call you. Then—' She's backing away from me, along the corridor, and I realise I'm supposed to follow her.

On the kitchen floor, the broken fragments of a mirror reflect the lamplight. I pick up the silver case from the dresser: it's all bent and the hinge is jammed. It's not like a scryer's irreplaceable, but there's a pile of paperwork and then someone's got to instantiate it . . .

'They took her.' Mrs M has begun to weep.

'Yeah.'

I never expected to find Marvo here. The trouble is, I couldn't risk being wrong.

That rat I mentioned to Charlie: I can see what colour it is now. I should have caught a whiff of it when we got out of the priory by climbing down a rope made of robes and trousers, but I wasn't . . . I guess I wasn't thinking straight. I definitely smelled it when Kazia ditched me down at the river. I heard it squeak when Marvo scried me, just a minute after Kazia made a secret call. I saw its shadow when Vannutelli's ugly gob showed up in my scryer.

Now it's sitting on my shoulder, nibbling at my ear with two very sharp front teeth.

'They'll be at my place,' I say.

'Why?'

'Someone's going to do some magic.'

I hear the rattle of iron-bound wheels outside the front door.

'Did you call the police?'

She nods. 'A neighbour . . .'

'Don't mention me. It won't help.' I open the back door. I feel strange asking this question: 'Will you be all right?'

'I can look after myself perfectly well,' she snorts. 'But I expect you to look after Magdalena.'

The street alongside the termite nest looks empty and I figure I'm first back . . . until I see a small, red point of light in the shadow behind one of the buttresses.

'The Knights are still around.' Charlie steps out.

'Yeah, I heard something clanking.'

His cigarette end fizzles out in a puddle. He pulls a

small package out of his pocket and tosses it to me. I head off towards the back of the monastery, pulling at the paper as I go.

Charlie's right behind me. 'All there,' he says.

'I owe you.'

He grabs me by the arm and swings me round to face him. 'Yes, you do, Frank.'

'Yeah, I know,' I say. 'I get it.'

'For now.' He smiles. 'So are you ready?'

He steps up to the wall and gets his fingers into a crack between two stones. He levers himself up—

'Charlie, no.'

He looks down at me.

'They've got Marvo in there. I'll have my work cut out, you know, with her . . .'

His face has fallen. 'You can't look after me too, that's what you mean.' I don't know what to say. He does. He drops to the ground. 'I'm a liability.'

I still don't know what to say. I watch him walk away.

'I'm sorry, Charlie.'

'Just wait till it's your turn.'

'If I live that long.'

But he doesn't smile. 'Good luck, Frank,' he says over his shoulder as he disappears round the corner.

If you were wondering where Dinny had got to, the answer is lying slumped on the steps leading up to my studio, where I can trip over him. He's dribbling. And yeah, he's been sick.

I'm tempted to leave him lying there, but I feel safer with him where I can see him. I get my shoulder under his arm and manage to lift him to his feet.

Inside, my studio door is rippling like the wind disturbing the surface of a lake. I touch it, and it whimpers.

'It's all right,' I say, and it opens.

OK, it all kicks off faster than I'd expected. I'm barely inside before the weight on my shoulder disappears, and by the time I've caught my balance, a figure in a black and white habit has got one arm locked round Dinny's neck and the other hand holding a knife to his throat.

So who's here? The two Dominicans, Lumpy and Hatchet Face, both looking very queasy. My blue-eared dog is scurrying around the floor, cheerfully licking up the contents of their stomachs – the after-effects of being dragged through a cloaking spell.

And there's the girl who did the dragging: Kazia, sitting on my mattress with her hands clasped tight between her knees. She doesn't look up, just stares down at the floor like she's spotted a few specks of dirt that the dog missed.

And the funny thing is: as I stumbled through the door with Dinny, there was still this stupid hope that it wouldn't be like this.

CHAPTER FORTY-ONE
The Bee's Knees

I've seen all sorts of weird stuff. Things appearing out of nowhere or vanishing in the blink of an eye, dropping out of the heavens like a stone or fizzling out in a shower of green sparks.

But I've never seen anybody tied up. I kind of imagined that it was one of those things that only happen in books, like breaking down a door by putting your shoulder to it, or knocking someone unconscious with a single crisp sock on the jaw.

It's Marvo, of course, who's on the receiving end of the tying-up. And I have to admit that, considering the sheltered lives they've led, the monks have done a beautiful job. None of this crap with winding a thick rope round and round her middle. She's got each ankle bound neatly to a leg of the chair, and her hands tied to the back of the chair behind her. She can move – she's been wriggling like hell ever since I fell in through the door. All she's managed to do is fall over sideways. She's still wriggling. Gives her something to concentrate on while I get my orders.

Yeah, sometimes I do the weirdest things. I don't mean weird like spells and stuff. I mean, things that I really don't expect. Things I never thought I'd do. Never thought I *could* do . . .

I kneel beside Marvo. In honour of the occasion, she's wearing her famous red duffel coat with the missing toggle – the one she was wearing the first time she ever came to my studio. And for some reason that breaks me up. I run the backs of my fingers down her cheek. I feel her shiver. Her eyes close.

'I won't let them hurt you,' I whisper.

I feel, I dunno, like this total fraud. We're talking demons here, even if Marvo doesn't know it yet. And once there's a demon in the room . . .

That's right. All bets are off.

Of course, the man giving the orders is still missing from the picture. But now I spot Vannutelli in the shadows beside the fireplace. He's dressed all in black, from the skullcap perched over his receding hairline to the neat, shiny black shoes.

He dances down the two steps like a ballerina. He skips across the floor towards me and holds out his right hand, palm down, fingers extended. I realise I'm expected to kiss the whacking great gold ring on his fourth finger.

'Show your respect.' He's staring at Marvo. 'Or your friend dies now.'

I kiss the ring.

'You know what I want. You can do?'

'I can do,' I say quietly.

I get these looks. Kazia, it's more of a glance, like she's afraid to catch my eye. I get this feeling that she's grateful, but maybe I'm imagining it.

Marvo, there's nothing to imagine. I'm quite glad that the hatchet-faced monk has got his hand over her mouth.

Vannutelli . . . it's a sort of smile. I think he thinks he can see right through me, and I'm hoping like hell that he can't.

'But it'll take a while,' I point out.

'How long?'

'Gimme six hours.'

He leans his head to one side and puts one finger to his fat lips while he thinks about it. 'Three,' he says. Which is two hours more than I'd expected.

It's something every sorcerer has to put up with: people sitting around tapping their feet, scratching and sighing.

A handful of cloves spit on red-hot charcoal.

'The prayers,' Kazia hisses.

'Don't need 'em.'

'Prayers?' says Vannutelli. 'What prayers?'

Kazia has got this anxious look on her face. 'We must ask God to bless the work.'

301

'You're trying to kill someone,' Marvo spits out, between Hatchet Face's fingers.

'Is God's work. He understands.' Vannutelli gives me his imperious look. 'You pray.'

'OK,' I say. 'Everybody on their knees.'

Marvo's excused, obviously.

'O Lord God Almighty, full of compassion,' I start. 'Aid us in this work which we are about to perform . . .'

Every time you summon a demon, you hit the fundamental paradox of sorcery: you're wheeling God out to force an evil being to do your dirty work. I'm running through the usual stuff, wondering what would happen if I just skipped it. Would I be damning myself? Not that I believe in damnation. Or should I get bonus heavenly points for at least being honest about what I'm up to?

When everybody's said 'Amen', I exorcise a couple of gallons of water. It's easy enough: you just toss in a handful of quicklime, mutter some more prayers and stir until everybody's yawning.

Which is when I give my arm a little shake. Something drops out of my sleeve onto the bench and I push it behind the scales.

Charlie's herbs.

I use most of the exorcised water to wash the floor; then I start messing around with a stick of chalk and some string. I'm going with a version of a Grand Honorian Circle. It's powerful and flexible, but kind of slippery and hard to control. At Saint Cyprian's they told us to steer clear of it, and the one time they caught me playing with one I got a month of detentions and an unpleasant ten minutes on the receiving end of a wet knotted rope.

So why go looking for trouble? Well, it's fast; you can get away with mucking about with the symbols; I know Kazia likes it, so she won't get her knickers in a twist . . .

. . . and it won't break if I make a few modifications.

After another half-hour, I've got a rat in a cage, I've purified a stack of cutlery, and I'm making smoke. I fill a silver basin. I stick my hand in my pocket and palm the banknote while I do my famous raw prawn imitation. Kit off, back to the audience, washing myself down with a sponge.

I notice that another symbol is fading from my sorcerer's mark.

Still wet, I open the wardrobe and haul out a clean linen robe and trousers. My Gift object slips into the pocket. Maybe it'll help me survive this.

I turn back to Kazia. 'Now you.'

She stares nervously around the studio. The two monks look far more interested in this than they should.

'Here.' I pull another robe out of the wardrobe and hold it up like a curtain. She's staring at me—

'All right.'

303

I close my eyes. I hear her shoes rattle on the floor. The soft whisper of her clothes. The splash of the water . . . Of course, I can't help looking. It's not, you know, just a chance to see a girl with nothing on, even if it's something I've never seen before.

But I've got to know: does she have any sort of sorcerer's mark?

At least, that's my story and I'm sticking to it.

And she doesn't. Have a mark, that is. Her skin is darker than I'd expected, with several moles down her back . . .

And one on the outside of her left breast. Medieval witch-finders used to think that was Satan's mark. I suppose, if you're looking for Satan's mark, that's a good place to start.

Anyway, she's caught me staring. I blush and close my eyes. But her body . . . it's kind of imprinted on my brain. She's not just darker than I'd expected, but stockier too. She looks tough. I don't know about magic, but if it came to a stand-up fight she could beat the crap out of me, both hands tied behind her back.

I feel her slip into the robe I'm holding. I let go and stand back while she ties the red cord around her waist.

One of the monks is cheerfully tying Dinny up in a neat bundle. I turn to Vannutelli. 'So remind me again. What've you got against this kid?'

As if I didn't know . . .

* * *

Picture this. A dark wet night, just over a year ago. A Ghost halted by the side of the road.

A uniformed elemental opens the luggage compartment. A cardinal and the Superior General of the Society of Sorcerers watch him drag a terrified boy out.

'Kill him!'

Vannutelli's problem, of course, was that he was fifty-five and getting very, very Blurry indeed. And the only way to fix that was by sorcery.

This is a world where all these guys know each other, even if they want to rip each other's faces off. Vannutelli originally came to Doughnut City to discuss the Concordat and the Society's submission to the Church. But while he was here he had a quiet word with his old fellow-novice Matthew. If he could get the Procedure done on the quiet, things might go easier with the Society . . .

And that's what Sean overheard them arguing about.

As a faithful son of the Church who wants to be the Big Man in a tiara one day, Vannutelli knows what a sin looks like when it sidles up behind him and pinches his bum. Even so, he wants Sean knocked off, and he tells Matthew to see to it.

But Matthew – and you might want to be sitting down for this – has scruples. So he goes hunting in the Closed Archive and comes up with this spell that everyone's forgotten about. Kazia rolls up her sleeves and, amazingly, it works. Sean goes to sleep, like the princess in the fairy tale, and gets bricked up in the crypt of the derelict church in the Hole. Matthew has no problem convincing himself that since nobody's actually dead, he hasn't done anything wrong – and even if he has, it's for the good of the Church and the greater glory of God.

Plus, the whole business has given him a useful hold over Vannutelli.

Everybody's happy.

Everybody who counts, anyway.

Of course it was always a stupid plan. Like Matthew said, convincing Marvo that Sean was dead just got her obsessed with finding out who killed him. A year down the line, he gets dug out of the crypt. The spell holds: he looks dead, Marvo falls over every time she tries to see him . . .

'What I have against the boy, Brother Tobias.' Vannutelli smiles. 'That is my business.' With his accent: 'That ees-a my-a bee's knees . . .'

'You're asking me to kill him.' I don't like being called 'Brother', especially by this arsehole; but I can't do much to stop him. 'That *is* my business.'

'I am not asking. I am telling.'

I shiver as Vannutelli's fingers stroke the side of my face.

'I know about sorcery,' he says. 'I know that your

Society lies when it says that magic is a gift from God. I know it is the work of the Devil.'

'So why did you make a deal with Matthew?'

'Saint Thomas Aquinas said that sometimes a Christian must work with the Devil *per far avanzare l'opera di Dio*.'

'To advance God's work.' We did Aquinas at Saint Cyprian's and I'm not sure that's quite what he said. But Vannutelli's the cardinal . . .

'You speak Italian?'

'Enough to read spells.' I smile. 'A demon taught me.'

Vannutelli shivers and starts to cross himself – then stops to make a slithery movement with his fingers. 'You try to be like a snake. Like Satan himself.' He completes the crossing action. 'Sorcery,' he says. 'I know it is evil. Tonight you must do an evil act so that your life will be better.' He points towards Marvo, still lashed to her chair, on her side on the floor, going round in circles. 'And so that your friend will live.'

'I can do it,' Kazia says.

Vannutelli shakes his head

'I'm more powerful than him.'

I look down at the floor. It's true, but I don't want to admit it.

'Perhaps,' Vannutelli says. 'But you failed me before.'

I suppose I could point out that it wasn't really her fault that Archasis popped out of hell malformed, but Marvo is wailing—

'Frank! Don't let him—'

Hatchet Face kicks her.

Vannutelli puts his arm round my shoulder and leads me up the steps to the fireplace, away from Kazia. 'It is late and I am tired of talking.' He smells of incense and peppermint. 'It is time for you to take your instruments and summon a demon to enter the mortuary and kill the boy.'

I'm still thinking about all this – and wondering whether I could actually summon a demon powerful enough to break through Ferdia's protective circle – when Marvo yells, 'Frank!'

'Shut up! I know what I'm doing.'

'But you can't—'

'The kid's in a coma.' I don't see any point in going through all the Sean stuff with her again. 'I don't think he's gonna wake up.'

Vannutelli smiles. 'You see, Brother Tobias has a choice. He can kill this boy he doesn't know, who will probably die anyway. Or . . .'

Lumpy has got hold of one of my spare knives. He runs his thumb along the edge and holds it up to show a thin, dark line.

'He can watch my associate kill someone he *does* know. Very slow. Very painful.'

'He means you, Marvo,' I point out. 'Just in case you hadn't realised.'

'Yeah, but what's the big deal?' She grunts as Hatchet Face kicks her again.

'Will you shut up and let me get on with it?'

'Who *is* he, though, the Crypt Boy?'

'Just some kid. Don't worry about it.' I turn back to Vannutelli. 'Will any demon do, or do you have a particular friend?'

Vannutelli gestures. Lumpy clouts me.

'You are the expert. I reward results. And if you do as I ask, your friend will live and I will absolve you of the sin you have committed.'

Don't you love the Church sometimes?

'But who'll absolve *you*?' I wonder.

'I have no need of absolution. God sees into my heart and knows it is pure, and dedicated to His holy work.'

I spend a few moments trying to get my head round that, then I wave in Marvo's direction. 'She's not really my friend.'

I'm getting to know Vannutelli's smile. It rises slightly at one side and involves some badly stained teeth. 'Then perhaps she does not need to live.'

I never imagined that she did. I don't give much for Dinny's and my chances either, if this doesn't work. Or even if it does . . .

CHAPTER FORTY-TWO
Judas's Heart

This is a mess. Circles and symbols all over the shop.

I'm in the middle, natch, standing in a triangle with a brazier at each corner. That's all inside five concentric circles, spattered with symbols.

It's further out that it all goes to hell. It's always good to have someone to give the responses and throw spices and brandy around when you're working magic. But this is too much of a good thing. I've got six of them, for God's sake. OK, so two of them are tied up, but all that means is that they can't really look after themselves.

Follow the geometry.

I've got eight crosses projecting from the main circle, like the spokes of a bicycle wheel. Each one leads to a double circle and a cluster of symbols. And six of these circles have got somebody inside them.

Vannutelli is to the north, where I can keep an eye on him. Hatchet Face is next to him, to the north-west.

I've got Marvo to the south-west and Dinny to the south. And Lumpy to the south-east, trying to look hard but just looking nervous.

I've sat the dog down in the north-eastern circle, with some extra symbols to compensate for the fact that it's an elemental. In my own head, I've expressed an intention for it to stay there. It might have been simpler to terminate it, but I've got used to having it around . . .

Vannutelli, Hatchet Face and Lumpy are each standing over a brazier with a knife and a silver shaker of spices, wearing a white linen robe and a paper hat with a name of God written on it in my blood. In a perfect world I'd have used 'Jehovah' or 'Tetragrammaton', for maximum effect; but the hats are small, and there's a limit to the amount of blood I can afford to lose right now . . . So I've gone with 'El'. Simple and to the point.

Marvo's still lashed to her chair and looking very pissed off. Dinny's just lying there. His eyes are open but he doesn't seem to be seeing anything.

The western circle is a bit larger than the others because, as well as a robe and a hat and a brazier to play with, Kazia has her very own cutlery and wand to wave around.

She also has the packet of herbs I got off Charlie. 'Just in case anything goes wrong,' I told her. I didn't say anything about the Judas's heart.

I'm ready to go. Paper hat. Linen robe with symbols

311

embroidered in gold thread and scrawled in my own blood—

Did I ever tell you about my laundry bills?

White linen trousers and kidskin slippers. Two wands, sachets of herbs and spices – Charlie's mandrake came in handy – two knives and a sword.

A disaster waiting to happen.

I turn to the audience. 'When I tap my wands together' – I demonstrate – 'I want spices and brandy in braziers, OK?' I turn to Marvo. 'You're excused, obviously.'

Candles flicker. Smoke rises from the braziers to form a cloud that spreads down the length of the studio, obscuring the ceiling.

'Seal your circles.'

There's a ragged chorus: 'In the name of the most high.' And the scrape of metal as they run the tips of their knives around the circles.

I know what you're thinking: if Marvo and Dinny are tied up, how can they join in the fun? Well, they can't.

I step across and stoop to run the tip of my knife around Dinny's circle. I see drops of liquid on the tiles. He's weeping quietly. I get it. Dinny used to be Gifted. He graduated from Saint Cyprian's a few years ahead of me and got a job out at the Ghost factory, conjuring up bright new ways of getting rich people from A to B. Woke up one morning and found that he wasn't Gifted any more. Stuck both hands in one of the machines.

It must be hell for him, watching the magic he can't do any more. I catch his eye for a moment—

'I'm sorry, Dinny.'

His eyes close. As I turn away, I notice that he's picking away at the rope holding him with the sharp tip of one hook . . .

Marvo's turn. The tip of my knife scrapes around the outside of her circle. 'In the name of he who is blessed.'

'You'd better know what you're doing,' she hisses.

No shit. 'Just stay calm. You're in a circle and nothing can touch you.' Except for what I said about demons in the room. 'In the name of the most high.' I straighten up. 'Don't move, that's all.'

Ten minutes later I've sealed everything off. The braziers crackle and pop, and the cloud of smoke above us thickens and lowers until it hangs just above my head.

I run a finger along the wooden bars of a small cage at my feet. The dish of the day, a plump white rat, stares nervously up at me, then goes back to scuttling round the sides of its prison. What is it about white rats? Do they remind demons of the good old days with wings and harps, before everything went all hot and dark and hellish?

Back to the audience: 'Right, everybody behave themselves!'

I catch Kazia's eyes. She nods. I'd vaguely hoped for

313

a smile, but there's no sign of one. I turn my back on her and face east. Beyond the outmost circle, in the flickering gloom of the candles, I can just make out a triangular shape on the floor. It's made out of strips of goatskin, pinned together with nails that I know came from dead children's coffins because I sneaked into various churches over the years and stole them myself.

Yeah, pretty creepy. But that's sorcery. And if a dead baby's got anything useful to do, it isn't counting nails.

I look over my shoulder, left then right. The gang stare back at me. Hatchet Face looks dead nervous, like he just wants to make a bolt for it.

So let's encourage him. I pull the wands out of my belt. My voice echoes around the studio, a bit shaky at first—

'Adonai, Tetragrammaton . . .'

I tap my wands together. All around me, brandy sizzles on red-hot charcoal.

All ritual magic involves some sort of Presence. Sometimes it hardly exists – it's just a thought that you've given a name to. But there's always got to be *something* there.

Instantiating an elemental is dead simple. The natural energies are out there and they're happy to be shaped into something that can help with the washing-up.

Angels are the good guys. At least, that's what they taught us at Saint Cyprian's.

314

Demons will do pretty much anything you force them to do, but that's the word: force. They don't want to help; they'd rather stay tucked up in a comfortable bed of fire feeling sorry for themselves. Maybe occasionally leaning out to snack off one of the damned.

Again, I'm just repeating what the Society taught me.

The thing is, anyway, you'd think demons would want a break from the heat and the boredom. But you always have to drag them up, kicking and screaming, and threaten them with a divine smacking.

'O Lord God Almighty, full of compassion, aid us in this work which we are about to perform.'

More brandy and spices. More sizzling. Thicker smoke. The studio darkens. Lightning flickers.

'I conjure thee, O Spirit Azazel, by the living and true God—'

I'm counting on Kazia not knowing all her demonic names.

'I invoke thee by all the names of God: Adonai, El, Elohim, Elohi . . .'

To my left, out of the corner of my eye, I can see Vannutelli. Maybe he's aware that there's something not quite right about invoking God to protect us while we summon up a demon to murder an unconscious boy. But he certainly doesn't show it. He's just standing there with his eyes half closed and a soft smile smeared across his mug.

315

The usual suspects: 'Ehyeh, Asher, Zabaoth, Elion, Iah, Tetragrammaton . . .'

It's a long list. I'm not taking any chances so I've got the names scrawled on a sheet of virgin parchment and it takes me a good ten minutes to get through them all. I glance around from time to time. Vannutelli's smile ripples lazily across his mouth like waves breaking on a sunlit beach. Lumpy is picking his nose. Fortunately, or not, he has the good sense to eat the bogies; if he flicked them out of his circle he'd be in dead trouble. Hatchet Face is running the same risk, nibbling anxiously at a fingernail. Beads of sweat run down his forehead into his eyes.

Kazia's face is a complete blank. Dinny lies there, closed up like a clam. Marvo glares back at me. My dog is licking its bollocks.

I click my wands together. 'Everybody—'

Another funny thing about ritual magic: you can break off the incantation to tell people what to do, or to scry your mum and ask her to put your underpants through the wash, and whatever demon you're summoning knows to ignore it. Just saying, that's all.

I wait for the sizzling to die away, then—

'I exorcise thee, O Azazel, and do most powerfully command thee, by Adonai, El, Elohim . . .' And I'm off through the list again. As I come to the end, I wave for Kazia to join in.

'. . . that thou dost appear before me in a fair human

shape, without noise, deformity or any companion. Come hither, come hither, come hither,' she chants along with me.

The smoke has descended to form a thick, choking fog. It smells of burning charcoal, of herbs and spices, of sulphur and rotting flesh.

Of very dirty, demonic magic.

To my left, Vannutelli is just an indistinct black shape. In front of me, beyond the outer circle, a ghostly phosphorescence seeps up from the goatskin triangle.

'Come forthwith, and without delay . . .'

I break off and crook my elbow across my mouth, like I'm muffling a coughing fit. Kazia continues the formula: '. . . from any part of the world, wherever thou mayest be . . .'

Actually, I know exactly where this Azazel bloke is. And, unlike Kazia, I know his real name. It's another of those escape clauses the Society teaches: you don't always want the punters to know who you're really summoning, so most demons have an alias or two.

Kazia's giving me this uncertain look. I've got one hand to my throat; I wave her on with the other—

'. . . and obey me in all the things that I shall demand of thee,' she chants. 'Come thou peaceably, affably—'

I don't think that's on the cards. I'm still coughing.

'Manifest that which I shall desire.' She's waving her wand in the air. 'I conjure thee, O Azazel—'

Good: she's said the name.

317

'By the living and true God!'

In the silence, the only sound is the rat scurrying around his cage at my feet. The gloom has thickened, and Kazia is just a vague silhouette topped by the pale, moon-like, open-mouthed disc of her face.

'How long is this going to take?' That's Lumpy.

The goatskin triangle has vanished into the smoke and I'm not even sure I'm facing the right way. I can still see the triangle at my feet. I shuffle a bit to my left.

'Are you ready?' I say into the darkness.

'Yes,' Kazia's voice comes back from behind me.

I put a silver disc to my lips. 'Behold—' I break off, coughing desperately – and, I hope, convincingly. 'You'll have to do it,' I croak. My voice really is drying up now. I'm shit scared. I may have bitten off more than I can chew.

'Behold the pentacle of Solomon which I have brought into thy presence.' Kazia's voice sinks into the gloom like blood into sawdust. 'I compel thee, O Azazel, by order of the great God: Adonai, Tetragrammaton, Jehovah. Come at once, without wile or falsehood, in the name of our Saviour Jesus Christ!'

Utter silence. Even the rat has stopped moving.

All I can see is darkness. And just as I'm thinking, oh hell! This isn't going to work—

There's a blinding flash of light, and a bolt of lightning punches a hole into the floor at the centre of the goatskin triangle. The smoke has gone from the

318

studio as if God himself had descended to suck it in with a single, almighty breath.

But there's no sign of God. No sign of anything holy.

For a minute the studio is illuminated by a dazzling white glare that wipes away any shadows and leaves everybody staring back at me like blindingly startled ghosts.

Next thing, there's a nauseating stench of decay and a roar like an avalanche as the floor shakes and thousands, then millions of black flies come pouring out of the hole in the floor, filling the studio with a solid, swirling, glinting mass.

'Stay in your circles!' I scream. Not that anyone can hear me.

One fly buzzes irritatingly. A million scream: a high-pitched, wailing roar that drills into your head and turns your brain to jelly. I've got my hands over my ears, praying that the din will stop before I explode, when the whirling mass of insects clears for a moment and I see a black shape stumbling across the floor towards the door.

It's human. Was human, anyway, when it left the safety of its circle and tried to make a run for it. Now it's just a throbbing mass of insects that moves in a vaguely human way: shambling legs, stumpy waving arms, a huge misshapen head.

I whirl round, heart in mouth. Marvo can't move,

but what about Kazia? I almost faint with relief when I see that the circle where I put Hatchet Face is empty.

He was quite a tall man, but halfway to the door he's suddenly less tall. I assume he's gone down on his knees at the heart of the living cloud. If he's screaming – and he has every reason to scream – I can't hear it over the roar of the insects.

The twitching mound on the floor gets bigger and bigger as all the flies pile in.

Marvo has her eyes screwed tight shut. Kazia's hands are clamped over her face. Lumpy watches with an expression of disgust. Vannutelli just stands in his circle, smiling grimly.

All the flies seem to have settled. The noise has softened to a throbbing hum and suddenly, amazingly, the studio is clear, still and silent.

'Now what?' That's Vannutelli.

'Make him transform.' That's Kazia.

'What happened?' That's Lumpy.

I wait for Hatchet Face to chime in, but the shifting heap of insects seems to have nothing to say.

'Frank?' Marvo's voice shakes.

'Make him transform,' Kazia says again.

'I can't.' I'm lying. I can but I don't want to. I want *her* to do the dirty work.

'What does she mean, "transform"?' Vannutelli asks.

'Demons don't have a physical body, at least not as

we understand it. They can manifest in any form – even in no form at all,' I say.

I've seen that happen and it can be deeply confusing. You know there's something there and you can almost see it, but you can't get your head round it. In my third year at Saint Cyprian's I managed to conjure up a Presence that manifested . . . well, I don't really know *what* it was but it kept turning inside out on itself and sent my eyes into a spin. Luckily, Matthew was there to force it to transform into something sensible – if you can call a rhinoceros with a red umbrella sensible – and save me. I was seeing double for a week.

'And this is not what you want?' Vannutelli gestures towards the mass of insects, which are beginning to dart and buzz restlessly.

It can't be long before it all kicks off again. And I still need Kazia to do her stuff.

'For God's sake, Frank!' she hisses.

'I can't.' I up-end all my herb sachets to show that they are empty. I hope I sound scared and confused. 'I've used everything up. I didn't have time—'

'Then I'll do it!' Her wand's in the air. Charlie's herbs sizzle in her brazier.

'In the name of God I command thee, O Azazel,' she chants. 'Adonai, Elohim, Tetragrammaton, Jehovah. Appear to me in fair human shape without deformity or deception—' She plunges her wand deep into the fire. 'Dissolve and be transformed!'

The active ingredient sizzling in her brazier – the one I neglected to tell her about – is the Judas's heart. It's an undistinguished-looking herb with hairy, almost grey leaves. But it's powerful when you want to betray somebody.

Flames flicker along the length of her wand. She tries to hold onto it, but it's too late. As she sucks her scorched fingertips, the wand turns to ash and collapses into the charcoal.

The flies have got the message. They're in the air, whirling and roaring. A few burn up as they fly into the candles. The flames spread as the tornado spins: a moving column of fire that twists across the floor, sending everybody diving for what little safety their circles provide.

The strips of goatskin flap and scatter, then come together again around the bottom of the black column.

There's nothing much left of Hatchet Face. A scattering of bones and flesh. A few trailing loops of offal. The tatters of his habit. Scraps of scalp with a few tufts of his tonsure attached.

I glance down at the cage at my feet. The rat looks up at me like it knows the sacrifice has been made and it's dead relieved. It curls up and goes to sleep.

Out on the dance floor, though, it's all go. The mass of flies has become a solid black column that spins faster and faster until suddenly, in a blaze of fire, it transforms into a glowing figure about seven feet tall, with goat's horns and bright, golden eyes like a bird's. And a feature that I haven't seen him with before: a long forked tail that coils and snaps like a snake.

He's not a pretty sight and, despite the tail, Kazia recognises him at once. She stutters, 'That's—'

'Azazel.' I smile.

'But—'

'Also known as Alastor.'

'What's happening?' Vannutelli can just about control his voice.

'He's tricked us.'

Confession time: I have. Oops.

As a general rule, demons only need one facial expression: hellishly pissed off. But Alastor doesn't look angry – just utterly freaked out, like he doesn't know how he got here. He stares around, eyes rolling wildly. His jaw hangs open, showing off a graveyardful of razor-sharp, yellow teeth that remind me, for a sad moment, of poor old Preston. No time to stroll down memory lane, though. Alastor spins round, like he's heard something behind him, hauls his axe out of the belt that's the only thing he's wearing, takes an almighty swipe—

And cuts off his own tail.

The clang of the axe is drowned out by his piercing scream. Another weapon comes out of his belt: the metal hooks of his scourge rip through one of the columns. Lumps of stone burst into flames as they bounce across the floor.

'What do you mean?' Vannutelli yells over the din. 'Tricked us how?'

Kazia gestures at Alastor. 'That's the demon I told you about. The one guarding Matthew!'

Alastor is out of his triangle, swinging away and mostly missing. This is one very confused demon.

'So Le Geyt can escape?' Vannutelli doesn't sound too pleased.

'No, Alastor must still be there.' Kazia turns to me, like she needs confirmation. 'This has to be another manifestation—'

'Does it matter?' Vannutelli yells.

'I don't know!'

Vannutelli glares at me like he's still running the show. 'What are you trying to do?'

I give him my most irritating leer. He snarls and pulls the knife out of his belt. 'I told you what would happen if you disobeyed me.'

'Did you? Remind me . . .'

'I said I'd kill her.'

'If you've got a problem, kill me.' I hold my arms out wide and stick my tongue out at him.

It's funny how you get these guys who control half the world, and all you've got to do is wind them up and they go off like a jumping jack. Because Vannutelli's out of his circle, red in the face, waving his knife . . .

324

But he's gone for Marvo. He kicks her chair and sends her sliding out of her circle—

There's a flash of spinning metal. Vannutelli is lying on the floor with an axe planted bang between his eyes.

Alastor reels across to him and, after several misses, sticks one taloned foot across his neck. The demon grabs the axe and pulls madly until it comes free, with a rush of blood, and he falls over on his back. He stares around glassily, then rolls over on top of Vannutelli and sucks his brains out.

'What's goin' on?'

It's a fair question, but Marvo's caught Alastor's attention. He's on his feet. And he's still got his axe—

CHAPTER FORTY-THREE
Cards in the Air

A crumpled, fire-blackened ten-quid note. Yellow and blue, folded in half. I pull my Gift object out of my pocket, but realise I don't have time to use it.

Alastor is heading in Marvo's direction . . .

I hear a roar of anger behind me and look round, just in time to see Dinny's ropes fall loosely to the floor. He's on his feet, hooks flailing, running at Alastor—

Who opens his mouth like a drawbridge and swallows him whole.

Dinny's given me the chance I need. But I'm staring stupidly at the banknote. I can hear a voice whispering urgently inside my head. It's my voice, reminding me that this is my Gift object. This is the charm that will save me from going post-peak.

No time to think. No time to remember my dad's face as I grabbed the banknote off him and the flames consumed him. The banknote is in the brazier. It curls up and turns brown—

The thing about demons: they're suckers for hard cash. As the paper catches fire, Alastor stumbles back from the very brink of Marvo's circle with a stupid grin on his face.

But demons get through money fast. I've only got a moment—

I'm out of my circle, sliding Marvo back into safety. I dance round the outside of her circle, scraping the tip of my knife along the floor and screaming, 'In the name of the most high!'

Alastor takes a wild swipe at me, but with his eyes still spinning in their sockets all he manages to do is take a chunk out of the floor.

'In the name of the most high!'

Alastor's coming at me again. I have a split second to form a desperate intention – which is answered as my dog flies out of its circle, barking madly, and leaps for his throat. It doesn't even get waist high before it disappears in a burst of flames. But it's earned me long enough to scream:

'In the name of the most high!'

And I'm back in my own circle, running the knife round with one hand and madly sprinkling brandy into the brazier with the other.

The rat in the cage opens one eye, then goes back to sleep.

Lumpy isn't taking it so well: he's thrown up all over himself. Kazia just stands there open-mouthed. Marvo is kicking away, trying to turn herself and the chair round to see what she's missing without leaving the protection of her circle.

The star of the show wipes his mouth with the back of his hand, but all he does is smear blood and stuff all over his face. He grins dementedly, and you really don't want to know what's stuck between his teeth. His long green tongue flicks out to lick away gore from between his eyebrows.

'Feeling better?' I ask.

He roars and takes a wild swipe at me with the scourge. I duck – not unreasonably, if you ask me. The whole building shakes like a steamboat has hit it. The hooks leave a series of bloody gashes in mid-air, above the line of my outer circle.

Alastor has gone purple all over and there's smoke blowing out of his ears, nose and mouth. And, since he's a demon, out of his arse of course. He's off again, around the studio, twitching and lashing out like he's seeing ghosts or something.

'Frank!' Marvo's managed to push herself round where she can see the fun. 'What's up with him?'

Before I can open my mouth, she gets an answer of sorts. My door blows back on its hinges and a yard-wide river of searing red fire comes rolling in, right up to Alastor's feet. A distant voice roars, 'Come and get me, shit-head!'

Alastor's confusion evaporates in an instant. His

skin changes colour, first to silver, then to burnished gold. He examines his weapons. The axe goes back in his belt. He pulls out his triple dagger and tests the sharpness of the longer middle blade by poking the tip through his tongue. He gives the scourge a few experimental sweeps, cutting swathes of gore through the air. He turns to me and snarls gobs of fire. I put my sleeve over my face as I feel the cold blast. When I look again, Alastor is disappearing out of the door. The flames roll up like a carpet behind him.

'Frank!' That's Marvo again. 'What've you done?'

I didn't plan any of this. I just gambled that if I threw all the cards up in the air they'd come down in a different order.

'Shut up. Haven't finished yet.'

There's one card that still hasn't landed. Alastor may have left the room, but he's not out of the game.

Here's how it's supposed to work. You conjure up a demon and give him something useful to do. It's stick and carrot. The stick is the power of magic and the divine names; the carrot is a small animal in a cage. When the demon's done what he was supposed to, you dismiss him and sever the affinity that the summoning created, so he can't come back and bite your head off.

What actually happened, though, is that Alastor snacked off Hatchet Face, Vannutelli and Dinny, then stormed off without even asking if I wanted him to bring me back a newspaper or a pint of milk.

Result? The affinity still exists and I'm in danger of spending the rest of my life – which promises to be very short – jumping every time something goes bump behind me.

'Aglon, Tetragrammaton! I charge thee, Alastor, to return whence thou camest, without noise or disturbance.'

'Yeah, right,' Marvo mutters. 'Some bloody chance!'

I've got my sword over my head. 'Begone in the names of Adonai and Eloim. Begone in the names of Ariel and Jehovah—'

At this point in a dismissal, I'd normally pay the Presence his fee in flesh and blood. I'm just going through the motions, but I may as well go through all of them. I open the cage, grab the startled rat and lob it out of the circle towards the east. It lands with a squeak in the smoking remains of the goatskin triangle and slides across the floor, its claws scrabbling desperately. It comes to a halt and jumps up on its back legs, staring around, twitching wildly.

'Begone!' I sweep the sword down, hoping – as the tip strikes sparks from the floor – for some sign.

Nothing. No bang. No blast of sulphur. Not even a damp fart or a handwritten note. Just the rat, scuttling up the leg of my trousers into my pocket.

I pull out my knife and start cutting my protective circles, one by one. A couple of minutes later, I'm outside, still in one piece and breathing successfully.

'It's safe,' I say.

Kazia watches me coldly from inside her circle.

'Suit yourself.'

I break Marvo's circle and cut the ropes. She rolls away from the chair and just lies there with her shoulders shaking.

'The word you're looking for,' I mutter, 'is "thanks".'

Bad idea. She jerks and kicks my legs out from under me. I hit the floor and my sword rattles away.

Marvo screams in agony. 'Cramp!' She makes a grab for her leg, but jerks back and clasps both hands to her head.

'Don't fight it—'

'Piss off!'

'Try to relax—'

Some hope. She's on her back, banging her head on the floor and going, 'Shit, shit, shit!'

And my sword? Lumpy has got it. I jump back as it whistles past my ear. 'Hey, what's your problem?'

No gratitude, some people. I duck as he takes another wild swipe at me. Where's a demon when you want one?

Lumpy is really getting the hang of waving the sword around. I'm hopping backwards around the place, thinking I could make a run for it, out of the door, if only—

'Get up, Marvo!'

I mean, it's my bloody sword, for Christ's sake. Forged, quenched and purified. You'd think it'd have the decency to turn red hot in his hands when he tried to use it on me. And there's always that problem with backing away from danger: you can't see what you're backing into.

I fall backwards over Marvo. She yells. The sharp end of the sword is pointing right at my gut and I'm wondering what being disembowelled will feel like—

When Kazia crashes into Lumpy and sends him flying. The sword spins off across the floor again—

'Get out,' Kazia screams. 'Go!'

CHAPTER FORTY-FOUR

Two Demons or One Demon Twice

Quiz time: how fast does a demon travel?

Correct! Two hundred and forty-seven miles per hour.

Me and Marvo, we're a lot slower than that, and by the time we get to the Bishop's Palace, we're both panting. Inside the library I can feel the floor shaking. The electric lamp bounces to the edge of the desk and crashes to the floor.

I make a move for the door in the corner, but Marvo's there first. She turns, arms wide. 'Not till you tell me what's down there.'

'Two instances of Alastor.'

While Marvo's struggling to get her head round that, the door mutters, 'Skinny cow!' She jumps and steps away from it.

'The reason you have to get authorisation from the Society to summon a demon—' I'm struggling to catch my breath. 'Look, there's all sorts of reasons, but the main one is that if some idiot summons a demon that's already up—'

'So you tricked Kazia.'

I nod. I've got a stitch in my side. My ankle still hurts. 'Nobody's ever really worked out exactly what happens, but it's always a mess.'

'What sort of mess?'

'Like when the first crusade turned up outside the walls of Jerusalem in 1099. That's ten thousand lunatics who've basically walked from Europe – they've been on the road for three years. They've eaten their own horses and drunk their own urine—'

'Ugh! You're making that up—'

'The point is, they're desperate – totally bonkers. Four months later, they're still outside Jerusalem and the walls aren't getting any thinner. So what do they do?'

'Yeah, yeah. Summon a demon.'

'Not just any demon, though: Beelzebub. Trouble is, the Muslim governor of Jerusalem, he's got a spy in the crusader camp who warns him what the Christians are up to. The governor has this bright idea: if the other side are going to summon Beelzebub, why don't I get there first? He's got a sorcerer in the city, so he puts him to it.'

'Who won?'

'Nobody. Two instances of Beelzebub popped up within a few minutes of each other. One outside the city, the other inside. After they'd finished beating the crap out of each other, there was no city left to conquer anyway.'

The floor hasn't stopped shaking. The door is still spitting curses.

'The Chinese made a habit of double summonings, right up to the seventeenth century. In 1747 the Society banned any further research and made double invocation a capital offence.'

'What is it with you and the Society? I mean, it's like you're deliberately trying to wind them up—'

'Not deliberately.'

'Oh yeah? Think about it, Frank.'

I'd rather not. I push past her. The handle of the door is warm.

'Arse!' says the door. Not unreasonably: that's exactly what I look like with my jerkin just slung on over my ritual robes.

'You don't have to come,' I point out.

Marvo's face is white. She struggles to stop her voice shaking. 'Think I'd miss this?'

She pulls her pentacle out of her coat pocket and drops it around her neck.

Down in the cellar, Alastor's going at it hammer and tongs. Axe and scourge, actually.

I don't think I'll ever get my head around demons. I'd rather not think of them as real, but these two sure act like it.

Yeah, there's two of them. Of him, strictly speaking, since these are identical instances of Alastor. They look exactly the same: same beady golden eyes, same razor-sharp yellow teeth, same goat's horns. And they must be thinking the same because they're each waving the same weapons and making the same moves. Only for some reason – and I guess this makes some sort of sense – they're doing it like they're mirror images of each other.

In all the smoke, I can't see which is the original instance that Kazia summoned to mash me all those weeks ago; or which is the new version that I tricked her into summoning earlier tonight. But one Alastor has the axe in his right hand and the scourge in his left. The other is all vice versa: axe in his left hand and scourge in the right. A bleeding gash opens in mid-air as Alastor A takes an almighty swipe with his axe. Alastor B does the mirror image, like I say: same weapon, same instant, same trail of blood.

The two axes meet.

You'd think there'd be some minute deviation, that the blades would glance off each other and there'd be fingers on the floor. No such luck. Razor-sharp. Dead on. Edge to edge. There's a deafening clang. Sparks and more smoke. The whole room compresses. Alastor and Alastor both reel back, emitting identical howls of rage. Both snarl and roll their eyes at each other. Both stick their axes back in their belts and pull out their three-bladed daggers. Both gnash their teeth and charge at each other.

Marvo's got her hands over her eyes. Me, I can't look away.

The daggers flash in the air and gouge out a rain of flesh and blood that sizzles on the black tiles of the floor. The tips of the longer middle blades meet, absolutely point to point. Another deafening bang. More sparks and smoke. The demons are face to face, pushing with all their might and blowing smoke out of every available orifice. The stink is unbelievable.

I'm wondering if this could go on for all eternity. One thing about demons: they never seem to get bored. They live in the moment . . . and drag it out for ever.

A voice: 'Come here, boy.'

My Master's voice.

It's a bit like all those names of God that I use on demons: you control things with names. As well as 'Frank', 'Sampson' and 'Brother Tobias', I answer to 'arsehole' and 'skinny little freak'. By calling me 'boy', Matthew's trying to turn me back into that scrawny little kid at Saint Cyprian's, with his mouth hanging open and a stupid, scared look in his eyes.

Does it work?

I step obediently forward, clutching my pentacle. Not that I need it: Alastor's too busy beating the crap out of himself to even notice me. Matthew smooths his tangled hair. He straightens his back so he's a good six inches taller than me.

'Are you responsible for this?'

I hang my head.

'I suppose you think you're clever . . .'

And you know what? I *do* think I'm clever. I look up at him. 'Wasn't me.'

'Who, then?'

'Kazia.'

'She's not that stupid.'

'Maybe nobody ever taught her about double summonings. Or that Alastor's other name is Azazel.'

'You tricked her. Why, though? I mean, where does this get anybody?'

'Got me and Marvo out of a hole.'

'But at what cost?'

'None to me and Marvo.' The Alastors are still pegging away at each other. 'Far as I can see.'

'So how do you propose to stop it?'

I smile. 'I'm not sure that I want to.'

When I was just a nipper I had this idea that grown-ups didn't get scared. I got over that the night my dad went up in flames and I watched him scream and yell and beg. We're all scared; the trick is how well we cover it up.

But I always thought Matthew was special. That he

338

really was as cool and in control as he always looked. That he could face up to stuff that scared the crap out of me . . . and just deal with it.

But now he transforms.

You know that formula I use; the one that goes: 'I exorcise thee and do powerfully command thee, that thou dost forthwith appear before me in a fair human shape . . .'

I've seen a lot of things transform into different things; but whatever that different thing is, it's never something you can get comfortable with. Matthew's whole body sags. He's not a grown-up any more; just this frightened kid who stares back at me and begs, 'Get rid of them. Please.' His hands move away from his body, palms facing me. He drops onto his knees. 'I can't take any more.'

It's like . . . I dunno. Like the Earth stopped turning. Like the sun came out in the middle of the night. Like the termites served me up a three-course meal . . .

Marvo nudges me. 'What's up with him?'

'There's a rule,' I say. 'Once there's a demon in the room, all bets are off.'

'Yeah, but—'

'Double that if you've been stuck down here for a month and suddenly there's two of them.'

'So what're you gonna do?'

I stick my hand in my pocket. Maybe the rat knows

what's coming, because it starts wriggling as I get my fingers round it, and when I manage to drag it out I've got to move fast before it can bite me. If a demon gets a taste of my blood, I'm sunk.

A moment later the rat is spinning through the air. Just for a split second it's the right way up, looking back at me with this reproachful expression on its gob. And then one of the Alastors has turned his head and flicked out his long, green tongue to wrap round the rat's middle and swallow it whole.

There's a brilliant flash of light and a gurgle like the plug being pulled out of the bottom of the Atlantic Ocean.

And a moment after that, there's just one Alastor in the cellar, who's in the middle of a wild swing with his scourge that carries him clear across the cellar into one of the columns. He bounces off, snarling and staring around in bewilderment.

'Where'd I go?'

Sorry, but I can't help it: 'He's behind you.'

Alastor jumps and swings. Another deafening crash. More flying chunks of stone. He hops around the place like water on a hotplate, spitting and lashing out.

Finally, the penny drops. He sighs, sticks the long blade of his dagger deep into his ear and wiggles it. When he pulls it out there's a white maggot twisting in agony on the tip. He stares at it for a moment, cross-eyed, then pops it into his mouth. He chews and swallows.

He looks up at me. 'I'll get you for this.'

I wave my pentacle. 'Gotta catch me first.'

'Shut up.' That's Marvo. 'Now what?'

CHAPTER FORTY-FIVE

Pentacle

'Frank finishes what he's started and I go free.' Matthew has transformed back into himself. He's on his feet again, stating this like it's the most obvious thing in the world.

'But I can't!' I wail. 'I mean, what am I supposed to do?'

'You're supposed to remember your oath of allegiance to the Society. You swore to submit yourself to the will of God and to serve the Society, even to the point of death and at the risk of your immortal soul. Well, now it's time to make good on that vow.' Matthew's got this gleam in his eye. 'Get rid of him' – he's pointing at Alastor, obviously – 'and we can resolve this.'

'You've got to let him out eventually,' Marvo points out.

'I'm bored,' says Alastor. 'Even if nobody else is.' He sticks all his weapons back in his belt.

So they're all ganging up on me. 'How?' I turn

back to Matthew. 'I mean, once you're free—'

'I'll sign a document, anything you like. I assume your licence has been revoked. I can have it re-instated.'

'Maybe you could sign a pact,' Marvo says. 'I've read about them.' She points at Alastor. 'He can guarantee it, yeah?'

Alastor grins. He pulls a small, golden snake out of his eye and bites its head off. 'It'll be an honour and a privilege, boss,' he says in Preston's voice.

I'm still staring at him when Matthew says, 'That's not a good idea. But listen to me, Frank. I'm serious about your obligation to the Society. Vannutelli wants to destroy us. One of the reasons I was prepared to make the Procedure available to him—'

'Yeah,' says Marvo. 'What *is* this Procedure thing anyway?'

I wave a hand for her to shut up, and turn back to Matthew. 'I suppose Kazia did that too.'

'It couldn't be done officially. But the whole point is, that gives me leverage on him. If it became known that he'd had the Procedure done, it would expose him as a hypocrite—'

'He's dead,' I say. And when Matthew just stares at me: 'Vannutelli. He's dead.'

'How?'

'He asked for it,' Alastor mutters through a grisly mouthful of half-chewed snake.

That's interesting. The instance of the demon that snaffled the rat must've been the one I tricked Kazia into summoning. Which means that this original instance knows what the copy did. But I have other priorities right now, because Matthew has suddenly gone bonkers again—

'You stupid boy!' he screams. 'Do you really think this is all some big muddy puddle you can jump into with both feet? The entire future of the Society is at stake and you manage—'

Words seem to fail him. Not for long, unfortunately. He's off again: 'Vannutelli would have been the next pope. That would've given us—'

'By "us", you mean you, right?'

'It's the same thing, don't you get it?' Matthew's gone red in the face. 'Oh, I've had enough of this.' The pissed-off look clears, like he knows what to do now. He smiles. 'I rather assumed that you would have explained to Detective Constable Marvell what the Procedure is . . .'

'No.' Marvo's doing her sullen face. 'He keeps clammin' up.'

Matthew smiles. 'That's understandable. You're *how* old . . . ?'

'Sixteen.'

'So you have . . . let's be reasonably optimistic, a twelve-year career ahead of you as a tatty, pointing out to Chief Inspector Caxton all the little things she can't see for herself. Sadly, the Lord giveth and the Lord taketh away. Your own decline will be sudden and catastrophic. It's not just the loss of your insights – of the talent that makes you such a valuable and highly regarded member of the police force – although I sometimes think it's as much a curse as a blessing—'

'You can say *that* again!'

'You go completely blind.'

'We know all this,' I mutter, like maybe it'll stop him.

Matthew's enjoying himself. 'So what if I told you that the Society has a Procedure to forestall or even reverse the Blur.'

'I knew it!' Marvo glares at me.

'I thought Frank would have told you.' Matthew grins. 'No? I imagined that, as a good friend, he told you everything . . .'

'I was going to,' is all I can manage.

'It's expensive, the Procedure,' Matthew continues. 'The principal ingredient is the eyeball of a particularly rare Tibetan wild cat. I'm sure I don't have to explain why it became so rare. The Procedure is performed upon all members of the Society upon the successful completion of their first year at Saint Cyprian's. That includes Frank, of course – like me, he will never need to wear spectacles. It can also be arranged for certain non-members of the Society for whom cost is not a problem. Although the Church has repeatedly condemned the Procedure as dealing with demons—'

Papal bull of 1957: *De magiae* . . . oh I dunno, something or other.

'—over the centuries many senior clerics, including Cardinal Vannutelli, have availed themselves of it. As have other non-members of the Society for whom cost is not a problem.' Matthew smiles down at Marvo. 'If you were rich, you need never go blind.'

'So how much?'

'More than you'd earn in a lifetime.'

'But it would save me . . .'

Matthew nods sympathetically. 'I'm truly surprised that Frank hasn't told you all this.'

'Yeah, me too,' Marvo mutters.

'So it occurs to me,' says Matthew, 'that maybe we have some basis for a deal. As Superior General of the Society I am in a position to make the Procedure available to you.'

'Not right now, you're not,' I point out.

He ignores me. He's watching Marvo. 'And I can tell you exactly what happened to your brother.'

'Oh please!' That's me. 'We know what happened—'

Marvo whacks me. 'Shut up, you! I'm talking to him.'

'Of course,' Matthew says, 'you'd have to let me go . . .'

Marvo's giving me this 'what now?' look. I'm giving her the same thing back.

Alastor, by the way, is leaning against a pillar, running the tip of one taloned finger down the edge of his axe.

Matthew is standing at the centre of his circle, hands on hips, looking down his nose at us. 'You haven't thought this through, have you? You've assumed you can just waltz in here and play games. Well, it doesn't work like that. What's in it for me? And don't tell me, better sandwiches. When do I get out of here?'

'Someone's gotta pay.' It's kind of weird, the way Marvo says it. Her voice is dull . . . expressionless, a bit like an elemental sounds. It's like she's stating this fact and because she's said it, it's got to happen . . .

'I don't think I'm prepared to go that far,' says Matthew.

'You'd rather be left stuck down here?' I say.

Marvo walks across to plant herself outside the circle. 'OK,' she says.

'Are you nuts?' I stammer.

She's still talking to Matthew. 'You write a confession – everything that happened, who this Vannutelli guy is, why you killed Sean—'

'Don't be stupid, Marvo! He's not gonna fall for that!'

'I can't do anything while I'm stuck in here.' Matthew gestures towards the chalk marks at his feet.

'All right then.' Marvo puts her hand in the pocket of her jeans and pulls out a small silver disc, swinging on a chain. My heart stops as I recognise the pentacle that I grabbed off Kazia, five days ago, in the summoning room.

'Where'd you get that?'

'Where you dropped it after you . . . what d'you call it? After you instantiated Preston.' She turns back to Matthew. 'Deal?'

'Don't be stupid, Marvo!' I make a dive for the pentacle, but she whips it away and tosses it to Matthew.

Alastor pushes himself off the pillar. We're all waiting to see what Matthew does next. He's holding the chain up with one hand. The reflected candlelight glides across his face as the pentacle revolves slowly.

He glares at me. 'Did you put her up to this?'

I shake my head.

'Put me up to what?' says Marvo.

'You do know what this is . . .'

'Yeah, it's a pentacle of Solomon. It'll get you past him—'

She's staring open-mouthed at Alastor, who has transformed into a wooden box, about two foot square.

Matthew turns to me. 'Yours?'

'Kazia's, actually.'

'Don't forget,' says Marvo. 'You promised.'

Matthew smiles, like a cat toying with a mouse. 'I am the Superior General of the Society of Sorcerers in England,' he says. 'I don't believe that an alleged promise to a very junior police officer carries any weight.'

'Yeah, but you promised!' Marvo looks round at me like she really doesn't understand.

I can only shrug. 'What'd I tell you? Should've listened . . .'

The wooden box opens. A long, grey worm emerges and weaves its way in and out of the pillars around the room . . .

The hand holding the pentacle is trembling. Beads of sweat run down Matthew's face. I know why he's hesitating, but I can't help this sinking feeling that all the resources of the Society are about to descend on my head.

'Anyway, the issue is academic.' Matthew sighs. 'This thing is useless as far as I'm concerned.'

Alastor has transformed back and is standing bang in front of him right on the edge of the circle, axe in one hand, knife in the other, and a huge grin plastered across his face. 'Looks good to me,' he says.

'Nice try, Marvo,' I say. 'But Kazia made it for her own use.'

Actually, I want to hit Marvo. I can't believe she could be so stupid. That she was prepared to betray me like that. If Matthew had got out—

'Come here, Sampson.' He's beckoning me over.

I step up to the edge of the circle, opposite Alastor.

Matthew lifts the lid of the lavatory bucket beside

349

him, and drops the pentacle in. 'You can go now.' He sits down and buries his head in his hands.

Alastor's grin has faded. He sticks his weapons back in his belt and wanders off into the gloom.

'Let's get out of here, Marvo.' I shove her towards the stairs, and I've stopped to check the symbols again when I hear the Boss say—

'It's hell down here.' He nods towards Alastor. 'With him.'

CHAPTER FORTY-SIX
Surprise

Out the back of the palace, it's daylight . . . of a sort. Marvo follows me down the garden towards the river.

'Are you really that stupid?' I say.

'How was I supposed to know all this pentacle crap?'

'I'm not talking about that. Suppose it *had* been good – suppose he'd got out—'

'I'd have arrested him as soon as we got outside.'

'Yeah, right. He's the Superior General—'

'He's not above the law.'

'Benefit of clergy. Ring any bells? He can't be tried in a secular court. The case'd go to an ecclesiastical court and it'd be packed with his chums.'

'So do *you* have it, this benefit of clergy?'

'Much good may it do me. The point is, when Matthew *does* get out—'

' "When" . . . ?'

'Can't keep him there for ever. And don't ask me what I'm going to do. Point is: you can't touch him, so don't try anything like that again.'

She's doing her disappointed look. The big eyes and all that. 'You said you'd help me,' she says. 'You *promised*.'

I scratch my head. I'm too tired and angry to care about unsightly red marks. 'I think I've helped quite a lot.'

'You still haven't found out what happened to Sean.'

There's nothing you can say to that, is there? It's a *great* spell, a pariah spell. We're down by the riverside gate. The security elemental beams at me. 'Lovely morning, Mr Sampson.' He opens the gate. In a perfect world it'd be like this all the time.

Beyond the trees, out on the river, a string of barges drifts downstream. I'm wondering what Kazia will do now, when Marvo says, 'Frank, what happens if you're swallowed by a demon?'

Yeah, poor old Dinny. He was a nutter, but he wasn't a bad bloke. Not evil, anyway. And he'd still be alive if I'd just left him lying on the steps outside my studio.

'He saved my life.' A tear glints on Marvo's cheek.

'What Matthew taught me,' I say. 'It's open and shut. If you're swallowed by a demon you go to hell.'

'Even a good person?'

'By definition, a good person can't be swallowed by

a demon. The Society would say you're confusing cause and effect.' I head off along the towpath. 'Crap like that,' I say over my shoulder. 'It's why me and the Society don't really hit it off.'

Marvo's trailing after me. 'I wasn't really goin' to, you know, let your boss go.'

'It's true what they say.'

'What?'

'Tatties are crap at lying.'

'Whatever. So what you gonna do?'

'Let me think.'

We're up the steps onto the bridge.

'Well,' she says, 'have you thought?'

'You don't let up, do you?'

'Why should I? Everybody else gets what they want – what about me? Frank, you promised!'

'No I didn't. You just assumed—'

'An' you let me.'

'Will you just shut up and listen for once?' I grab her arm, just above the elbow. She's so scrawny, my middle finger and thumb meet.

'That hurts!' She pulls away. 'I'm going home.'

'Good.'

And for a few moments, that seems to be that. But ten yards up the road, she turns and says, 'You know your problem?'

'Which one specifically?'

'You're jealous.'

353

'Jealous of who?'

'Jealous of your boss. You're not sure what he had going with Kazia.'

'Huh!'

'And you're jealous of her coz she did magic for him and you're afraid she was better than you.'

'Nark off.'

'It's not just that you're scared of him—'

'I'm not scared of him. Just don't know what to do with him.'

'The real reason you've got him trapped down there isn't so he can't get at you. It's so Kazia can't get to him. What do you think of *that* for an insight?'

She turns away. I watch her stomp off up the road towards the railway station. She's still small and skinny. Her hair's still a mess. She's so wrecked she can't walk straight.

I'm cold and I can't hang around here all day. After a bit I follow her, careful to keep my distance. She looks back once and sees me. She walks faster. I walk slower. Her red duffel coat disappears round a corner.

I think I prefer Marvo without the insights. That's what I think.

You expected my studio to be empty, didn't you? Apart from a couple of dead bodies, obviously.

But Kazia's still there. Yeah, I'm as surprised as you are. There she is, though, fast asleep on the mattress.

354

Alastor is still whining away in my head, but quieter than before. Maybe all the fun tired him out.

I get the chair that Marvo was tied to and turn it the right way up. I sit down and watch Kazia. She's just lying there on her back with one arm across her eyes. One leg twitches. Maybe she's dreaming about me . . .

OK, maybe not.

There's just enough room that someone could lie down beside her and maybe put his arms around her without waking her. But I'm not quite that person. It isn't something they taught us at Saint Cyprian's.

I realise I kind of wish she had just made herself scarce. I sit there and wonder what I'm going to do about her.

She made a decision to stay here and wait for me. Why do I have this stupid idea that I owe her something? It's like I feel responsible for all the shit that's happened to her. I mean, if I imagine I'm standing back where I can see myself perched on the chair staring at her . . . I dunno, I reckon she's doing OK. She gets to run wild playing with magic and knocking people off; and any time she gets in over her head, all she has to do is whistle and here comes Frank! Charging to the rescue like a knight in rusty armour on a moth-eaten donkey.

I realise that when I look at her it's not the real Kazia that I see. It's this stupid fantasy – and I can't let go of it.

I get up out of the chair, quietly so I don't wake her

up. I look back to see that she isn't secretly watching me. Then I step into my broom cupboard and start hunting through my books.

This part of my studio, it isn't physically partitioned off; it's hidden behind another cloaking spell. A space about ten feet across, lined with glass cabinets, cupboards and shelves. I run my finger along the spines of old, leather-bound books: the *Grande grimoire*, the *Liber Honorius*, the *Receuil des signes magiques* . . .

I look up from time to time. There's this one time I catch Kazia moving, but she just turns over on her side, so she's facing away from me, and curls up in a ball.

After an hour or so, I've figured out what to do. I write it all down on virgin parchment and put the books back in the shelves. I step out of the broom cupboard and stand over Kazia.

For a moment I let pictures of her form in my head. I really need to be careful about those. I lean down and shake her shoulder. Her eyes flash open and she almost falls off the other side of the mattress.

'It's all right,' I say. 'It's just me.'

'What's happening?'

'You broke Marvo's brother. So you're going to help me fix him.'

CHAPTER FORTY-SEVEN

A New Leaf

L et's talk about resurrection. Because obviously that's what Marvo's brother needs. Not literally, thank God – we've been down that road before and it wasn't an experience I care to repeat. But I've scratched my head some more, and I think I've come up with a ritual that might fix him.

Earth. Air. Water. Fire.

The four classical elements. It was a simple idea when the medieval alchemists stole it from the Ancient Greeks; but, being alchemists, they immediately started finding ways to make it more complicated. Adding new and more exciting elements. Thinking up numbers and multiplying them. I'm tired and easily bored, so I decide to stick to the original four.

I've got four sheets of paper, one for each element. I'm making lists and drawing little diagrams.

Earth. Jesus spent three days in the tomb before he came bouncing back. Maybe if I could come up with

357

the right way to bury the kid alive . . . and the right magic to stop him turning from buried and unconscious into buried and dead . . . that might work.

Some Indian sorcerers make a big performance of this. We had one who came to Saint Cyprian's once. I can't remember whether it was a recruitment drive, or he was trying to raise money, or just showing off. Anyway, he got us to bury him in the rhododendron beds and when we dug him up three days later . . . Well, good thing he hadn't bought a return ticket.

Air. That one beats me. What am I supposed to do? Tie the kid to a flock of pigeons?

Water? Nope, one wetting's quite enough, thank you.

Fire? There's this story in the Bible about how these three guys – Shadrach, Meshach and Abednego – got so far up King Nebuchadnezzar's nose that he tossed them into a blazing fiery furnace. But when he opened the door to check how the cremation was going, he saw not three, but *four* men in the furnace, walking around, happy as Larry.

The fourth guy? The Archangel Michael, sent down to rescue them. Obviously, he's the man to call.

I can't do a full-blown blazing fiery furnace. But there's a building I can set alight: the shed out in Wytham Wood, just down the hill from the three Weird Sisters and the crater where I instantiated poor old Preston.

It's two days since I got a couple of resurrection men I know to cart away the bodies from my studio. Then I grabbed everything I could think of, just in case the Knights of Saint Cyprian came back and worked out how to break the cloaking spell.

Since then, I've been camped out, gathering wood and drawing things on the ground. It's difficult, working out in the open and on this scale. For a start, how do you draw a circle when you've got a building in the middle? Normally, I'd just hammer a peg into the ground and run round with a length of string. But I need the shed slap bang in the centre of the circle and the walls are in the way. It takes me a while to work it out. But finally I knock a hole in the roof; then me and Charlie chop down the flagpole in one of the local schools and set it up so the top sticks out through the roof of the shed, and tie the string to that.

The geometry is complicated and pretty damned peculiar. More alchemy than magic. But then what I'm trying to do is transform the kid . . .

It's a double circle, fifteen yards across. And it's like there's an equilateral triangle behind it, with just the corners sticking out. And then inside the circle is a seven-pointed star, which was another nightmare to draw, with all sorts of stuff splattered around the place. And another circle, tight around the shed.

I drew all this by knocking a nail through the bottom

of a tin of white paint – several tins, actually – and letting it drip out.

Like I said, two days.

I'm at Charlie's place now, with Kazia. We've ploughed through the prayers and doused ourselves in cold exorcised water. We've purified the last few instruments and wrapped them in black silk.

I didn't really expect her to see it through. You know, I thought she'd just tiptoe quietly away, sometime when I wasn't looking. I kind of wish she had, because it's hopeless. Can't trust her; can't turn her in; can't bring myself to tell her to go away.

She acts like she's seen the light. Turned over a new leaf. Repented of all her sins and wickednesses. She's told me everything she remembers about how she cast the pariah spell, and she's helped me work out all the materials, planetary influences and symbols to undo it. That's one of the reasons the geometry is so peculiar: I get the alchemical bits, but there's a lot of Baltic magic here that doesn't mean a thing to me.

She helped me and Charlie kick a hole through the back wall of the shed and pack the inside with brush-wood and dead branches, leaving a clear passage down the middle. Then we sat around for three hours together, poking holes in ourselves and drawing the major symbols in blood on linen squares.

But we haven't talked about anything. It's like there's this box with all this stuff inside it that really matters – but if I open the lid even the tiniest crack, it'll all burst out. And I get a picture in my head of millions and millions of black flies, whirling and screaming . . .

So I leave the box shut tight.

I pack the wrapped instruments into my satchel. I fasten the straps and look at Kazia, and it seems like she's got smaller.

That's partly because she's shaved her head. OK, it's an archangel, not a demon, that we're invoking, so there's no risk of being grabbed by the hair and dragged off to hell. But, to be honest, I don't trust archangels either – there is such a thing as Too Good To Be True. And anyway we need human hair as part of the burnt offering

Maybe she's sick. She seems to move slower than I remember. Her eyes . . . it's like the blue's faded and that film across them – the thing that always seemed to shield what she was really thinking – it's got more opaque.

I've said it over and over again, until you must be sick of it: I love her.

Only I don't. Not any more, anyway . . . and I don't think I ever really did. At least, that's what I tell myself. On the other hand, I'm only fifteen so what do *I* know?

I guess I feel sorry for her. Like she's messed everything up and maybe if I'd done something different . . . you know, maybe we wouldn't be here dripping blood onto linen squares and not talking to each other.

Yeah, I know: I should stop whining. It's Marvo's brother who's going to get set alight.

Marvo herself? Haven't seen her since she walked off. To tell the truth, there've been a few times over the last couple of days when I've been tempted to call it all off and leave her to it.

I still can't believe that she was prepared to make a deal with Matthew. But she was. And I guess that's a sign . . . I dunno, of how desperate she is. I could just go off and sulk and let her sort it all out for herself. It wouldn't be right, though.

So Charlie's been round to the jack shack to tell her to be outside the mortuary in a police van. It's after dark and I can see her silhouette as I duck past, keeping to the shadows. Kazia's behind me. Charlie's waiting for us in the yard round the back, with the deliveries door open.

Smash and grab. Me and Charlie bust into the amphitheatre and push a startled diener out of the way. Charlie gets the Crypt Boy over his shoulder, Kazia's holding the door open, and we just run out with him.

I dash ahead, through the lobby, past the open-mouthed receptionist, and out of the front door. I'm first

362

into the van because I know what's coming: seeing the kid will send Marvo into a spin. She just has time to splutter, 'What are you playin' at?' before Kazia and Charlie toss him in and her eyes go all wild.

She's still kicking as we bang off up the Woodstock Road.

CHAPTER FORTY-EIGHT

A Secret Optimist

A Presence is a Presence. You draw the shapes and symbols, you dress up like a birthday cake. If it's demons, you stamp your foot, scream the names of God, and poke your wand in the fire. You compel them.

If it's angels, you plead and grovel. And if it's archangels, you plead and grovel like hell.

Thank God it hasn't rained. We've got the shed packed with firewood and ready to blow. We've got this bloody great circle painted all around it. The linen squares with the symbols that Kazia and I drew with our blood are pinned to the ground with nails from a dead baby's coffin. In the three corners of the big triangle we've got the sun, the moon and the *corpus*, the body. In the seven tips of the star I've got the sun, the moon and the five planets Mercury, Venus, Mars, Jupiter and Saturn.

I can't do candles because they'd only blow out. But north, south, east and west I've got four lamps that

Charlie rustled up. They're burning consecrated oil that I siphoned off from the barrel in the cellar of the termite nest, so I'm hoping that the fact that it was nicked doesn't deconsecrate it. Something else we didn't cover at Saint Cyprian's.

I've managed to get seven braziers; one at every tip of the star. They symbolise the seven stars, the seven colours of the rainbow, the seven stages of alchemical transformation. You name it, they symbolise it – so long as there's seven of whatever it is.

In an ideal world, the shed would've been built on an east–west axis. But of course it wasn't, so I've got precious stones representing the planets, the sun and the moon arranged all around the circle to rotate the magic space into a favourable orientation.

All this in only two days? I'm impressed, even if you're not.

I'm ritually clean. I feel sick. But I can make this work. I'm a secret optimist. Secret even from myself, most of the time.

Let's get down to the grovelling.

Everybody's got a small circle inside one of the arms of the seven-pointed star. OK, so Marvo's still passed out cold in hers. To be honest, I'd prefer to do all this without her – I know she's going to be more trouble than she's worth. But it seems like she's got the right to be here. At least Kazia, Charlie and me are all wide awake. And on our knees.

The kid is curled up in his circle, right outside the shed. We've wrapped him in a white linen cloth, like a shroud, and slapped a pair of slippers on his feet.

Let's go, then. These things always start pretty much the same way. Feel free to skip ahead . . .

'In the name of Adonai the most high. In the name of Jehovah the most holy.'

I've got a bowl of black ash in front of me. I dip my finger in, and smear a cross on my forehead. As Charlie and Kazia copy me, I recite: 'In the name of the Lord, Amen. In the name of the Lord who is blessed. In the name of the Lord, Amen.' I pick up the bowl, and I'm off! 'Adonai, Tetragrammaton, Jehovah, Tetragrammaton, Adonai, Jehovah, Otheos . . .'

The wind has dropped. The owls have shut up.

'O Lord God, full of compassion, look with favour upon the work which we are about to perform. I do most numbly beseech thee—'

'Frank!' That's Charlie. 'Numbly?'

Oops – an old joke from Saint Cyprian's come back to haunt me. I nod and go again: 'I do most *humbly* beseech thee: assist us mercifully, O Lord, in these our supplications and prayers . . .'

There's a lot of this until I get to a bit you might know: 'Earth to earth. Ashes to ashes.' I close my eyes. 'Dust to dust.' I tip the entire bowl of ash over my head.

I can hear coughing. I open one eye and see Charlie

struggling in a thick cloud of ash. I give him my fierce look and manage to get crap in my own eye. I can't make any attempt to wipe it away: the ash must fall or lie as it sees fit. At least, that's what Kazia's recipe seems to say, and who am I to doubt her?

Time to rustle up an archangel.

'O blessed Michael, angel of the Lord, I beseech thee by God the Father Almighty who created us out of nothing and by the virtues of all the holy names of God: Eli, Eloe, Sabaoth, Adonai, Elion, Sother, Emanuel . . .'

Eventually, I run out of names. I toss a handful of sulphur into the brazier and get a rush of brilliant blue flames.

'In this, by this, and with this, which I burn before thy face . . .'

I throw in a couple of drops of mercury and some salt and get a lot of sizzling and spitting.

'O Eternal! O King Eternal! Deign to look upon thy most unworthy servant and upon this my intention. Vouchsafe to me thine archangel Michael, that in thy name he may judge and act justly in all that I shall request of him.'

Next up, some metal filings: silver, copper, gold, iron, tin and lead. They spit in the fire—

And we've got light. Lots of light. It doesn't seem to come from any particular direction and doesn't cast any shadows. It's like everything's being illuminated from within. Kazia's holding her hand up, staring at it open-mouthed. Charlie catches my eye and draws his finger across his throat. I read that as, 'Stop now, while you still can.' I shrug apologetically and drop the wad of Kazia's hair into the brazier. It sizzles and burns and gives off a horrible smell.

'O great Lord Michael, who will defend us in battle; who will rescue us from the power of the enemy, especially at the hour of death; who will cast down the Antichrist and bring our souls to judgement—'

With archangels, flattery gets you everywhere.

'I conjure thee by the living and true God. I invoke thee—'

The bigger the Presence, the louder the bang. There's a detonation like someone's fetched the entire planet a whack with a spade. I just manage not to go flat on my face. Kazia nearly topples out of her circle. Marvo's rolled over . . . .

What can I tell you? He's an archangel. Golden hair and pearl-white skin. Robes that shimmer with every colour of the rainbow. And, for some reason, red shoes with pale blue bows and two-inch heels. Wings too, of course. You can't have an archangel without wings. That'd be like a chocolate biscuit without chocolate. Or my dad without a glass in his hand.

I try to hit him with more flattery. 'O great Lord Michael—'

He just holds up one hand. He turns. Marvo has

rolled over again and is lying outside her circle.

I remember telling her once: the main difference between demons and angels. Demons want to do damage. Angels . . . they seem to want to help. Like they feel sorry for us.

Michael walks over to Marvo – none of this floaty crap, thank God – and goes down on one knee beside her. He takes her head between his hands. Her eyes flutter open and she stares at him, open-mouthed. He draws her up until she's sitting, and lays her head on his shoulder. He strokes her hair. She smiles . . .

And you know what? I get this pang of jealousy, a physical pain in my heart like when I burn a wand after a ritual. And I'm thinking: why couldn't it've been me?

I look round. Charlie and Kazia, they've both got the same resentful frown plastered across their faces.

A mixed blessing, archangels. I say, if you can't please everyone, don't bother.

Anyway, down to business. My ears are still ringing and my voice is unsteady, but I say, 'Behold the pentacle of Solomon, which I have brought into thy presence. Thou hast healed the sick—'

He holds up his hand. 'Yes, we know all that.' He sounds pleased with himself. He lays Marvo down in her circle and gets to his feet, brushing dirt from his robe. 'Shall we get this over with? I haven't got all night . . .'

He sounds exactly like Matthew. My throat has gone dry. I point to the kid.

'And you want me to do what, exactly?' Michael says. 'Sort out your mess for you again?'

I want to say that it's his mess – Matthew's – not mine. And that it's not for me, it's for Marvo—

'Come here, boy!'

My Master's voice. I step out of the circle. I've got a moment to think that I'm done for.

'Hold out your hand.'

I feel a sharp pain across my palm, and I'm still staring at the cane in his hand when he turns to Kazia.

'And you.' Not just Vannutelli's voice: the toad-like *head* with the skullcap perched on top.

She blinks and steps out of the circle. No cane this time; he slaps her hard, across the face. A trickle of blood runs from her nose.

He turns to Charlie. 'I can't be bothered with you.' And a moment later he has transformed back: wings and red shoes with blue bows.

A shower of falling stars streaks across the sky overhead.

Michael says, 'And I saw a great white throne, and Him that sat on it, from whose face the earth and the heaven fled away. And I saw the dead, small and great, stand before God; and the books were opened and the dead were judged out of those things which were written in the books, according to their works. And whosoever was not found written in the book of life was cast into the lake of fire.'

He picks the kid up and cradles him in his arms. 'I could take you all out,' he says. 'One flick of my wrist. But I'm in a generous mood tonight.' He looks down at the kid. His voice softens. 'And this child has suffered enough.' He stares me right in the eyes. 'So can we have some fire?'

I just stand there blinking like a fool.

'Come on, somebody must have a light!' He sighs ostentatiously. 'If you want a job doing, do it yourself.'

The shed bursts into flames.

As he disappears into the inferno with the kid in his arms, it's like Marvo finally wakes up. She screams, 'Sean!' and dives after him. I take a flying leap and grab her by the foot and we both go flat in the dirt. She's kicking and wriggling, struggling to get free. I just hang on in there and take my knocks.

Maybe she gets tired. Maybe Michael has something to do with it. She just goes limp on me. The shed is blazing away like all of hell has been tossed inside it. The flames leap towards heaven in a dancing whirlwind of sparks. The roof falls in. The fire gives a final rush. The walls stand for a moment like blackened teeth. Then everything collapses in on itself and Michael is stepping out of the other side of a field of glowing embers with the kid, apparently unsinged, still cradled in his arms.

371

He drops him on the ground, like a rag doll.

'Well?' he says.

It takes me a moment to catch up. I dive into my circle, grab my black-handled knife and reseal it behind me—

'In the name of the Lord, Amen.' I grab my sword. 'I thank thee, Lord Michael, because thou hast appeared—'

'Get on with it, boy.'

I sweep my sword across my toes. 'Do thou therefore depart in peace—'

But he's already gone.

So I'm standing there with my mouth open, and you know what? I think I found Michael scarier . . . OK, maybe not actually scarier, but certainly more *unsettling* than any demon I've ever met. Demons, it's like a firework display: 'I can go off any moment with a whizz and a bang and I'll take you with me . . .'

Angels, it's like they're under your skin and you don't even know they're there – or what they're burrowing towards.

Enough, anyway. Let's wrap this up. 'Marvo,' I say.

'What is it this time?' She climbs unsteadily to her feet. 'I don't feel well.' She stares at the glowing shell of the shed and the twist of smoke disappearing among the stars. 'What the hell's goin' on?'

'Over here . . .'

'Oh yes,' she says at last. She sounds only slightly

surprised. 'Sean.' Her hand flies to her mouth. Tears run down her cheeks. 'What happened to him?' She's on her knees beside him . . .

Sean gives this violent spasm that almost lifts him off the floor.

Marvo whirls round and whacks me one. 'Did you do this to him?'

CHAPTER FORTY-NINE

Repentance

I'll spare you the touching reunion scene because actually it isn't as touching as all that. Marvo's up for some serious weeping and wailing, but although Sean's eyes are wide open and he's breathing steadily since he did that big twitch, he isn't exactly in touch with the big wide world yet.

Mostly – for now, at least – he just dribbles. So we take him home, where his mum waves her amulet around and refuses to believe that this is her beloved boy. Finally, Marvo convinces her and we leave her clutching him while he dribbles gently on her shoulder.

An hour later, the rising sun is reflected in the black water of the canal across the road from the jack shack. Marvo's shivering, despite her coat and my jerkin over her shoulders. I step out of harm's way as she blows a cloud of cigarette smoke. 'I can't stand it, Frank.' Her voice shakes. 'The thought of him just lying there, all that time . . .'

'Don't think about it.' I'm a fountain of good advice. 'He'll be OK. A decent healer can fix the scars.'

'You sure?'

'Yeah. Good as new. Just like the picture on your mum's piano.'

Kazia is sitting on the edge of the canal, watching a rat swim past. Marvo leans close to my ear and whispers, 'So how did she make it work? I mean me, my mum, everybody who knew Sean . . . how did she figure out all the details?'

'She didn't need to. You and your mum did all the hard work. Put together the story, filled in the details. You thought there'd been a funeral and that certain people turned out. Obviously they didn't, but you'd treat them like they did and the spell'd ripple out, I dunno, sort of like an infection, and make them believe it.'

'What about the headstone?'

'Matthew must've organised it.' And got Kazia to extend the spell to it. Hence the buzz of magic I got off it.

'"Our beloved boy". Maybe he felt guilty.'

Yeah, maybe.

Kazia looks round as Marvo tosses her cigarette into the water. 'OK,' says Marvo. 'Let's see what Doctor Death says . . .'

'Sean *Michael* Marvell,' says Marvo.

Squeezed into his corner, in his tiny den at the top of

the jack shack, Doctor Death closes his eyes. There's a sound like sheets of paper being shuffled: elementals can really take the piss sometimes. He looks up with an apologetic smile. 'Sean Michael Marvell is not known.'

I turn to Marvo. 'All straight now? No pariah spell. No police record. Nothing.'

I push my chair back. The gas light fades. Doctor Death's head falls forward onto his chest.

I'm halfway down the spiral staircase when Marvo says, 'I asked him about your dad.'

'Huh?'

'Yesterday.' She's a couple of steps behind me, one hand on the rail. 'What he knew about him.'

'It's none of your business.'

'If it was an accident, like you said—'

'When'd I say?'

'You told me once, your dad fell asleep with a lighted cigarette.'

Maybe I did. I can't remember. 'Can we just get out of here?' I head on down the stairs.

'But that'd get the fire brigade out, and the police would investigate.' Marvo's right behind me and I realise she isn't going to shut up. 'So why didn't Doctor Death know about it?'

'Maybe it's like you said, he's getting past it.' I can't help sniggering. 'Needs new batteries.'

'Or maybe it wasn't an accident and it was one of your stupid magic things . . .' She trails off. Her footsteps have stopped. I look round and she's just standing there by the window over the canal. Her face has gone white. She's staring blankly back at me. She shakes like breaking china . . .

Heads down, everybody! Insight coming in: 'Frank?'

'What?'

'You killed him.'

That's the trouble with fixing Sean: Marvo's fixed too. I turn and head off along the corridor, but she calls after me, 'Why, Frank?'

'I told you, it was an accident.'

'Like hell it was.'

I sigh. When Marvo's on a roll, there's no point in fighting her. 'I was a fire-starter, OK? As a kid. You know, I could just set things alight—'

'Yeah, but *why*?'

'I'd get angry. Boom! That's how they found out I was Gifted. My dad . . . I dunno, must've whacked me once too often when he came home pissed. I don't remember, OK?'

'But how come Doctor Death doesn't know about it?'

'The Society wanted me. They probably had a quiet word.'

'Does it ever occur to you that maybe you're not as important as you think you are?'

Of course it does. But if I don't talk myself up, who

else will? I'm dead on my feet, and I still have to decide what to do with Kazia. At the bottom of the stairs, I push through the door into reception—

Straight into Caxton, standing there, hands on hips, face like thunder. Ferdia's right behind her, clutching his sorcerer's case and looking pleased with himself.

'I've been looking for you,' Caxton snarls.

I really don't need this; I'm so tired I can barely stand up. I try to push past her, but she grabs me by the collar of my jerkin and slams me back against the wall. 'Kidnapping, assault . . .'

She runs out of steam, so Ferdia adds helpfully, 'God knows what else.'

'Ouch.' I rub the back of my head.

That gets me a shaking. 'The Crypt Boy, where is he?'

I can't move, but I can twist my head round to Marvo. 'Do you want to tell her?'

Ferdia's parked his case on the desk. He makes a grab for Marvo's arm. 'Are you all right?' he asks in this weaselly voice.

She pulls away. 'He's at my house.'

Caxton's turn: 'Who is?'

'My brother. Frank found him.'

'Alive,' I point out.

Ferdia stutters, 'But he's—'

'Not as dead as everybody thought he was.'

'You're saying—'

'I fixed him.'

Caxton and Ferdia, they're not the sharpest knives in the drawer, so it takes a while to convince them. Crypt Boy. Sean Marvell. One and the same. But I know we've finally got there when the door opens and Mr Memory steps up to stand beside Caxton. With the spell broken, there's no case to solve – no data to be remembered. He's got a sad smile on his face, and I can see the wall through him. He'll soon be gone.

'I want to see the boy,' Caxton announces.

'Beryl,' I say quietly. 'Give him a couple of days.'

She looks at me. Not fierce, but like she's staring into a clock or something, trying to figure out how it works. 'Why on earth didn't you tell me you knew who he was?'

'I'm sorry.' I shrug. 'I should've.'

And while everybody's still standing there with their mouths open, I dodge round Caxton and head for the outside door. I'm halfway across the street when I hear Marvo's voice—

'You do realise she's taking the piss.'

'Caxton?'

'Don't be a prat – *Kazia*!' Marvo's heading down the steps after me. Washed out. Hair all over the shop. 'You know she doesn't love you.'

'Think I'm stupid?' But I can't help asking: 'Why shouldn't she, though?'

'She just doesn't, that's all.'

'It's funny,' I say, although it isn't. 'I know you'd

have to be mad to want anything to do with me—'

Marvo blinks.

'So you're right: she must be taking the piss. But I can't stop myself. She acts like she – well, there's something . . .' I wish I really knew what it was. 'So I've got to help her.'

'And that's what she's countin' on.'

'Doesn't mean she's not in trouble.'

'Frank—' Marvo's caught up with me. Her fingers are heading for my cheek, but I turn away and head off round the corner towards the canal. She really doesn't know when to give up. 'I'm not saying she doesn't want something from you.' Marvo's right behind me. 'Just saying, it's not what you're hoping for.'

I'm telling myself that she's just jealous when she goes on—

'I know what you're thinking.'

'Oh yeah?' I try to imagine a zebra in a pork-pie hat.

'That I'm just jealous. Well, I am. I don't get you, Frank. You know she's trouble—'

'And that's what I'm trying to tell you. I know what she's done. I know she'd be mad to love me and since she's not mad—'

'There's something not right with her.'

'You'd be a bit bonkers if you'd been through what she's been through—'

'So is that all you're worth, Frank? A girl that's not

380

right in the head?' Marvo's lost another toggle on her duffel coat, and her shoes are all scraped and spattered with mud. Not just washed out, a Montgolfier crash.

'I just need to know she'll be all right,' I say. 'Don't you get it?'

'You didn't answer my question.'

You know what? I mean, it's kind of pathetic, but all this makes me feel like a real person who's worth worrying about. I don't really want to hear what Marvo thinks about Kazia. It's obvious she's got it in for her; it's pretty obvious why, and I ought to be flattered and all that.

But the thing about Marvo is, I owe her. She kind of told me once she was in love with me. I don't believe that – like I said, you'd have to be mad, you know? But it's been fun working with her again.

Interesting, anyway.

And if I've enjoyed it, well, maybe she has too and I suppose, yeah, she's going to miss me . . .

I realise I'll miss her.

'Are you going to stop hitting me now?' I ask.

'What?'

'You know, now I've found Sean for you. Are you going to stop—'

She smiles. 'Last time.' And whacks me. 'OK?'

'Right,' I say. 'Deep breath. Kazia.'

But when we reach the canal, Kazia has gone and I get to watch Marvo trying not to look pleased.

* * *

There's really only one way this can end.

A few hours later, two Knights of Saint Cyprian throw me into a chair. Ignacio Gresh, the Society's Grand Inquisitor, looks up from his desk. He's wearing his usual black suit. His black tie has a simple pentagram embroidered on it in gold thread. The scarring across his face looks like he was in a fire, but nobody seems to know exactly, and he's not telling.

The room is lined with books and files and it's not exactly cheerful. A big, grisly ivory crucifix on one wall. A glass case stuffed with holy relics: teeth, bones and bits of hair that fell off dead saints. There's a window with a view over the town, and a small door in the corner leading to a chamber that nobody I know ever got into – but the novices all used to say it contained chains and sharp things for Gresh to cheer himself up with during the long winter evenings.

It's ten minutes since I strolled up to the front gate of the Society's headquarters and turned myself in.

'Mr Sampson.' Gresh's smile would curdle blood. 'To what do I owe this unexpected pleasure?'

'I've been a fool,' I say, in what I hope sounds like a tone of repentance.

'You're still a fool.' He nods to the Knights. As the door closes behind them, he pushes his chair back and walks round the desk until he is standing behind me. I feel his hands press down on my shoulders. 'So tell me: where is the Superior General?'

All the time it took me to walk here from Oxford, I wondered how I'd answer this question. The good news is that the Inquisition won't torture me or use magic to get the answer out of me: any spell to extract the truth from somebody only tells you what you want to hear.

'He's dead,' I say. 'A demon.'

'And who summoned this demon? You . . . or the girl, Kazia Siménas?'

OK, that came as a surprise. But at least it means there's no reason to be coy. I tell him all about Kazia and Matthew and Alastor. When he asks me where Kazia is, I tell him the truth: I've no idea.

I'm still trying to convince myself that I don't care.

As far as Gresh is concerned, the only lie – the only really massive whopper – is not admitting that Matthew's still there, stuck down in the cellar with Alastor. I dunno, I've got no idea what to do about him. Maybe I'll think of something . . .

Meanwhile, either Gresh buys my story or he's just pleased to get me out of the way. Two days later I have a pilgrim's emblem pinned to my woolly hat and I'm on my way to Rome.

On foot.

Acknowledgements

A big, big thank-you to my agent, Stephanie Thwaites, at the Curtis Brown literary agency; to Ruth Knowles and Kirsten Armstrong at Random House Children's Publishers; and to everybody else who has helped make *Pariah* far more coherent than it would otherwise have been.

Thanks also to all the gang at *The Economist*, and especially Penny Garrett, for keeping me in gainful employment; and the staff in the Canterbury High Street branch of Caffè Nero, for all the caffeine.

Eternal thanks to Cecily Macnamara, David Simmons, Tim Williams and Chris Bidmead. (And apologies to Bidmead, who is still waiting for the lunch I promised him after *Gifted*.)

The titles of chapters fifteen and forty-four were lifted from an art installation (*Two Seagulls or One Seagull Twice*, 1973–4) by my old Dublin chum James Coleman.

Pariah was written with the help of two excellent writing applications: *Scrivener* and *Ulysses*.

Finally, I should like to apologise to the real Dominicans who, I am absolutely sure, have never had *any* sort of truck with demons.

Glossary

ASB   The Anti-Sorcery Brotherhood.
Founded 1898; membership
unknown. It does what it says on the
tin: it's a brotherhood (so no girls)
and it's dedicated (if you can describe
a crowd of arseholes as dedicated) to
the destruction of the *Society of
Sorcerers*.

CID   The police Criminal Investigation
Department, easily recognisable by
their bleached hair and bewildered
expressions.

College wars   1927–31. For centuries the various
colleges of Oxford University were
happy to compete on the sports field.
Then someone came up with the
bright idea that real weapons and
live ammunition would liven things
up a bit. By the time everyone got

bored, most of the university was a
pile of ashes.

**The
Concordat**   The Church formally recognised the
Society of Sorcerers as a religious order
in 1563. But it was a match made on
earth, not in heaven. The Society
kept hauling demons up out of hell to
make things explode. The Church
complained about the noise, but the
Society was having too much fun to
care. After the Society turned the
pope into a piano, both sides agreed
that enough was enough; and in 1908
they finally signed the Concordat, a
document the size of an encyclopaedia
in which everybody promised to
behave. Some hope . . .

Contiguity   See *Sympathetic magic*.

**Dictionnaire
infernal**   An (incomplete) encyclopaedia of
demons, written by Jacques Auguste
Simon Collin de Plancy and first
published in 1818.

Doughnut City   Oxford. So-called because of the
burned-out Hole in the middle
where there used to be a university
(see *College wars*).

Elemental A form of natural energy that even a post-peak sorcerer can channel and convert to physical form, usually resembling a human being or an animal. They have purpose, but – unlike angels and demons – no consciousness. Basically they're slaves, except that you don't have to feed or shelter them, or look after them in old age, since they can be made to disappear at the flick of a finger.

Ghost Magically powered vehicle that allows the rich and powerful to get from point A to point B without having to smell horseshit.

Grimoire A book containing a collection of magical procedures. Because we don't make this stuff up as we go along, you know. We get it out of books written by dead guys who made it up as *they* went along . . .

The Hole The burned-out wasteland in the centre of *Doughnut City*, left behind after the *College wars*.

Inquisition If you've built yourself a religion, you've got to have rules. And if

anyone breaks those rules you have
to set them straight. Pain seems to
work. Pope Leo XVII gave the
Society of Sorcerers permission to set
up its own private inquisition in 1787.

Jack   Policeman, uniformed or plain
clothes.

Mandrake   A thick plant root with magical
properties, often branched so that it
resembles a small human figure with
arms and legs. Sort of. According to
legend, when dug up it emits a
scream that will kill anyone who
hears it; so people used to tie a dog
to the plant and retire to a safe
distance before calling the animal.

Montgolfier   The Montgolfier brothers, Joseph-
Michel and Jacques-Étienne, made
the first public ascent in a hot-air
balloon in 1783. After that people
started using lighter-than-air gases
like hydrogen, and added engines.
Very quickly they realised you could
drop explosives from them.

Nekker   General term of abuse for sorcerers,
a contraction of necromancer.

Necromancy – from the Ancient Greek νεκρός (nekrós), 'dead body', and μαντεία (manteía), 'prophecy or divination' – is the art of raising the dead to foretell the future. As if dead people care about football results.

Pentacle
A design written on paper or parchment, or engraved on metal, and used to command or to protect against demonic forces. There's good money to be made selling protection from disease and sure-fire winners at the races. Also known as an amulet or talisman.

Pentagram
A five-pointed star, drawn without lifting the pencil from the paper and a symbol of . . . well, pretty much anything you like.

Post-peak
The Gift – the ability to work magic – appears in early childhood and peaks around the age of seventeen. As it fades after that point, a sorcerer is said to be 'post-peak'. The Gift becomes undetectable after about twenty-five.

Presbyopia
The age-related inability to focus clearly on near objects. It starts to

391

kick in around twenty and is acute by twenty-five. Symptoms are eye-strain and headaches, and difficulty seeing in dim light or focusing on small objects or fine print. Spectacles help, but not very much. Gardeners, for example, can see enough to work; but they need a kid to read the instructions on the packet of seeds.

Scryer

A magic mirror. Some sorcerers have claimed to be able to see the future this way; but its general use is for communicating over long distances.

Society of Sorcerers

Founded as a secret religious confraternity in 1513, partly to share ideas, but mainly to prevent arguments between rival sorcerers turning into Armageddon. Officially recognised by the Church in 1563. Relations have deteriorated over the last fifty years or so. The Church has accused the Society of heresy. The Society is rumoured to be sharpening its wands.

Sympathetic magic

The principle that physical objects are invisibly linked by magical forces

392

that a sorcerer can detect and analyse. *Contiguity* (also known as *contagion*) is the affinity that persists eternally between any two objects that have ever touched each other, or between the individual fragments of a single object. *Simultaneity* is the link between all events occurring at the same moment in time, anywhere in the physical universe. *Similarity* is the relationship between objects that physically resemble each other.

Tatty

The police force is run by idiots whose *Presbyopia* makes them effectively blind. Any kid under twenty can still see clearly, but tatties are special: they're incredibly sharp and they get 'insights' that tell them stuff nobody else could have worked out. The downside is that they go completely blind aged around thirty.

Thomas Aquinas

Born 1225, died 1274. Philosopher, theologian, saint.

Tonsure

A silly haircut. Sorcerers adopted it to prevent demons grabbing them by the hair. Monks took it up because they thought it made them look cool. To be fair, standards of what constitutes 'cool' have changed since the Middle Ages.

The Vatican   Also known as the Holy See. The pope's business empire, based in Rome.

ABOUT THE AUTHOR

Donald Hounam grew up just outside Oxford. He toyed
with Medieval history at St Andrews University, and wrote
a PhD thesis on apocalyptic beliefs in the early Crusades.
He threw paint around at the Ruskin School of Drawing in
Oxford, then found himself in Dublin where he threw more
paint around and reviewed films until his flatmate set the
building alight one Christmas, whereupon he scuttled back
to England and started making up stories . . .

ALSO BY DONALD HOUNAM

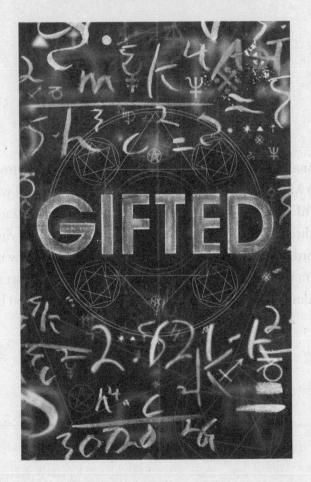

'A fresh, thrill-packed magic and mystery story that delivers a new twist . . . Hounam could be onto something very big here.' – *South China Morning Herald*